A
FATEFUL
OCCURRENCE

A NOVEL *by*
Marie Shields

To May
Love Marie
x x

ORIGINAL WRITING

ISBN: 978-1-78237-164-9

A CIP catalogue for this book is available from the National Library.

Published by ORIGINAL WRITING LTD., Dublin, 2012.
Printed by CLONDALKIN GROUP, Glasnevin, Dublin 11

This Novel is dedicated to my four children,

Anthony, Maureen, Thérèse and Paul.

Also to my grandchildren and great-grandchildren

PART 1

Kate O'Hara's fingers were stiff with cold. It was very freezing in the outside dairy. She lifted the wet linen cloth and squeezed out the icy water and wrapped it around the last cheese and placed it in the box already prepared for it. Kate checked the butter then covered all the boxes with clean flour sacks. The damp cloths would keep the cheeses and butter cool until all the produce was delivered later that morning. Tightening the shawl around her shoulders she heaved a sigh of relief, she had finished. She returned to the warmth of the kitchen and stood in front of the fire and warmed her hands for a few minutes, then glanced up at the clock on the mantelpiece, the hands showed 4.30 am. The water in the big old iron kettle, which hung over the fire was hot, so she brewed a pot of strong tea. After she had poured herself a large cupful, she sat down to enjoy it and wondered if Molly had remembered to come early, then she heard the outside door close with a bang and Molly called out, 'It's me, Mrs. O'Hara'.

Molly removed her boots and left them outside the door. She flung her shawl onto a nail in the wall and walked down the short passage to the kitchen in her stocking feet. Molly knew Mrs. O'Hara dearly loved her farm, but not chunks of farm mud on the kitchen floor! 'Sure it's a cold morning, Molly' said Kate. 'Pour yourself a cup of tea'. Kate watched her as she did so and wondered what would become of her. Molly was very pretty and a good worker, but unfortunately, she was, as the 'locals' put it, 'not quite right'. While Molly drank her tea, Kate told her to collect all the eggs she could find and to look under the hedges around the henhouses. 'Chickens don't always lay their eggs in the hen-house, take the large basket'. After Molly had left to collect the eggs, Kate bustled about the kitchen; a large breakfast was needed to feed her son Michael, the Murphy twins Sean and Patrick, Molly, her daughter Clare and herself.

Kate was a widow and had been so for many years. Now 60 years old, her once lovely auburn hair was now quite white, however, her deep blue eyes still sparkled with vitality, she was a very handsome woman. Kate had worked hard all her life from a very early age and saw no reason to stop now. Although she always helped on the farm, mainly she looked after the family and ran the house efficiently, with Molly's help. Her motto had always been 'the devil finds work for idle hands' and to the best of her ability she made sure no hands were idle! She lifted the last batch of Soda bread from the skillet and placed them on the table, walking over to the fire she gave the pot of porridge a stir, the thick rashers of bacon were 'doing' nicely in the oven, she would cook the eggs when the family returned for breakfast. Kate looked at the clock; it was now 5.00 am and wondered how much longer it would be before the family finished packing the vegetables etc., into the crates and loading them onto the two carts. All the produce had to be delivered to the Connaught Hotel in Dublin by 7.00 am. Molly should be finished feeding the chickens and pigs by now, she thought? Kate glanced around the kitchen once again, and then satisfied that everything was 'as it should be' she walked down the passage to the outside door. Opening the top half of the door she looked out, then unlocked the bottom half, taking down her shawl from the nail on the wall she wrapped it around her shoulders and stepped outside. Walking down the path Kate surveyed the farm; she loved it dearly and never tired of the view as it was soft and peaceful. Invisible hands drew aside the early morning mist and revealed patches of sky. It promised greater beauty. Kate walked a little further along the path and scooped up a handful of soil and ran it through her fingers, it was good soil now. Martin was never very far from her thoughts and she wished he had lived to enjoy all the benefits of his hard work. She still missed him and remembered the night he was thrown from his horse and was killed as if it was yesterday. She shivered a little and drew her shawl closer around her and decided to return to the house allowing her thoughts to drift as she walked alone and remembered how she had met Martin, all those years ago.

It was during the 1846 Potato Famine that swept through Ireland. She lived with her Da, and Ma and two little brothers, Patrick and Eamonn on a bit of land in a small cottage. They were very poor. One evening after a very poor meal of nearly rotten potatoes, her Da told her they would be evicted from the cottage because he could no longer pay the rent due to the Famine. Kate remembered how her Ma had wiped away the tears from her eyes. There was nothing anyone could do to stop the eviction from happening. Tenants-at-Will had no rights; they were owned body and soul by the English Landlords. Agents carried out the landlords orders with the help of the English soldiers. They even regarded the women in the family as their property, to do with as they pleased. Needless to say, in that respect, many an Agent had met with an unexplained accident! As the tears ran down her face she remembered how she had looked at the faces of Patrick and Eamonn as they slept peacefully beside the turf fire. The glow from the fired adding colour to their small faces which were pale and pinched from constant hunger. Sobbing loudly her Da and Ma tried to comfort her but she knew what to expect and the Agent and English soldiers were nothing, if not merciless, in the way they carried out their duties.

Thud! Bang! Thud! Bang! Crash!. The door of the cottage fell in and four soldiers burst in, rifles pointed at the family. With prods from the rifles and physical abuse, it was only a matter of minutes before the family were outside their home. The look of terror on the faces of her two little brothers in the light from the blazing thatched roof will haunt her as long as she lived. An almost palpable feeling of rage engulfed her against the English and their supporters who made the terrible laws under which they had to live. In that moment, she vowed she would survive somehow, although she knew the family had been given a death sentence. Her Da led his family away on their long walk to 'nowhere'. There was hardly any food at all, little as it was they gave to the little boys. Sometimes they were lucky and found a few berries and some seaweed. But they all grew gradually weaker, day by day their movements became more sluggish. Patrick and Eamonn could hardly put one foot in front of the other. One evening, her Da insisted they all sit down in a corner of the field under a wide hedgerow to rest. Holding Patrick on his knee and Ma holding Eamonn in her arms, she remembered how they all cuddled up close to keep warm and soon fell asleep from exhaustion. Kate remembered the terrible scream so vividly as it pierced the air, and her Ma. sobbing loudly. Patrick and Eamonn had died in their parents arms.

Kate, her Ma and Da kissed Patrick and Eamonn goodbye and said a 'Hail Mary' over them and covered their tiny bodies with stones, leaves, branches, anything that would prevent the rats and dogs from tearing their bodies apart and continued on their journey to 'nowhere'. In their hearts they were sure the two little boys were better off in Heaven, with Jesus, away from the cruelty and inhumanity they had endured in their very short lives. Putting her shawl on the nail she still remembered the terror she felt over the loss of her parents who also dropped dead on the road to 'nowhere' and how she had covered their bodies as best she could, and said a prayer for them although she knew they didn't need it and solemnly took an oath that she would survive somehow, if only to live long enough to tell her future children and grandchildren about the heartbreak, grief, misery, poverty, hunger and death she and millions of others had endured. She walked on.............

It was Martin's Da who had found her, half dead under a clump of bushes and although it was against the law to help people who had been evicted from their homes, in any way at all, on penalty of eviction themselves, he had brought her to live in his home with his wife and son Martin. She thought how lucky they had been, Martin and herself, to have a son. As his heir, Michael had been old enough to take over the leasehold of the farm on the death of his father. Otherwise, the land would have been reclaimed by the owner, even though the leasehold didn't run out until 1893. During the Famine, she and Martin had always believed that it was deliberate Policy of the English Parliament to mishandle the situation. Ireland and England were separated by a 'strip of water' so to speak, and boat loads of potatoes could have been shipped over in hours. Instead, The English Government shipped grain out of Ireland. They talked and talked about how they could help, until millions of people either died of starvation, fever and dysentery or emigrated to

America or Australia in the 'coffin ships'.

Years later, when she and Martin were courting, they had decided to emigrate to Australia. Martin believed there was plenty of land and that way, they had a future. Then a miracle happened! The Duke of Lancaster, the owner of the land, made a decision which completely altered the course of their lives. The Duke didn't like Ireland, in fact he never visited, he left his property etc., in the hands of his Agent, hence the tag 'Absentee Landlord'. The Duke was constantly informed by his Agent that his 'tenants at will' were refusing to pay unjustified rent increases, he was furious. It also upset him to be told of the ill-feeling towards him that spread like wild fire among his tenants; especially those evicted from their homes and regarded all of them as 'trouble makers' he believed his tenants were shiftless drunkards, incapable and unwilling to do a day's work. He thought they would be grateful to him for a diet of potatoes and a hovel to live in. The constant problems were all the fault of 'those damned Irish Peasants'. His personal comfort was very important to him and did not appreciate the inconvenience and turmoil his tenants created in his life. The Potato Blight and subsequent Famine of 1846/48 was, for him, the last straw. Something had to be done to keep these tenants quiet so The Duke devised a way of dealing with the situation which would allow him to pay his gambling debts and wine bills. He would offer a long leasehold on certain pieces of land to young men whom he considered would be a good risk. Martin was offered a leasehold of 45 years on a derelict farm. The condition was that the farm would be improved each year and that the 'ground rent' was paid promptly, Martin accepted. Kate and Martin were married shortly afterwards and moved in immediately.

Many years later, Martin signed an agreement with the Connaught Hotel to supply vegetables, butter, cheese, eggs and whatever other produce he could supply, ham and bacon etc., as long as it was of high quality. Kate remembered how some nights they had been so tired, the only clothes they had the energy to take off were their boots. She wiped away her tears with the back of her hand as Molly was coming along swinging the pig-swill kettle backwards and forwards. There was still no sign of the others when she arrived at the house and after washing out the pig-swill kettle, washed her own hands under the pump in the yard and put the kettle to one side. Kate asked her to fill the water jugs in the bedrooms with the hot water from the iron kettle. 'Fill an extra jug for Paddy and Sean and leave it in Michael's room'. When Molly had finished Kate said 'after breakfast Molly you can spend the rest of the day with your family'. The sound of horses hooves and voices outside told Kate it would not be long before four ravenous people walked into the kitchen asking if breakfast was ready. Michael, Paddy, Sean and Clare walked into the kitchen in their stocking feet – they knew the rules, and sat down at the large table. 'I've collected the boxes from the dairy and stacked them on the cart, Ma' said Michael. After they had finished eating their breakfast of porridge, bacon and eggs, Molly placed a large teapot full of strong hot tea on the table and they helped themselves to the freshly made soda bread. 'Sure no one makes soda bread like you Mrs. O'Hara' said Paddy with his mouth full. 'That's probably why the bacon tastes so good, the pigs get the leftovers' joked Sean. Everyone laughed; they were all in a good humour. The men finished breakfast and raced upstairs to wash and change their clothes while the women cleared the table and generally tidied up the kitchen. They were nearly finished when Michael came into the kitchen, washed and changed and looking devastatingly handsome. Michael was 6ft 2, with very broad shoulders and not an ounce of surplus flesh on him. His hair was raven black and he had the biggest, bluest eyes possible. Smiling at Kate and Clare, showing his even white teeth, Michael said 'have a good day in Dublin' crossed the kitchen floor and kissed them both on the cheek. Paddy and Sean had washed and changed and were also ready to leave. They did everything together; they looked so alike it was hardly possible to tell them apart. They had red hair and freckles and didn't take life too seriously; they always seemed to have a good time. Saying goodbye to Kate and Clare they followed Michael outside. Michael gave one final check that the crates were securely fastened and jumped up onto the first cart. Paddy and Sean followed suit on the second cart and with a slap of the reins the horses moved off at a quick trot. The farm was only a few miles outside of Dublin so they would be there in plenty of time.

While Kate spoke to Molly, Clare went upstairs to wash and change her clothes. She decided to wear her dark green dress with the short fitted jacket. The high neck was trimmed with pale green silk and matching buttons marched down the front. Looking at herself in the long mirror she liked what she saw. Her bonnet complimented her outfit and allowed some of her beautiful auburn hair to be seen; her green eyes seemed larger than ever. Pulling on her gloves she went downstairs to wait for her mother. Kate came downstairs shortly afterwards looking very distinguished in her brown dress and matching cape. The edge of the cape and the hem of her dress were trimmed with pale primrose coloured braid and the cameo brooch put the finished touch to her outfit. Molly stood looking admiringly at both of them. 'We will see you tomorrow morning' said Kate 'Take the basket of food home to your mammy and be careful not to break the eggs'. Kate knew that Molly's mother, Mrs. Kelly, would be glad of the food, feeding a large family in Ireland was not easy. Molly left carrying the basket carefully and shortly afterwards the sound of wheels crunching on the gravel outside could be heard. 'The cab's here' declared Kate and they both left the house, closing the door behind them. Arrangements had been made with Molly's family to keep an eye on the farm. Lifting their long skirts they climbed up into the cab as the cabbie lifted their luggage and with a flicker of the reins the cab moved off.

After delivering the produce to the hotel, Paddy, Sean and Michael arranged to meet late at Tommy Doyle's pub. After calling into the bank, and the horses stabled they set off for the pub. Doyle saw them and came over for a chat. While they were talking, an argument erupted and looked around he looked to see where the noise came from. Although a big man, he moved quickly and threw them out. Doyle liked 'a quiet house. Paddy 'slipped away' then Sean and Michael followed to a back room.

Rory was already inside the room. Rory spoke first, arguing forcibly that unless they carried out their plan soon, it would be too late and the quarry would have flown. 'Is Friday soon enough?' asked Michael. The four men discussed details of the plan agreed, it was a good one – it had to be, their lives depended on it. Rory left first by the back door. 'Take the two carts home by yourselves' said Michael to Paddy and Sean I'll see you both at the farm tomorrow'. After Michael had left, also by the back door, Paddy and Sean made their way back into the bar and settled down for a good convivial day. Michael knew Dublin like the palm of his hand; he had finished his education there. Walking for some time until reaching the street he was looking for he knocked on the door. The lace curtains moved slightly at the window and then the front door opened and a voice said 'come in'. Stepping inside Rosie declared 'sure you're a fine figure of a man, Michael O'Hara'. Michael laughed easily as she led the way to the front parlour and asked if he would like a drink. Shaking his head, Michael replied 'maybe later'. She nodded her head and left the room, he followed her upstairs. Later, he reached over and pulled a packet of cigarettes from his jacket pocket. As he lit one, Rosie lay back on the pillows and watched him. She wondered, as she had often done many times before, why he was not married? Most men in their late thirties were usually married or at least thought about it. 'Rosie, I need your help" he said. She looked at him sharply and decided whatever it was he wanted to discuss with her, it was serious. Slipping out of bed she dressed quickly. 'I'll be downstairs when you need me, I'll make a pot of strong tea' she said as she left the room. Michael followed soon afterwards and sat on the nearest chair in the kitchen. Rosie waited for him to explain why he needed her help. 'Indeed, it's not easy to talk about, but you need to know the whole story before you decide whether or not, you want to help?'

'Three years ago, I was engaged to be married, her name was Moira Flanagan, I loved her very much. Moira lived in Dublin with her parents but she spent a good few weekends with me and my ma and sister at the farm. She was happy, great fun to be with, I considered myself a very lucky man'. The last time she and I were together, was on a Sunday after Mass, three years ago. She suggested a picnic in the fields, so that is what we did. We strolled through the fields until we reached 'our spot' beside a small stream and settled down to enjoy the day and the picnic'. Michael stopped speaking and as Rose watched him she realised something terrible had happened. 'She had an old school friend who invited her to some family celebration, I don't know the details'. Rosie waited for him to explain why he needed her help. 'During the evening, Moira was introduced to a young man called John Blunt. The family had met him on many social occasions; he worked in a book shop in Dublin'. 'Michael drifted away'! 'A few days later Moira's mother asked her to take her place on a charity stall for a church situated in a rather rough neighbourhood, you know it yourself. It's always a hot bed of resentment against the English and soldiers patrol the streets. As Moira and another lady got into a cab two soldiers passed them. She recognised the young man, she had previously met him at her friend's house; and Moira knew he had recognised her'. Michael lit another cigarette while Rosie waited for him to continue: 'Moira contacted her friend and explained the situation, they were both very frightened. If he was an English soldier, why was he working in a book shop as a civilian? Sure the answer is obvious, he was an informer, a spy for the English They decided to tell Moira's brother Rory, who contacted me and began making enquiries from various sources and were given confirmation that he was indeed a soldier, but his name was not John Blunt, there was no such name listed on the army personnel files. A few days later, Moira's body was found not far from her home, she had been battered beyond recognition. We believe Blunt' killed her, if he didn't kill her himself, he was responsible for it. When I saw her I was filled with such rage and vowed to find whoever had killed her I would make him pay'.

'Moira's family had called their doctor. He informed the Authorities and this included the army. While he examined her clothes he found a small button, exactly the same as those on the tunics of the English soldiers. Blunt killed her because she had recognised him for what he was – an informer!' Rosie offered him a little whisky, he nodded, she waited for him to continue, as she had no idea what he wanted of her. Michael told her an appointment was made with the Commanding Officer stationed nearby. 'Mr. Flanagan, Rory and myself went to see him. We explained the situation and asked him for his assistance. He posted him back to England, he didn't care, after all she was only an Irish girl' he said angrily. 'However' said Michael 'a few weeks ago one of Rory's friends thought he saw Blunt in Dublin and was certain it was him. Rory and I spent days through our various sources trying to find out if it really was him seen in Dublin and it was confirmed, he is also a high ranking officer. We have no idea why he is back again though? and believe he will be returning to England shortly'. After lighting another cigarette he told Rosie that a 'special dance' is being held for soldiers, their wives and girlfriends on Friday. 'We know he isn't married that's where you can help, only of course if you want to?' he explained.

'Mother of God!' exclaimed Rosie, 'what true Irish woman could resist'.

'This is what I want you to do, it is vitally important' said Michael. 'I want you to draw Blunt outside into the grounds of the building where the dance is being held, beginning at 9.00 pm. A little after 9.00 pm make some excuse and go inside. I'm sure you will think of something? But leave him waiting outside for you, go inside and close the door and don't come out again'. 'How in God's name am I to get into the dance, I don't know what he looks like' said Rosie urgently. Michael pulled an envelope out of his pocket and handed it to her, taking it from him she opened it, inside was an official invitation to the dance. 'So I'm Agnes Ryan am I? she said and laughed. 'One of my friends will escort you to the dance and escort you home again, no explanations will be necessary. Do you think you could arrange to be in the grounds with Blunt at 9.00pm?' he asked anxiously. Rosie looked at him and smiled 'Sure that's no trouble at all' she answered.

'Here is a sketch of Blunt, it's a good likeness, Rory says, but we don't know his real name, we have to rely on you recognising him. When you feel you can do so, burn the sketch, we don't want any suspicion to fall on you' explained Michael. 'To be sure then that's all you need to know, you're a grand girl, sure you are'. Handing her another envelope he said 'there is enough money here for your expenses, I want you to buy yourself a new dress, you must look your best for Mr. Blunt'. As he was leaving, Rosie said 'God speed Michael, I'll be saying a prayer for you'. He nodded and left the house. After he had left, Rosie sat down and thought about all she had heard. She concentrated on what Michael had asked her to do on Friday and then memorised the sketch of Blunt carefully, first his eyes as they didn't change much except with age. The nose wasn't too clear but she knew she would recognise the mouth, it was very full. She decided she could recognise him and threw the sketch into the fire and watched it burn. Putting the invitation in a safe place she put the money in her purse, dressed herself in her outdoor clothes and set off to buy a dress for the 'special occasion'.

'Whoa!' said the cab driver as he brought the cab to a standstill outside the Connaught Hotel, he tethered the horse and jumped down onto the pavement. After helping Kate and Clare down from the cab, he lifted their luggage and set it down on the pavement beside them. Kate paid the fare, he touched his hat and the cab moved off. A porter from the hotel descended down the steps and carried their luggage into the hotel across the foyer to the Reception Desk and waited until Kate and Clare had registered, the Duty Clerk handed him the key to their room and led the way upstairs along a carpeted hall until he reached the room which had been reserved for them. Standing aside to allow them to enter the room he handed the key to Kate and then placed their luggage on a wooden chest at the foot of the nearest bed. Kate gave him a tip, they removed their bonnets and gloves and dropped them on a nearby chair and looked around the room. The furniture was Mahogany, highly polished. Two comfortable armchairs were placed either side of the fireplace. They were upholstered in dusty rose pink velvet. A gilt clock stood on the mantelpiece and hanging above was a gilt ornate mirror. In the hearth were brass fire-irons ready for use. A large floral rug covered most of the polished floor boards and the colours were mainly grey, soft rose and pale green. 'It looks very comfortable' said Kate. 'Yes it looks lovely' answered Clare, still looking around the room. On one side of the room there was a large wardrobe and on the opposite side of the room a large dressing table on which were set out two crystal candlesticks and a matching trinket set. The bed hangings on the beds were identical. Each had a shirred valance and curtains made from dove grey silk, edged with a dusty rose pink bobble fringe, the pillows and sheets were crisp white linen and a patchwork quilt made from pieces of the same dove grey silk as the bed hangings, with an occasional patch of dusty rose pink and soft green covered the bed. I love the colours' Clare said and walked over to a connecting door and opened it. 'A bathroom!' she exclaimed. Turning on the hot and cold water taps she joyfully watched as the water flowed freely into the bath. Turning off the taps she turned to her mother and said. 'All that lovely running water, sure I'll be soaking in a lovely hot bath tonight, it's just wonderful, wonderful'.

Kate looked up from unpacking her clothes and said 'yes dear, I'm sure it is, but shouldn't you unpack your clothes?' There was a knock on the door and Kate called 'come in'. Matthew Quinn, the Hotel Manager, walked into the room smiling as Kate shook his hand. 'Sure it's lovely to see you both again, and you look so well, would you like a pot of tea sent up to your room?' 'That would be lovely,' Kate answered. 'I'll be seeing you both before you leave tomorrow and I will arrange to have a cab waiting'. As he turned to leave he said 'I hope you enjoy your visit'. Kate and Clare finished unpacking and sat down to wait for the tea and toast. They didn't have to wait long, a waiter entered carrying a tray and placed it on a nearby table. As Kate poured the tea and Clare munched her toast, Kate asked her what plans she had made for the day. 'I wrote to Bridget O'Reilly and have arranged to meet and perhaps do some shopping and as Bridget loves music we might go to a concert. Declan will escort us back to the hotel and concert and I have invited them to dinner tonight.' 'I have a lot of business to attend to this morning' she explained. 'I'll see you all at dinner this evening'. When the cab stopped in front of Bridget's home, Clare made her way to Bridget's door, they were so happy to see each other. Mrs. O'Reilly heard a noise and met Clare in the hall. 'Now let me look at you, sure you're a sight for sore eyes, so you are' she declared. I'm always telling Bridget that the pair of you work too hard. 'Thank you' Clare answered 'you look very well yourself'. Mammy has arranged for Bridget and Declan to have dinner with us tonight in the Hotel, as we return to the farm tomorrow morning'.

'Now tell me' queried Mrs. O'Reilly, 'how is Michael these days? Dear God! that was a terrible thing that happened to Moira. Has he heard any more from the Authorities concerned?' 'No' she answered sorrowfully, you know Michael, he doesn't talk about it a lot and when he does he gets very upset and angry. Mammy has to calm him down, she is always telling him 'let it be, let it be'.........Clare didn't really want to talk about it either, it distressed her. However, Mrs. O'Reilly had other ideas. 'What villain would want to kill an innocent girl like Moira? She never did any harm to anyone; I don't suppose we will ever find out who killed her. God rest her soul'. Clare just shook her head, thankful for the knock on the front door and hoped it was the cab driver. It was!. As the cab moved off Bridget asked Clare where she would like to go first. 'I need some more books and slates and sewing materials for the children, there aren't enough' said Clare. I think if every child had a slate each, they would try harder. You know some of them are very bright indeed, but sometimes I wonder if they even get enough to eat. What do you think?' . 'Well, I really only help out with the music, but sometimes I do take a class if a teacher is unwell. From what I can see we don't have that problem because the Parish Priest organises special collections. The people are very poor and the children aren't clothed or fed properly, sometimes it is partly the parents fault, Drink is a curse'. 'Where do they get the money to drink, I wonder?' asked Clare. 'Ah! There is always a 'bum' willing to buy another 'bum' a drink' Bridget said scornfully. Bridget rapped on the divider and told the driver they had decided to get off. After paying him they walked quickly towards the bookshop. 'Do you mind the noise of the traffic?' queried Bridget. 'No, I quite enjoy the hustle and bustle of the City, it's a nice change from the quiet countryside', she answered. Clare bought the slates and books and arranged to have them delivered to the farm, looking around the shop for Bridget, she spotted her and asked 'what is so interesting, you seem to be a thousand miles away?' said Clare. Bridget looked up from the book she was reading and said 'it's written in Irish. God knows how it got to be here on the shelves. I'm going to buy it, I hope the salesman isn't too curious?'. 'There is still plenty of time before the Concert starts, let's go and have lunch' suggested Bridget, 'lead the way, I'm ravenous' replied Clare. After lunch they caught a cab to the Concert Hall. As they set off Clare thought about Declan, it was months since she had seen him. 'Is Declan very busy these days?' she asked. Bridget glanced at her, as she was watching the traffic. 'Yes, he seems to be, but he is looking forward to seeing you and your mam tonight'. The Concert was just about to begin when they took their seats. Music was Bridget's life; she was really looking forward to this evening. As the lights dimmed the members of the orchestra took their places. The sound of instruments being tuned fill the hall. 'Isn't this magic, I love Chopin, don't you Clare?' Bridget whispered. 'Indeed it is' she replied. The Conductor took his place in front of the orchestra, lifted his baton. The Concert had begun.Kate meanwhile, spent most of the morning dealing with business matters. She ordered supplies for the farm and arranged delivery as soon as possible. She checked the time on her fob watch, time for lunch she thought. After lunch Kate spent most of the afternoon in the fashionable shops. She bought new trimmings and furnishings for the farm and a few personal items. She bought a new bonnet and decided to wear it. Then remembering the morning rush and Molly. 'I must get her a present' she thought. Deciding on a new shawl for Molly, she wanted her to have something new when she returned. Molly's wages were spent on the family, they helped to keep them all alive. The Kelly's were a large family and Molly was a proud woman. The cab stopped outside the Connaught Hotel. Kate paid the cabbie and entered the hotel, she asked for her key and if some tea could be sent up to her room. She also told him there would be two extra guests at their table for dinner. The breakfast tray had been removed and a fire burned brightly in the fireplace. Autumn could be rather chilly in the evening. She removed most of her clothes and slipped beneath the quilt for a well earned nap.

Bridget and Clare clapped their hands with the rest of the audience at the end of the Concert. 'Wasn't that just wonderful?' said Bridget and Clare agreed. However, she was looking for Declan and she couldn't see him in the crowd. She searched the crowd again. He wasn't there! hiding her disappointment she asked Bridget, 'do you see Declan', but she couldn't see him either. As she was wondering what had happened to him she grabbed Clare's arm and weaved her way through the throng and stopped in front of a young man standing alone near the entrance.

'Finbar!' exclaimed Bridget, 'what are you doing here and where's Declan?' Finbar was looking at Clare. 'Miss Clare O'Hara, Mr. Finbar Delaney' said Bridget. 'Declan was called away urgently, something about a sick cow, he sends his apologies and asked me to escort you home' explained Finbar. 'Declan and I have been invited to dinner with Clare and Mrs. O'Hara at the Hotel where they are staying'. Turning to Clare, Bridget asked 'would your mam mind if Finbar came instead of Declan? 'she wouldn't mind at all' answered Clare. Finbar asked Clare and Bridget to wait until he could get a cab. 'Do you like Finbar?' Clare asked Bridget. 'Well enough' she answered. Finbar returned and escorted them to a waiting cab and sat opposite Clare, 'Do you come to Dublin very often?' 'not very often' answered Clare. We have a farm a few miles outside of Dublin and come here from time to time'. On their arrival at the Hotel, Clare asked the Duty Clerk if her mother had returned, he replied yes, she returned earlier this afternoon'.Opening the door Bridget flew across the room to give Kate a Kiss and introduced Finbar to her. 'Declan couldn't come, he was called away. Clare thought you wouldn't mind if Finbar came to dinner instead' she added. As the girls freshened up Kate asked Finbar how long he had known Declan? Finbar told her that he went to school with him and their friendship had continued into their adult life. When they reached the dining room a waiter moved forward and led them to a table which had been reserved for them. Clare looked around the room, It was lovely. The walls were panelled wood and a moss green carpet covered most of the polished wooden floor. Silver cutlery and crystal glasses were set out on a crisp white linen tablecloth.

They chatted happily over dinner and during the course of the conversation, Bridget said 'Isn't strange, you and Declan are such good friends Finbar, and yet, you seem to be quite different?' 'Sure, I spend quite a bit of time in Connemara or Galway. My friends and I work with the children through the 'Hedge Schools'. We teach them to read and write. I feel very strongly that the English Government shouldn't win in its attempt to keep them, or indeed, anyone who is within their reach, illiterate. They believe that if they succeed they will have less problems. They are mistaken of course, eventually justice will demand that the Tenants-at-Will have a normal degree of security one way or another!'.

It was getting late and Kate thought it was time to leave the dining room and return to their room. Finbar thanked Kate for a lovely evening. Clare asked 'are you tired mam?' 'Yes a little, but it's pleasant tiredness, if that is possible, it was a lovely dinner and has gone well. I'll not belong in the bathroom dear, so you won't have to wait too long to get into that lovely bath you're so looking forward to' she answered jokingly. Shortly after, Kate emerged from the bathroom and kissed Clare goodnight. 'I'll see you in the morning dear, 'Goodnight Mam, sleep well' answered Clare as she made her way across the room to the bathroom. She ran the water until it nearly filled the bath and then stepped carefully into the water. She slipped down until only her head was visible, this is wonderful! She thought, just wonderful!

The following morning Kate and Clare went downstairs for

breakfast, Kate locked the door behind her and handed the Duty Clerk the key and asked him to arrange for their luggage to be brought down, 'We shall be leaving in about one hour' she said. They had both nearly finished their breakfast when Mr. Quinn joined them. 'I have arranged for a cab for you and hope everything has been satisfactory?' He and Kate discussed a few business details then he stood up and shook hands with both of them. Kate and Clare arrived home; Molly helped to carry their luggage upstairs. Knocking on her mother's bedroom door Clare poked her head around 'I'm off to see Father O'Connor mammy she said. I need to talk to him about the slates and books etc., I bought for the school'. 'While you are there, ask him to dinner on Sunday' Kate replied. 'I'll do that' answered Clare and left the house.

Kate went downstairs into the kitchen. The only sound was the ticking of the clock on the mantelpiece. She was alone. She sat down on a chair by the fire and looked around her. The kitchen was quite large, very warm and comfortable. The multi coloured rag rug she had pegged herself added a touch of colour to the blue/black slate floor. An old rocking chair stood near the window and an old oak dresser took up most of the opposite wall. A miscellaneous collection of dishes, plates, cups and saucers etc., were displayed on the shelves above it. A large oak table and six chairs stood in the middle of the floor.

She closed her eyes and memories of the past came tumbling over each other. The kitchen had been the scene of so many happenings in her and Martin's life, how she wished he was here now to share the life she had. After they married all their money was spent on the farm. The marital bed had been a present from his family, a rickety old table and a couple of rickety chairs were the only furniture they possessed. The oak dresser, table and chairs had been bought cheaply at an auction at least 10 years after they married. They could only afford one fire and as the bedroom was too cold without a fire, they had set up the bed in the corner of the kitchen by the fireplace. It was cosy and warm when they held each other close; they were the happiest couple in the whole of Ireland. Martin had made the rocking chair and also a cradle when Michael was born. They didn't think they would have any more children, but then when they least expected it, Clare was conceived, God had blessed them with another child. She could still see him clearly, as he lifted Michael or Clare when they were babies, his large hands calloused with hard work. Many a time he had carried the baby in the cradle down to the fields, she and Martin had to do all the work themselves in those days. It had been very hard, but their love for each other grew stronger and that made everything worthwhile. I'll ask Father O'Conner to say some Masses for Martin and I'll put fresh flowers on his grave, Kate promised herself. She could hear Molly banging around in the yard and went out to see what she was doing. 'Have you fed the chickens and the pigs Molly?' she asked 'Yes, she replied and I have some eggs too'. 'Good girl, leave them in the dairy and come down with me to the fields, I may need some help with the cows'. When Kate and Molly returned to the house, Kate gave Molly her present she bought while in Dublin. Molly's face lit up as she wrapped the shawl around her shoulders. Dinner was ready; Michael came into the kitchen and gave his mam a kiss. Paddy and Sean had already left. 'Michael did you and the twins have a good time in Dublin? she asked. I suppose you spent most of the time in Doyle's pub?' 'Yes sure, we did just that he replied. We had a grand time. How did you and Clare spend your day?' 'We did some shopping and Clare and Bridget spent the afternoon at a concert and then we had dinner together. Declan couldn't make it, he was called away so a friend of his, Finbar Delaney escorted them home.. I spent most of the morning on business, arranging supplies. Clare arrived home a few minutes later and sat down at the table. Kate then sat down herself and they enjoyed the potatoes, bacon and cabbage especially Michael, who had heaps. Clare said teasingly 'it's a wonder you're not fat with all the food you eat, you must have hollow legs'. Michael just laughed and continued eating, he was hungry.

When dinner was finished Clare tidied up the kitchen. Michael heaped more peat on the fire and banked it so it would burn slowly throughout the night. Kate picked up a lamp 'I'm rather tired son, I think I will go to bed, God Bless'. Clare decided she also would retire to bed. Michael settled down for a final cigarette, he had a lot of things to think about.

It wasn't difficult for Michael, Paddy and Sean to get away on Friday night. Friday was the night they played cards in the backroom of Doyle's' pub until the early hours of the morning. They left at their usual time so that no questions would be asked. They had plenty of time to pick up Rory where they had arranged to meet. They should be at the place where the dance was being held just before 9.00pm. They didn't want to arrive too early in case they were spotted. Time was important. Sean drove the cart around the back of the building and hoped no-one would notice. What they had to do wouldn't take too long if everything went to plan? 'Remember now, we stick to the plan and from now on not one whisper said Michael. Blunt is a highly trained soldier, he might recognise our voices and we might just let slip a name'. Sean stayed with the cart and the other three climbed over the wall, landing on the other side on their hands and knees. Fortunately for them, they were in a garden. It was quite dark but they could hear music wafting through the open windows. Michael took out his watch, it was nearly 9.00 pm. They crawled forward towards the front of the building, keeping well into the shadows as they needed to be able to see the front door. As Michael was crawling along he was hoping Rosie had been successful, if she had, Blunt should be standing near the front door. Michael could see them now, they were both laughing.

Shortly afterwards, they saw Rosie say something to him and turn around and go inside. They waited until the door closed behind her and luck was with them, Blunt had turned to look at her and had his back to them. The boys moved swiftly, Michael stuffed a gag in his mouth and locked his arm around Blunt's throat. Rory tied the blindfold and Paddy tied his hands behind his back. Blunt struggled but it wasn't much use with Paddy on one side of him and Rory on the other. Michael pushed him from behind when they thought it necessary. Sean had tethered the horse and stood on the cart waiting for them. As Michael was the tallest he climbed over the wall, landing on the cart. Michael and Sean then leaned over the wall and as Rory and Paddy pushed Blunt, they pulled him over the wall into the cart, then helped the other two over the wall into the cart. Sean drove off in silence out of Dublin and once on the country road turned down a lane that led to nowhere. It was a cul-de-sac and surrounded by fields, not a house was in sight. Sean tethered the horse and the four men jumped down off the cart and dragged Blunt after them. They 'frog marched' him to the end of the field, out of sight. Michael pulled an old sock over his head; he had cut slits in it for his eyes, nose and mouth and then motioned to them to go away and waited until they were out of sight. After untying Blunt's hands, Michael removed the gag from his mouth and finally the blindfold. The two men faced each other and Michael unleashed his fury! And left Blunt lying there. When they were out of earshot, Michael remarked 'I'm thinking Blunt will have a bit of explaining to do, if and when, he returns to the Barracks. I wish I could have killed him, I wanted to but we had all agreed to stick with the plan and it's better this way. We can all work harder for the 'Cause' and there may be another time'. Paddy and Sean agreed. 'I feel that my sister's death has been partly avenged, God rest her soul Rory said'. The boys made good time to Doyle's arriving at their usual time and after ordering drinks they made their way to the back room and joined a card game. Doyle brought the drinks himself and as he set them down on the table he looked questioningly at Michael. Michael nodded his head slightly and carried on playing cards. Doyle understood!

Later, as Michael thought about everything that had happened, he wondered if there would be an outcry by the Army if Blunt was found or turned up. After considering all the possibilities he decided it was too risky for them to do too much. The Commanding Officer of the Battalion stationed in the area would probably suspect he and Rory had something to do with it? After all, they had suggested a connection between one of his soldiers and the murder. An English soldier, Michael reasoned, hated by all the Irish people, had been battered unconscious to within an inch of his life but he had not been killed, there was the difference. The Commanding Officer would go through the motions of an investigation and then let the matter drop. As everyone knows, in any army, the golden rule is 'don't get caught'.

Clare sorted through the letters. Most of them were business letters, one addressed to her but she couldn't recognise the handwriting. Turning the envelope over to see if there was a forwarding address. There was none. As she opened the letter it began, Dear Clare, before reading it she looked at the signature. Declan's! why would Declan be writing to her, she wondered? After reading the letter a second time to make sure she had read it correctly, she wondered why Declan had said he had something very important to discuss with her and would see her on Sunday. What on earth could it be? she asked herself. She gave up guessing and went into the kitchen and gave the letter to her mother. Kate read the letter and a thought crossed her mind. Perhaps Declan was interested in Clare, other than as a friend? She dismissed the thought as wishful thinking and asked 'did Bridget say anything which would give you any idea what he wants to talk to you about?' 'No, answered Clare. Sure we'll find out soon enough'.

Clare chose her outfit very carefully on Sunday morning. She liked Declan and wanted to look her best. She finally chose a navy blue dress and jacket trimmed with pale blue and a bonnet to match. The previous night she had spent extra time brushing her long, thick hair until it shone like burnished copper. She finished dressing and went downstairs to join the family. After Mass, Clare spent some time chatting to a group of young people all dressed in their 'Sunday Best' then joined her mother who was chatting to Mrs. Kelly. They said their goodbye's and walked home. Kate needed to put the final touches to the dinner she had prepared. Clare set the table using the matching china and the best cutlery; she was satisfied with the result and sat down to wait for Declan. Clare heard the sound of horse's hooves past the kitchen window and went out to meet him. Declan greeted her as he normally did and teased her, as usual, about her 'red hair'. She laughed and walked with him as he led the horse to the field. Declan walked over to Dusty who was 'in foal' and ran his hand over her belly. 'I'll take another look at her the next time I'm over' he said.

Michael had finished whatever he was doing in the barn and came over to join them. They all walked back to the house together. Kate greeted Declan warmly and after a few minutes chat served lunch. After lunch, Clare and Declan left her mother and brother in the kitchen and went into the front parlour. This was Kate's pride and joy. All her best furniture and ornaments were displayed there. Clare poured Declan a cup of tea and waited for him to explain his letter. 'Clare he began, I've decided to make some changes in my life and I'm wondering if you would think about being part of it? I need more time for myself, at the moment I seem to be working night and day. I've decided to take a partner into my practice, that way, I should halve my work'. Clare listened politely and wondered what all this had to do with her. She realised he was still speaking so she tried to concentrate. 'We've known each other for some years now, to be sure only as friends but I have always held you in high regard and admired you, not only for your beauty, you are very dear to me'. He stopped speaking for a few minutes then asked, 'Clare, will you marry me?' She nearly dropped the cup and saucer she held in her hand and looked at him in astonishment and disbelief. 'Indeed, I know you will need time to think about it, there is no rush. I don't expect you to give me an answer right now he exclaimed. I'm thinking we should see much of each other over the next six months, with the understanding that at the end of that period, you will give me your answer'. Clare just stared at him, she was speechless. Holy Mother of God help me, she silently prayed. She could hardly think as she walked over to the window and looked out at the farm. What had Declan actually said? I have always admired you and you are very dear to me, Not I love you or I'm in love with you. Was friendship enough, she wondered? She knew she had always wanted more from Declan than friendship and had no doubt, given the right circumstances, she would fall in love with him before they married. What about Declan? what if his feelings for her didn't change and he only 'admired' her? That was what she had to find out. She knew other men found her beautiful and attractive, at 19 years of age she had attended many social functions. She had a choice. Clare turned around and walked over to where he sat, smiled at him and stretched out both hands. Declan stood up and grasped hold of them firmly in his. 'I've thought about what you have suggested and I agree to see more of you. During that time, I will decide whether I want to marry you. In six months time, I will give you my answer'. 'Thank you Clare' he said. 'Shall we tell the family our news?' Clare asked. Walking into the kitchen, smiling at each other, Clare explained the situation, both Kate and Michael were very pleased. It was good news! Michael gave his sister a bear hug and said 'see that you take good care of her Declan' as he shook his hand. 'It will be nice seeing you more often Declan', Kate said. Clare waited until Declan returned from bringing his horse around to the front of the house, then joined him outside. Declan took Clare's hand in his and kissed them mounted his horse and said. 'I'll be over to see you next week'. Clare watched him until he was out of sight.

Declan had arranged to go home for dinner on the Monday evening following his visit to Clare and looked forward to telling his family the news. When dinner was nearly finished he said 'I have some news'. I'm going to take a partner. I have asked Clare to marry me'. Astonishment, surprise and pleasure showed on their faces. Bridget was the first to react and jumped up from the table and hugged him saying 'my best friend is going to marry my favourite brother'. Declan laughed 'You only have one brother Bridget' he said. Declan's mother and father were delighted and congratulated him. They were all convinced Clare would say Yes!.

The O'Reilly's were a close-knit family. Mary and John were proud of their children and only wanted the best for them. 'Clare's a lovely girl, I couldn't ask for a more suitable daughter-in-law, don't you agree John?' 'yes, she is a beautiful girl, I know

Bridget is delighted' he answered. 'I wonder what I will wear to the wedding?' 'I'm sure you will find something nice, goodnight dear' he remarked. It was very strange, he thought as he drifted off to sleep, that the most sensible of women seemed to go into a spin when a wedding was in the offing. Thank God all I have to wear is a suit!.

Finbar and Declan met at their usual place, Doyle's, during the week and looked forward to a relaxing evening. After a few drinks Declan said 'I've some news for you'. 'What sort of news?' Finbar asked. 'I've decided to get married'. Finbar thought it was a very sound idea and asked when all of this will happen. 'Probably sometime next year, I want to look around for a suitable house. I have saved the best bit of news until the last though said Declan. It is Clare O'Hara that I asked to marry me and I hope she will give me her answer in six months'. 'I wish you all the best, Clare is a lovely girl' Finbar said, 'now let's have another drink to celebrate'.

Michael and the twins were on their way to Doyle's, it was Friday night and Paddy said 'We haven't heard a whisper about Blunt, do you think he got back to the barracks?' 'Well one way or another I'm sure he got back. Perhaps Doyle will have some news for us' answered Michael. Finding a vacant table at Doyle's they sat down and ordered drinks. The Pub was full on Friday night so Doyle brought the drinks over himself. He chatted and joked with them for a few minutes and as he turned to leave slipped a note into Michael's hand. Michael finished his drink and made his way to the toilet outside. He looked around carefully to see if there was anyone else there but he couldn't see anyone. By the dim light shining through the window he read the note.

The Army have been asking questions, wrote Doyle. I told them you were all here playing cards. They know nothing, but you can expect a visit. Michael tore the note into shreds and flushed it down the toilet and made his way back to the table and spoke quietly to Paddy and Sean. 'The Army has been asking questions about Blunt. Doyle told them we were all here playing cards, but said we could expect a visit'.

Suddenly the level of noise in the bar dropped. Michael looked around and saw two Military Policemen walk through the door. Looking at Paddy and Sean he said 'remember boyo's, they know nothing!' Everyone watched as the two M.P's approached Doyle and spoke to him. He turned and nodded his head in Michael's direction. When the two M.P's reached their table, the three men looked up enquiringly.

'Which one of you is Michael O'Hara?' one MP asked. 'Ah! Sure that's me' Michael replied. 'I need to ask you some questions, come with me' the M.P' said. Michael looked at him and asked 'what kind of questions and about what?' 'We will tell you in private' the M.P. replied. 'Indeed, you'll tell me now, or I'll not move from this table', Michael replied angrily. The M.P. moved threatenly towards Michael but his companion stopped him, saying 'It's a routine matter, a soldier was hurt recently and our Commanding Officer remembered you and thought you might be able to help us in our enquiries'. 'You're Commanding Officer thought I could help you? 'I'll come with you' he said smoothly. Michael and the two M.P's made their way to the back room. He could feel all eyes on him as he crossed the floor and sat down and lit a cigarette. 'When you came to our C.O. you were with two other men, who were they?' the M.P. asked. 'One was the father of my fiancé Mr. Flanagan. the other was her brother' Michael exclaimed. 'So what was the connection between your fiancé's death and the Army?' 'When they examined her body, they found among her clothes a small button, exactly the same as those on a soldier's uniforms. Your Commanding Officer was very polite and anxious to help in any way he could and said he would make some enquiries and inform us if necessary, we were very grateful to him'. Michael explained. He noticed a glance pass between the two M.P's. 'Another question, do you and your friends come to Doyle's often?'. 'To be sure we do, we play cards here every Friday night'. 'I see', the M.P. said and turned to his companion. 'I think we have finished here'. The two M.P's left the room and Michael followed them, as they reached the bar all eyes turned on them. The two M.P's left the pub and Michael rejoined Sean and Paddy and explained the M.P's wanted to know why and who? had been at the interview with their Commanding Officer. 'Sure they know nothing, they're only fishing, I even said we were grateful to the Commanding Officer for his help 'God forgive me. I need this', he said as he finished his drink.

The danger had passed- for the moment he thought. Michael, Paddy and Sean entered the kitchen and sat down at the table ready for the breakfast Kate had already prepared for them. The conversation centred on various aspects of the farm. i.e. How the piglets were doing, the new calves and the potatoes and vegetables. Suddenly, Michael jumped up from the table and said 'Ma, I've a letter for you from Mr. O'Shaughnessy, I'll run upstairs and get it' Kate opened the envelope and pulled out an Invitation 'We are invited to a private 18th birthday party for their daughter Eileen. It will be held at the Connaught Hotel'. 'It's only two weeks away ' said Clare'. I'll ask Declan to escort me and maybe Finbar could escort Bridget?' 'Will you be going Ma' Michael asked?' 'No, I don't think so son, I'm getting a bit old for jaunts' Kate answered. 'Will you ask your Da to come in to help on that afternoon? she asked the twins. 'I'll do that Mrs. O'Hara' Paddy answered. They all knew that the party was to raise funds for 'The Cause'. It was necessary for many reasons to disguise that fact. Donations would be forwarded through the usual channels.

It was Saturday afternoon and Kate sat down to rest. Declan was calling for Clare and they off to Dublin for the weekend to attend the birthday party the family had been invited to. She heard Clare call 'mammy for God's sake come up here and help me, I'm struggling to pack my evening gown, it will be so creased. I'll never be able to wear it and Declan should be here soon'. 'There now that should do the trick' Kate said as she closed the case, just remember to hang it up as soon as you get to Declan's, any creases will have dropped out by the party on Monday'. They carried the cases downstairs and Clare helped herself to a cup of tea. Declan arrived and walked into the kitchen, he greeted Kate and kissed Clare on the head. Declan took the luggage to the carriage as Clare said goodbye to her mam. Kate watched as the carriage disappeared down the road to Dublin. After Declan had carried Clare's luggage to the bedroom he came running down the stairs, kissed her on the cheek and said 'I'll be back in time for dinner, I've a few calls to make' and left the house. Bridget helped Clare unpack her clothes and admired her beautiful gown. Bridget held up her own gown 'sure Finbar won't be able to take his eyes off you Clare said'. 'Is Michael going to the party?' asked Mrs. O'Reilly. 'Of course, Michael wouldn't miss a chance of enjoying himself, he loves parties and lots of people. Paddy and Sean are also invited, that means everyone will have a good time' Clare answered. 'I've not been to a party with Finbar before'. Bridget said. I hope when we are dancing, he dances on the floor and not on my feet!. They all laughed then Bridget played the piano for them, she was an excellent pianist. After Mass on Sunday Declan took Clare to see the house he had leased. As he helped her down from the carriage, Clare looked at it. It was tall and narrow, three stories high. A short flight of steps led up to the front door. 'Let's just take a walk around the area, so that you have some idea of what it's like', Declan said and tucked her arm in his. They walked for some time and then returned to the house. Declan unlocked the door and stepped inside, holding the door open for Clare. The hall was quite long and narrow, on either side of the hall were two large rooms and door at the end. Declan opened it and Clare saw a small walled garden. 'How lovely Declan, I'll plant more trees and flowers, sure it will be a grand place to sit when the weather is warm. They climbed the stairs to the 1st floor, the rooms were very large and Declan explained that they would be altered to provide a bathroom and sitting room as well as a bedroom. They climbed the next flight of stairs and explained that two of the rooms would be turned into a large bedroom for Tom. his partner in the Practice. The attic would be renovated to provide a bedroom so the local girl could live-in as a maid and he has arranged for a local woman Ms. Casey to come in every day. 'You will meet all of them when you come up again next weekend.' Clare walked over to the window and looked out over the chimneys and roof tops of Dublin. In the distance she caught a glimpse of the Liffey river. 'It's a grand house Declan' she said.

Bridget and Clare spent the next afternoon preparing for the party. They both wanted to look their best. They laced each other's corsets and chose the jewellery they would wear. They pirouetted in front of the mirror and were very pleased with their reflections. 'You both look beautiful,' sure Declan and Finbar will be proud of you' Bridget's mother said. I'll let the boys know you are ready'. Clare giggled and said 'let's show them how poised we are and descend the stairs slowly, we'll make an entrance'. They both stood on the landing looking down on Declan and Finbar.

Declan was average height and his hair, his very fair. Finbar on the other hand was tall and broad with very dark hair. The both looked very distinguished in their evening clothes. Bridget and Clare descended the stairs as slowly and gracefully as they could, they wanted the men to really notice them. They did!. Declan thought Clare looked dazzling. Her gown of Ivory silk complimented her creamy complexion and beautiful hair. She wore a single strand of pearls around her throat and a matching pearl ornament in her hair. Walking quickly over to the foot of the stairs he said 'I've never seen you look so beautiful Clare'. 'Thank you Declan' she said giving him a dazzling smile.

Finbar looked stunned. This beautiful woman wasn't the same Bridget he had known for years. In her gown of white lace and satin she looked radiant. She wore a necklace of crystal and a matching hair ornament. Taking hold of her gloved hand Finbar said 'you look lovely'. They joined Michael and his friends and after speaking to Mr. & Mrs. O'Shaughnessy Michael whisked Clare away to introduce her to more of his friends, including 'The Tommy Doyle'. Clare realised he was not at all what she had expected him to be but was very charming. They had wonderful night and danced the night away. Soon it was time to take leave of their hosts. Declan and Finbar collected Clare and Bridget's evening shawls and made their way to the front of the hotel to wait for a cab.

After arriving home the girls climbed the stairs to their bedroom. 'Wasn't that a grand party Bridget did you enjoy yourself? asked Clare. 'I had a wonderful time Clare but do you understand men? I don't know what to make of them at all'. Clare looked at her and wondered what she was trying to say, 'Finbar has asked me to marry him, he is going to speak to Da. tomorrow morning Bridget said. Clare put down her brush and hugged her friend and said. 'Sure that's the best news I've heard since Declan asked me to marry him'. 'In answer to your earlier question about men, No! I don't understand them either'. They both laughed and slipped into their beds. As soon as their heads touched the pillows, they were both asleep.

Clare sat down at the small table in her bedroom and picked up her pen. She opened her Diary and wrote:

December 1st 1888

It is now three months since Declan asked me to marry him. We have spent as much time as possible together. His behaviour towards me is different, although he still treats me as a dear friend. However, there is much more warmth in our relationship. He laughs a lot more and seems to be more relaxed when he is with me. All is going well, I have, as I knew I would, fallen in love. I have decided to accept Declan's offer of marriage. Of course, I shall not tell him of my decision until the six months have passed.

The weeks leading up to Christmas were always hectic on the farm. Michael, Paddy and Sean worked day and night to fill Christmas orders, a well as the standing order for the Connaught Hotel. Molly helped by plucking the feathers off the chickens and packing the eggs in boxes. Clare and Kate helped as much as they could but each had their own work to do. Kate was especially busy, she always cooked extra puddings and cakes to give to the Priest to distribute to some of the villagers as well as a few chickens and eggs. She was always acutely aware of the poverty in the village, she had been there, so to speak, many times herself and little enough as it was that she provided she knew it was better than nothing. It was pitiful how some of the families struggled. However, it did not mean that because they were poor, they had lost their dignity. She always remembered how poor she and Martin had been when they were first married – only their families knew 'how' poor!.

Clare stood on a stool as she placed Holly with lots of red berries, behind the picture in the front parlour. 'Mam she said. Declan will be over to see me sometime tomorrow, I'll be asking him to spend Christmas with us here at the farm. There is something magical about Christmas and I want to spend this Christmas at home, with all the people I love'. Kate smiled, she hadn't realised what she said, but Kate now knew that she would say 'Yes' to Declan when the time came. They finished arranging the room and then stood back to admire their handiwork. 'Doesn't it look lovely' Clare said. 'Indeed it does' Kate answered.

The following afternoon, Declan arrived as promised and suggested to Clare they take a stroll around the farm. She wrapped a shawl around her shoulders before going outside. It was a cold day, but a dry winter sun did it's best to shine as they walked arm in arm for some time. Clare caught up with all the news regarding Bridget. 'Declan, Christmas is very special to me, I love every minute of it. I was wondering if you would spend Christmas with me, here at the farm?' Declan looked down at her, smiled and said 'Indeed I will' he put his arms around her and held her close. Looking into Clare's face, what he saw there told him all he needed to know and kissed her on the forehead. Clare then pulled away and looked up at him and said 'I love you Declan' They held each other close for a few more minutes then Declan burst out laughing. 'Sure I can't even remember what we were talking about'. Clare laughed and said 'Christmas Declan, Christmas.' They walked together for some time and chatted about their future. Declan explained he loved the countryside and his job as a Veterinary Surgeon, he loved working with animals. 'I think we should go back to the house now, it's rather cold' Clare said. They walked into the kitchen together and sat down by the fire. Clare told her mam that she had asked Declan to spend Christmas with the family and he had accepted. Kate was delighted. Suddenly Declan stood up and handed a letter to Kate and apologised for not giving it to her earlier. After reading the letter Kate asked Declan to take her reply to his parents as they have invited her to spend New Year with them, 'they are very kind'.

Kate was very proud of the fact that she could read and write. When she and Martin married, they were both illiterate. Neither of them had attended school. They both had to work from an early age. Martin had signed the Leasehold with an X. She remembered the evening when it all changed for the better. Martin had brought a present home from Dublin for Michael, he was 7 years old. It was a children's book on animals. Michael had been attending the village school since he was five years old and could read and write. He had been so excited, he couldn't wait to read it himself and then asked his father to read it to him. Martin told him he was busy, but would read it to him later. Michael then asked her to read it to him. She and Martin had looked at each other, an unspoken question hung in the air. She decided to tell him the truth, after all, it wasn't their fault they couldn't read or write.

She had explained to Michael that she and his father were very, very, poor and their help had been needed to keep the family's body and soul together so they could not attend school. Michael had looked at her and then at his father and said. 'I'll teach you and Da. how to read and write It's easy'. Some weeks later Martin brought home three slates and some chalk and each evening for an hour or so, Michael wrote out the alphabet on his slate and they copied it on their slates. Michael sounded the letters for them. Gradually and laboriously over the months they made progress. Soon they were able to write simple words and read them. Michael didn't seem to notice that it was an unusual situation, he was very pleased they could read and write a little. Kate remembered the first time she and Martin had signed their names to a business agreement, it had made such a difference to them. Over the years they had become avid readers of anything and everything until eventually they became selective in their choice of reading. Kate sat down at the table and wrote a very nice letter to Declan's parents accepting their kind invitation to spend New Year with them, then handed it to Declan.

It was cold and frosty, the night air was sharp on their faces as the family and Declan walked to Church on Christmas Eve to attend Midnight Mass. Clare and Declan walked arm in arm and chatted happily. 'Don't you just love Christmas' Clare asked Declan. 'Well, to be sure this Christmas is very different, I'm beginning to realise all I have missed'. They reached the small grey stone Church and Michael opened the door for them. The church was nearly full, but they found seats and sat down, most of the population of the village were already seated. There would be stragglers as usual, but they would stand at the back, trying to merge with the stonework hoping that Fr. O'Connor would not recognise them.

The small church was lit by candles, it seemed to shimmer in the candlelight. Large ones were placed each side of the altar, smaller ones on the altar, and much smaller one in front of a statue of Our Lady and of course, lots in front of a statue of St.Patrick. The lingering scent of Incense hung in the air. At the foot of the Altar was placed a small wooden crib filled with straw. At midnight, Fr. O'Connor would place a small figure of the Christ child in it. The congregation would sing a hymn and the Mass of Christmas 1888, would begin.

Christmas passed very pleasantly for the whole family. Kate entertained a few guests and Clare and Declan spent as much time together as possible. A few days after Christmas a few of Michael's friends, including Paddy and Sean popped in for a few 'jars'. Bridget's parents, Mary and John made Kate and of course Clare, very welcome. It was the first time both families had spent time together since Declan had proposed to Clare, and Finbar and Bridget were now officially courting. New Years Day 1889 was celebrated with a toast to the New Year and to the future of the two young couples. It was a very happy occasion. Molly's father always kept his eye on the farm, he fed the pigs, chickens and milked the cows, leaving Michael free to spend New Year in Dublin.

'Wake up! Ma. Wake up!' Michael said and shook his mother by the shoulders. Kate opened her eyes and saw Michael by her bed, a lamp in his hand. She sat up and asked 'What's wrong son?' 'Sure it's Dusty, she can't deliver her foal, I need help Ma'. Kate was fully awake now and told him to take the old red blanket from the chest and fill a bucket with hot water. 'Go back to her and do nothing except hold her head and talk to her I'll be down as soon as I'm dressed, Oh! leave the lantern on the table for me'.

Kate slipped an old dress over her nightgown, wrapped a thick shawl around her shoulders and went downstairs as quickly as she could. Taking a large jar of goose fat from the kitchen cupboard and putting some old towels in a basket. She picked up the lantern and walked to the door, pulled her boots up then set off for Dusty's stall. Hanging the lantern on a nail, she took over from Michael. Speaking soothingly to Dusty and stroking her head she then ran her hand over the mare's belly. Dusty struggled but she was too exhausted to do much harm. Kate moved her hand over Dusty's belly again, this time she pressed very hard. She stopped and said. 'I know what it is son, the foal's legs are stuck. I'll have to try and turn it, talk to her and hold her down'. Kate rolled up her sleeves and rubbed grease on her hands and arms, then set to work. She pushed and pulled as firmly as possible. Michael had a hard time with Dusty. Suddenly Kate felt the foal move and said. 'let her go son'. Fifteen minutes later, the foal dropped out. They watched as it struggled to it's feet. Dusty took over, she licked her foal lovingly and soon the foal was nuzzling at Dusty's teats, all was well!. As she closed the stall behind her Kate asked 'what shall we call him?' 'Sure he's lucky to be here at all, we'll call him 'Lucky' he answered. They both looked over at 'Mother and Son' doing what came naturally. Michael put his arm around his mother's shoulders and said 'Ma, sure you're a wonder! how in

God's name did you know what to do ?'

'Well son! you're Da and I couldn't pay for a Vet, if anything went wrong when we were first married and had the farm, we learnt the hard way . We lost some calves and foals, but we kept on trying and learnt as we went along. We had nothing to lose, without our help the animals would have died anyway'. Kate took off her outdoor clothes and filled a basin with hot water from the kettle. She washed her arms and hands thoroughly. 'Goodnight son', she said as she climbed the stairs, 'Goodnight Ma' he replied.

One morning Kate, Michael, Sean, Paddy and Molly had nearly finished breakfast when Michael asked to be left alone with his mam to discuss some business. Kate looked quizzically at her son and asked. 'What business do we have to discuss Michael?' 'Ma! I have some grand news. The Irish National League are giving a party in honour of Mr. Parnell, here, in Dublin. I have been invited and I'll take you with me', he declared. 'Holy Mother of God! Kate exclaimed and blessed herself. Throwing her hands up in the air in surprise and delight she said with a twinkle in her eye: 'Sure he's a great patriot.

Michael smiled and explained: 'It's a private party to be held in a large house in Dublin. The Irish National League want to pay tribute to Mr. Parnell for all the work he has done to help the tenants resist the pressure of eviction by the absentee landlords. All donations go to the usual cause'. 'When is the party?' she asked. 'Next Friday evening, I've booked two rooms for us at the Connaught Hotel, we will stay the night in Dublin. No-one is to know about Mr. Parnell's presence, not even Clare. I'll think of some other reason, perhaps a business function?', he answered. 'It will be an honour to meet the great man. I have always admired his courage, sure he's a man after my own heart' she declared with conviction. Michael left the table and walked towards the door just as Molly entered the kitchen carrying a large cheese. 'Here Molly, let me carry that cheese for you' he said as he took the cheese and placed it on the dresser. Molly followed him 'you're a lovely man, Michael sure you are'. 'You're a grand girl yourself Molly' he said gently and left the house.

Knocking on the door of his mother's room in the hotel Michael walked in. 'Ma are you nearly dressed, it's time to leave?' 'In a minute' she called from the small dressing room. Kate looked in the mirror and checked her reflection, she wanted Michael to be proud of her tonight. She pirouetted to check her skirt and petticoat length and was satisfied, then picked up her evening shawl and purse and walked into the bedroom where Michael waited for her. As he looked at his mother, he thought she looked beautiful and felt so proud and told her so. Kate just smiled. 'I've a cab waiting for us' he said as they left the room and closed the door behind them. Kate locked the door and they went downstairs filled with anticipation of the magical evening ahead of them.

March 1st, 1889

Diary Entry

(Clare)

It is now six months since Declan asked me to marry him. Soon he will come and ask me again formally. I shall say yes. I love Declan, and I hope I make his life full and happy. I am his first girl friend perhaps that is why he seems to be holding back? I do hope he will tell me he loves me, in his own words. I know I shouldn't be thinking about babies, but I want a large family, and as Declan is a good strong man there will be no problem with that!.

Clare left school a little earlier than usual. She knew Declan would ride over to see her today, sometime in the afternoon. Today she will give him her answer. When she entered the house, there was no-one there. Outside she could see Molly feeding the chickens and Michael, Paddy and Sean moving among the cows in one of the fields. I wonder where mother is, she thought? as she climbed the stairs to remove her outdoor clothes and freshen up. Hearing the sound of horses outside she looked out and Declan walked into the kitchen and came over to where she was sitting, gave her a kiss on the cheek then took both of hands and said 'Clare, will you marry me?' 'Yes, Declan I will', she answered. Taking a small box from his pocket he handed it to her. Clare tried to open it but her fingers didn't seem to work very well. Finally she managed and nestling inside was a beautiful ring. A large Emerald surrounded by sparkling diamonds. 'Here, let me put it on your finger where it belongs' and took her in his arms and hugged her. Clare clung to him, leaving no doubt in his mind about her feelings for him.

Molly walked into the kitchen, Clare showed her the ring. 'It's lovely so it is' she said admiringly.. When Kate returned, Clare stretched out her hand to show off the ring. 'Sure it's beautiful dear, I'm delighted for you both' she said and hugged her. Taking a bottle of wine out of the cupboard Kate poured a little into three glasses. She lifted her glass saying 'I wish you both every happiness and may you always be as happy as you are today'. Kate prepared dinner while Clare and Declan discussed their future plans. When Michael walked into the kitchen Clare stretched out her hand to show him her ring. 'So! he said 'my baby sister is to be married, is she?' as he picked her up and swung her around. She laughed and said 'put me down Michael, sure you're making me dizzy'. Michael shook hands with Declan and said half jokingly , 'See now that you take good care of her. A toast' Michael said as he lifted his glass 'Slainte, may God Bless you both'. During dinner Declan explained that the alterations to the house would be finished by the end of the month and he proposed to move in with Tom, his partner in the office.

'Have you decided on a date for your wedding?' Kate enquired. 'Yes Mam' Clare answered 'August 16th. 'Sure a Summer wedding will be lovely, so soon, I won't have my young sister nagging me about the amount of food I eat' Michael teased. 'Ah! go on with you now' she answered and laughed. Michael looked at her as she smiled at something Declan said. He had never seen her look so beautiful and so happy. He had always taken care of her because he was so much older. I'll miss her very much he thought.

Memories of the past flooded back and suddenly Michael felt empty hearted, he missed Moira so much. No other girl could ever take her place. Declan left soon after dinner and Clare walked with him to the door. Taking her in his arms, he kissed her on the cheek then mounted his horse and said 'My family will be delighted that you have said Yes'. 'God speed ' she said fervently.

Looking at her ring sparkling in the lamp light she thought it's really going to happen. I am soon to be Mrs. Declan O'Reilly. Later, as Kate brushed her hair she thought about Clare. She was very pleased Clare was happy and nearly settled. Declan was a good man and would give her a good home and eventually a family of her own, but there is something I can't put my finger on, she thought to herself, and then pushed it to the back of her mind. Thank God she would never know the poverty she had endured when she was first married. I'll miss her all the same she thought, as she wiped the tears from her eyes. Her last thought was how pleased Martin would be as she drifted off to sleep.

Clare spent a lot of time in Dublin during the six months before her wedding. She chose furnishings for their new home and Declan gave her a free hand and was delighted with the result. She stayed with her future in-laws and shared Bridget's bedroom, as usual. The talked long into the night about wedding dresses, going away outfits and Bridget's bridesmaid dress. The also talked about men, in particular, the marriage act. They both understood what it entailed, but were not looking forward to it – at all. It was something good wives did for their husbands. As a close friend, Clare promised to tell Bridget 'Ah! Well, said Bridget. It can't be all that bad, sure you only have to look around at all the children there are in Ireland to know that'. They both laughed so much, it hurt!.

Clare's mother arranged to have the Wedding Breakfast at the Connaught Hotel. Mr. Quinn was delighted and promised the best the hotel could provide. They chose the menu and left the rest in his capable hands Clare also spent time having fittings for her wedding dress and going-away outfit. Declan had already organised the honeymoon, but was keeping it a secret.

The months flew past and soon it was time to send out the Invitations to the wedding. Clare and her mother discussed whom to invite. There was no problem with their immediate friends or Declan's. However, it was their neighbours in the village, Clare had known them all her life. Obviously it would be impossible to invite them all. They decided they would ask the Headmaster, with Father O'Connor's permission to use the school for a separate celebration. 'I'm sure they will say yes', she declared.

The week before her wedding Clare and Bridget had the final fittings of their dresses. Clare's wedding dress and going-away outfit fitted perfectly. Bridget was pleased with her dress also, she had chosen a very pale pink silk and it suited her colouring. Clare arranged for all the clothes to be delivered to the farm during the week, she wanted to be sure they were in safe keeping. Bridget would stay with her to help in the preparation. During the afternoon on the eve of her wedding, Clare, her mother and Bridget arranged the flowers in the church. When they had finished, the altar looked beautiful, the candles adding their own special charm. Clare placed a special vase of white roses in front of Our Lady's statue with a silent prayer. Everything was ready. Clare felt wonderful. Tomorrow she would marry Declan, her heart nearly burst at the thought of it.

August 16th dawned. It was a perfect summer day, the sun shone in a blue, cloudless sky. Clare awoke early and was wide awake when her mother came into her room to call her, slipping out of bed Clare gave her mother a big hug. 'I love you mammy' she said. 'Sure I know you do darlin, I love you too'. Molly has the water ready for your bath, I'll go and see if Bridget is awake' she replied. Her mother and Bridget put the final touches to her train and veil and stood back to admire her. Clare's beautiful auburn hair was piled high on top of her head and her veil was secured by a delightful head-dress of lily of the valley. The dress was white satin with a lace overlay, high necked with a fitted bodice and long tight sleeves. The beautifully draped skirt formed a train and around her throat she wore a choker of pearls, a gift from Michael. She carried a bouquet of pink roses and lily of the valley she looked absolutely beautiful. Choking back her tears her mother said 'sure there's not a more beautiful bride in all Ireland'. Bridget joined Michael, who looked very handsome, and Molly at the foot of the stairs to wait for Clare. They all watched as she slowly descended the stairs. Michael kissed her on the cheek and said proudly. 'Mother of God, but you're a picture Clare', Molly burst into tears 'Sure you look lovely so you do. I' have to be off now, I'll see you in the church darlin' Kate said..

Clare left her home on Michael's arm, Bridget followed behind holding her train for the short walk to the church. Bridget straightened her train and veil, she looked perfect. She could see Father O'Connor on the altar steps and walked down the aisle on Michael's arm to meet Declan. Father O'Conner began the Nuptial Mass. After saying their vows, Fr. O'Conner asked 'Who gives this woman to be married to this man?' Michael stepped forward and said 'I do'. Fr. O'Conner asked ' do you know of any impediment why you may not be lawfully joined together in Holy Matrimony, speak now'. There was no reply from Clare and Declan and he placed the ring on Clare's finger. Bridget handed Clare her bouquet and on Declan's arm she walked down the aisle of the little stone church, radiantly happy as Mrs. Declan O'Reilly. When she reached the doorway of the church, a little girl handed her a small posy of wild flowers.

The bride and groom left for Dublin with the sound of cheers and best wishes ringing in their ears. When they reached the Hotel Clare gasped in astonishment at the floral decorations. On a table in the centre of the room, stood a magnificent wedding cake, surrounded by place settings. After the photographs had been taken, Mr. Quinn escorted them to their places then signalled his staff to serve the food and wine. Later, Clare and Declan led the way into an adjoining room where a String Quartet played very softly. She lifted her train and veil and slipped into Declan's arms as they led their guests onto the dance floor. Clare and Bridget slipped away into a room which had been placed at their disposal. Clare changed into a lilac silk outfit. The family all kissed Clare goodbye, then returned to the other guests, leaving the couple to slip away on their honeymoon. Michael and his mother left for home and agreed it had been a truly wonderful day.

As the carriage turned into the last stretch of road Clare caught sight of the sea. 'Declan!, she exclaimed, I've always wanted to visit Bray, how wonderful!' After dinner, they returned to their suite of rooms. Declan considered it more appropriate for the occasion that there should be more than just a bedroom. Declan handed Clare a glass of wine and sat down beside her on the sofa, raising his glass he toasted 'to us'. 'It's getting late Clare, I'm sure you are tired after today's events. I'll undress in the dressing room, I won't be very long'. He kissed her and left the room. When he returned, Clare was wearing a beautiful cream silk nightdress and peignoir, trimmed with lace and satin ribbon. She had loosened her hair and brushed it. It fell like a cloak below her waist. She was everything any man could ever desire in a woman. 'You look lovely' Declan said as he led her to the bed and climbed in after her. He blew out the lamp and took her into his arms. Sometime later, he whispered. 'hold on to me Clare'. When he entered her she buried her face in his shoulder, it wasn't quite what she thought it would be, but she was part of him now and she loved him so much. They both drifted off to sleep.

Molly was ready to leave when Kate said 'will you ask your Ma to come and see me tomorrow, Molly?' Mrs. Kelly arrived with Molly the next morning. She walked into the kitchen Kate asked her to sit down. Molly didn't wait to hear what Mrs. O'Hara had to say to her Ma, she had her work to do and that was more important to her. 'Has Molly done something wrong Mrs. O'Hara?' she asked anxiously. 'Molly is no problem at all, sure she's a grand girl, works hard and I'm very fond of her'. Kate assured her. 'It's yourself I want to speak to'. Mrs. Kelly heaved a sigh of relief and wondered what she wanted with her. 'I know you have plenty to do at home, but I need help in the house now that Clare is married and there is too much for one person. Molly can only help a little, she has plenty to do with work outside on the farm. I need someone to do the washing and help with the cleaning two days a week. Do you think you could manage that?' Mrs. Kelly thought a miracle had happened. 'To be sure I can she answered quickly. 'When would you want me to come?' 'Monday and Tuesday, as early as possible' Kate said as she walked her to the door.

As Kate cleaned Clare's room, she thought how much she missed her, but she was now married and was very happy. Maybe soon she would have a grandchild, it would be lovely to hold a baby in her arms again. Her thoughts turned to Michael, he still hadn't got over Moira's death and it nearly destroyed him. She wondered if he would ever marry? he now held the responsibility of the Leasehold on the farm. Martin's death had changed their lives in more ways than one.

Clare and Declan arrived home two weeks later. Mrs. Casey had everything in order, Clare thought her home looked beautiful and was glad to be home again. Tom joined them for dinner, he was a great raconteur, his stories of funny things that had happened to him as a Vet made them all laugh. Michael, Paddy and Sean surprised her on Friday night by calling in to see her on their way to Doyle's, she was delighted, she missed them so much. Bridget came over as soon as she could. They laughed and talked as they had always done before Clare was married. When Clare explained to her, as discreetly as a lady could, the marriage act, Bridget agreed that if that was all there was to it, she would be glad to marry Finbar. 'Let's have a family party' Clare said one evening when she and Declan were alone. We'll invite all the family'. Declan thought it would be lovely and he would check his diary. It was all arranged. Clare, Nora and Mrs. Casey went to a great deal of trouble to ensure that everything would be as perfect as possible. Clare wanted her first dinner party, in her own home to be a success and it was.

Kate was very proud of her daughter, she had proved to be a good hostess and Declan seemed very agreeable. Eight months had passed since Clare and Declan had married and Clare wondered if you would ever conceive a baby. They had not discussed a family and Clare wanted baby, it would be wonderful.

A few months later, Clare felt the need to see her mother; she hurried downstairs to the surgery and wondered if Declan had already left on his rounds. 'Declan, if you're using the carriage today, could you drop me off at the farm and pick me up on your way home?', she asked. She rushed upstairs and put on her outdoor clothes then picked up a few small gifts she had bought for the family while shopping in Dublin. Declan had only the time to greet Kate as he dropped Clare off, promising to call for her later in the afternoon. Kate was delighted to see Clare and when they were inside she said, 'you look wonderful, marriage certainly agrees with you. We've got seven new piglets and ten new calves, come with me down to the fields and take a look at them' Kate suggested. Clare tucked her arm inside her mother's and they strolled along, eventually they reached the sow. Clare watched as the piglets suckled. 'Aren't they just beautiful' she declared. 'let's go and see the new calves'. Kate pointed out a cow and her calf. They stood a little distance from the others. 'That calf is just a few hours old', Kate said. Clare watched as the cow moved away from her suckling calf, but the calf just followed her and when she stopped to graze, it began to suckle again. Clare and her mother sat down on the old bench as Clare looked around her. It was beautiful! There was new birth all around her she felt part of it. Soon, she thought, I will give birth to a child and provide another line in the timeless chain which linked generation to generation. past, present and future would all be embodied in the new gift of life. 'Mammy!' she exclaimed. 'I am having a baby, I'm so happy I think I'll burst', she threw her arms around her mother and hugged her. 'That's the best news I've had for years said Kate. At last I will soon be a grandmother, that's grand news, sure I'm delighted for you both' she said lovingly. 'It's our secret Mammy, I'll tell Declan tonight'.

When they were alone in their bedroom, Clare put her arms around Declan's neck and kissed him. She looked up at him and said, 'I've got some grand news for you'. 'Come on then, let's hear it' he said with a smile. 'I'm having a baby' she said joyfully. Clare felt his body stiffen and saw an expression on his face so fleeting, one blink of an eyelid and she would have missed it. Her heart nearly stopped beating, this wasn't the response she had expected from him. Something's wrong, she thought, but what? he released her, then turned away. When he turned to face her, she saw a hostile stranger. The blood drained from her body, she felt faint. Pulling herself together she waited for what was to come. 'Babies make a mess. They are always crying, always demanding attention' he declared savagely. 'It's your child Declan, I thought you would be pleased?' she said through her tears. 'Well!, I'm not pleased at all, I don't like babies, I didn't want a child', he shouted. Clare was no shrinking violet, she had been brought up by a mother who had fought to survive and the two men in her life, her father and her brother, had always treated her with the utmost respect. She would take nothing less from the husband who supposedly loved her. 'Don't you dare shout at me, I'm not deaf, sure it's a bit late to say you don't want a child Declan, you should have thought about the consequences of your actions a lot earlier, shouldn't you?' she answered sarcastically. 'I don't know why I ever married you? he replied. 'Well now, that's something I'm wondering myself'. He lifted his hand to strike her, then dropped it, Clare felt sick to her stomach. 'Well!, you have made yourself quite clear, you don't want a child. I don't know why you ever married me? obviously you don't want me. now, let me tell you something, I don't want you, this is the only child I will ever have by you. I will be your wife in name only from this night on. I don't care where you sleep , but to be sure, you'll not sleep in my bed again. If you ever raise your hand to me again, I will tell Michael the whole story, he will believe me'. His face was a cold mask of dislike for her. If he doesn't go soon, she thought, I will collapse.

Declan turned away and left the room. She locked the door behind him and collapsed on the bed sobbing until she could cry no more. She didn't understand what had happened, she felt confused. What sort of man didn't want his own child. However, that was not the point of the argument. It was the contempt and naked dislike she had seen on his face that distressed her. What had she done to deserve this treatment? she asked herself.

She knew the answer, nothing! It came solely from Declan. She thought they were happy together, now she was exhausted and wondered why he married her, he obviously did not love her. She wondered what to do, she couldn't leave him, no woman could survive socially if she left her husband. Holy Mother of God Help me, she prayed. The next morning she dressed very carefully, she did not want him to see her in anyway distressed from the previous night's events. Declan behaved as though nothing had happened when they met during the day. How could I not have seen him for the fraud that he is, she wondered?. After dinner, she excused herself saying she had a headache. She locked her bedroom door behind her and sat for some time in a chair, wondering if he would try to come in. He didn't and she eventually undressed and fell asleep.

Everyone was delighted when she announced she was having a baby. She watched Declan go through a pantomime of accepting congratulations. He let it be known that in future he would use the spare room, so that he would not disturb Clare, he was anxious about her health. Declan behaved as though nothing had ever ruffled the matrimonial waters and never lay with her again, presumably because she was thickening at the waist, she thought bitterly. She took comfort in the knowledge that at the end of the nine months, she would either hold a son or daughter in her arms, God willing, and no-one could take that away from her. The family did not suspect there was an estrangement between Clare and Declan, they both played their parts very well indeed.

She and Bridget shopped for material for maternity dresses and silk and satin for baby dresses and baby necessities. Clare ordered three dresses in different colours and also embroidered a beautiful Christening Gown, she was determined that their child would be welcomed into the world with love. The two doting grandmothers, Kate and Mary were busy crocheting and the spare room was being painted by Tom. The months passed quickly enough and soon the time of her confinement drew near so Mary, her mother-in-law came to stay. Kate couldn't leave the farm for too long, she would come when the baby decided it was time.

Clare was delivered a son on 18th January 1891 with a minimum of trouble. She immediately named him Daniel. Bridget's wedding went off beautifully. Clare invited her mother to stay for a day or two, she knew she loved being with Daniel. There was a strong bond already between grandmother and grandson. Finbar and Bridget had decided to live with her parents as the house was big enough. So the marriage of the two friends had not altered the situation between them. In fact, Clare realised she would see a lot more of Bridget now she was married. Finbar told Bridget he was going out with his colleague Des and a few friends for a few drinks at Doyle's and would hopefully not be too late and left the girls to do what girls do.

Doyle's was the favourite watering place of most of them, but Finbar, changed his mind' 'Let's just wander from pub to pub' he suggested. They ended up in a small pub tucked away in a cul-de-sac in a district near the Liffey. It was packed, a fiddler played jigs and reels. Then a young man with a wonderful voice sang a lovely ballad. They sat down and ordered drinks. During the course of the evening, for one reason or another, they had all changed places and Finbar found himself eventually, on the opposite side of the table. He lifted his glass to his mouth and stopped in mid air. Sitting in the far corner of the room was Declan with a young man about eighteen years of age. They were laughing and talking like old friends. He just stared at them until he felt a tug on his sleeve. 'God boyo!' you look as if you have seen a ghost' Des said. 'Ah! It's only the drink he replied. There was something about the two of them that disturbed him. He kept his eye on them and when he saw the young man say something to Declan, who nodded his head, he decided to wait for Declan outside. Finbar finished his drink and said 'I'm off, I've had enough drink for one night, I'll see you tomorrow.' Waiting outside, Finbar saw Declan come out with the youth, his arm around his shoulder. Declan didn't notice him and they continued up the street. Finbar expected Declan to leave him and then he could have caught up with him. They didn't separate, the young man unlocked the door of a nearby house and they both went in. 'Holy Mother of God', he thought.

Over the next few weeks he watched the house from time to time and Declan was a frequent visitor and made discreet enquiries about the young man from one of the waiters in the pub who told him 'he is one of those, you know' and often came into the pub with his friend and were always together.' He could hardly believe the evidence of his own eyes. All the years he had known Declan, there had never once been any indication that he was homosexual. 'God what a mess, he thought distractedly. What the bloody hell shall I do? What about Clare and his family?

He thought about tackling Declan then decided to speak to Michael first. He didn't know him very well but he knew he was a sensible man and between them they could decide what to do. He left a note for Michael at Doyle's asking him to meet him at a certain pub. Finbar arrived in good time and hoped that Michael had received his note. He was delighted when he saw him and sat down as Finbar ordered drinks. After he had explained the situation to Michael, his reaction was predictable. At first total disbelief and then as he realised the implications for Clare, absolute rage. Finbar asked Michael if he had noticed anything wrong between Declan and Clare, or has she said anything to you at all?' 'No. he replied but sometimes Clare does seem deep in thought'. 'God! Michael!, what are we to do. I keep hoping it's a nightmare and I'll wake up'. I'll have to work out a plan to deal with it, but the families must not find out, it would kill his sister and parents, not to mention Clare if she knew that we had found out', he said. 'Why in God's name did he ever marry Clare? how I'll keep from murdering him when I see him, I don't know? I think it would be best if you stayed out of it Finbar, it wouldn't do any good for him to know you are aware of his peccadilloes. We'll let him think I'm the only one who knows his secret'. 'Meet me at Doyle's' next Friday night I'll be with Paddy, Sean and Rory, so make some excuse so I can leave with you, we'll take a cab to the pub to see if he is there and if he is I'll decide what I must do'. 'alright Michael, I'll see you next Friday' he said.

‘Who shall we invite Finbar?' Bridget asked as they discussed the plans for their dinner party. 'Keep it small and don't forget I've a meeting on Friday night' he answered. 'Sure I've not forgotten, I think Saturday night is more suitable, don't you agree?' she replied. Finbar didn't answer, he would have agreed to any night except Friday night.

Finbar joined Michael and his friends at Doyle's and chatted for some time. He had few drinks with them and then asked Michael, as casually as he could, if he could discuss a business proposition with him some time. 'Sure there's no time like the present' Michael answered and got up from the table. 'I'll be back later for the cards, keep a place for me boyo's'. They took a cab to the pub and Michael suggested it would be better if he went in alone in case Declan was there and spotted him. 'Wait out of sight, I'll come out again as soon as I can' Michael explained.

The pub was packed and very noisy. Michael took his time looking for Declan and eventually saw him sitting in a corner with his 'friend'. Walking outside to Finbar he said bitterly 'He's in there alright, the both of them nice and cosy together. You take a cab home, I've a plan and if it works out, I won't need to contact you again'. 'For God's sake Michael be careful' he said anxiously. 'I promise you I won't lay a finger on him, I won't need to touch him'. 'Goodnight' Michael replied. Michael waited out of sight and sometime later they came out of the pub walking towards the house. He watched them go inside together and waited impatiently for about 15 minutes, then hammered as hard as he could on the door and soon the door was opened by the young man. He pushed him aside and looked around, there was no light in the downstairs room, so he took the stairs two at a time and walked into the bedroom.

Declan was in bed and turned his head when he heard the footsteps, no doubt he thought his 'friend' had returned. An expression of astonishment, then fear, crossed his face as he saw Michael standing there. 'Who are you and what do you want?' the youth shouted at Michael as he entered the bedroom. 'You keep that mouth of yours closed, or I'll close it for you' he said threateningly. He turned to Declan and said 'Get dressed, I'll wait'. The youth sat and watched the whole proceedings in silence. When Declan was dressed, Michael took hold of his arm and they walked downstairs and out into the street. The walked in silence for some time until they found a cab. Michael gave the driver the address of another pub on the other side of the City. They sat in silence until they arrived at the pub. Michael chose a quiet corner and ordered drinks. When their drinks were served Michael took a drink then said icily to Declan. 'Why did you marry my sister?'

'I wanted to try and live a conventional life, I thought if was married everything would work out' Declan stammered. 'Why did you choose my sister?' Michael asked stony faced. 'Because I knew her, she was a nice girl and I thought she would make an excellent wife' Declan explained. 'I see', he said softly. 'So you married my sister under false pretences, you bloody selfish bastard'. You didn't have to marry her at all, you should have stayed with your boyfriend all your life if that is what you wanted.. 'Do you realise what you have done? my sister has to spend her life with you, I could murder you right now. You had better pray that when we leave here I don't smash you to pieces. You planned it all, you used my sister as a cover for your behaviour. 'Tell me, Michael asked sarcastically how in God's name did you ever father a child?'

Declan was furious. 'I never wanted a child'. 'Mother of God, sure I've heard everything now' Michael said. Bringing his face close to Declan's he asked 'does Clare know how you feel about the child?' He knew from Declan's expression that she did. 'You bloody arrogant, callous bastard, how dare you treat my sister like a common slut. Listen to me boyo and hear me well. If you weren't married to my sister I wouldn't give a damn what you did, but you are, and that's the difference. If I find out that you have hurt Clare again, by God, I promise you will be sorry. I'll tell her and your family your little secret, do you understand?'

'Yes' was all he could stammer. You stop seeing him from now on, and do not go to that pub again. Does he know your real name?' he asked. 'No, I use another name' Declan answered. 'If I hear any gossip regarding your activities, someone will find you dead in a ditch. 'I never really trusted you Declan, but Ma and Clare were happy enough and that's how it has to stay, if you value your life. 'I'll be watching your behaviour from now on like a hawk, and if I hear any gossip regarding your activities, someone will find you dead in a ditch. Do I make myself clear?'

Declan was very scared now that Michael knew his secret and didn't want to go home until he had composed himself. He hailed a cab and asked the driver to drive around for a while. Eventually, he decided to call in to see his mother and father. By the time he arrived at their home he had composed himself, outwardly at least. Bridget, Finbar and his parents were all enjoying a cup of tea and were delighted to see him and told them he had finished his calls early. Finbar was very shocked when he saw him and watched him as he laughed and joked with Bridget as though nothing had happened. He knew something had happened, Michael's rage would ensure that, he had obviously kept his promise not to lay a finger on him. Sure, I never knew him at all, he thought bitterly. Some time later Finbar discussed his plans to teach in the Old Hedge Schools during the summer break with Bridget. 'I'd like to come with you this year, I've never seen Connemara'. Bridget said. 'Sure I'd love you to come with me' he replied, but it's not like Dublin, it's very primitive. A cottage is placed at our disposal but it has only two rooms. The men sleep in the kitchen and the women share the bedroom, it accommodates two couples usually. It would give you a chance to use your Gaelic; most of the villagers speak only a smattering of English'. 'Two couples you say, why don't we ask Declan and Clare to come with us?' Bridget suggested. Finbar hesitated for a moment then said 'it would be nicer for you if Clare came with us, and of course Declan could be a great help'. 'Ill ask him the next time we visit them'. A few weeks later Bridget called on Clare and the two friends spent a very pleasant afternoon together. Bridget was such fun to be with,

Clare valued her friendship more than ever now. Daniel was of course, the centre of their attention. Bridget loved him, he was her first nephew and was so proud of him.

Daniel was now eight months old, he had grown into a beautiful baby boy and had inherited Clare's lovely green eyes and her curly hair, except that it was not auburn, it was nut-brown. On most mornings when Clare went into the nursery to pick him up he was usually standing at the end of the cot. When he saw her, his little face broke into a delightful toothless smile of welcome. She couldn't get enough of him, everything he did, every noise he made was a miracle to her. She always referred to him as 'God's little gift'. Daniel gurgled quite happily as Bridget played with him on his rug, which Clare had put down for him. 'Why don't you and Finbar come to dinner tomorrow night?' Clare asked. 'There will only be yourselves and Tom, unless he is out on call'. 'Sure that would be grand, I'll ask Finbar tonight'. 'I don't think there is a meeting this week', Bridget replied. Mrs Casey and Nora helped Clare prepare something special for dinner and Tom kept everyone amused with his funny stories, and told one about a funny incident that happened at a meeting he had recently attended.

'The hall was packed with people who had come to hear a well known speaker on Peasants Land Rights. Tom explained during the course of the evening a man got carried away by the atmosphere as he stood on the platform addressing the crowd. He suddenly thumped his chest with his big fist and declared. 'I'm a ' Pheas*ant*, I was born a *Pheasant* and I'll die a *Pheasant*'. A man, standing at the back of the hall who'd had more than a few drinks called our loudly, 'For God's sake man, will you come down off that platform and not be making a FOWL of yourself'. When everyone had stopped laughing Finbar thought it was a good time to mention Connemara. 'Bridget is coming with me to Connemara this year, why don't you and Clare come with us?' he asked Declan. 'To be sure I'd love to come with you, but I can't leave Tom to take all the calls while I'll away. 'Would you like to come Clare?' Bridget asked. 'Oh, Yes, I've always wanted to see the west of Ireland and especially Connemara with its dolphins and seals'. 'If it's only the calls that are stopping you Declan?'. Tom said, 'Sure I'd be happy to take them, there won't be that many and I can ask Mrs. Casey to keep and eye on the place'. 'What about Daniel?' Declan asked Clare. 'I wouldn't take Daniel with me. I'll leave him with Mammy'.' How long will we be away?' Declan asked Finbar. 'About a week' he replied. 'Well! that's settled then, let us know the dates in plenty of time so that we can make suitable arrangements' Declan declared.

A week before she and Declan were due to leave, Clare visited her mother and asked her to look after Daniel, she was delighted. 'I'll ask Mrs. Kelly to come in every morning so that I can look after him properly, sure it will be lovely to have him here at the farm', Kate said. Mrs. Casey was delighted to be left in charge of the household while Clare was away and promised to take care of everything just as Clare wished. Declan drove Clare and Daniel to the farm the day before they were due to leave, with all Daniel's necessities. After dropping Clare off he said he would collect her later in the afternoon. Michael set-up Daniel's cot in Clare's old bedroom, and Kate put his clothes in the drawers and thought about all the happy years spent here with Clare. Clare explained to her mother Daniel's routine, and knew love and attention would be plentiful. Clare was ready to leave when Declan called to pick her up. As he walked into the kitchen Michael was holding a gurgling Daniel above his head and watched him. Clare laughed and said 'let me have him now Michael, sure you can have him for a week'. Michael handed Daniel to Clare and turned to Declan and asked 'have you taken part in the Hedge School scheme before?' 'No, but I'm looking forward to it, it should be an experience', he answered pleasantly. Clare kissed and hugged Daniel then handed him to her mother, secure in the knowledge that he would be well looked after until she returned. 'It's time to leave, Declan said' Michael hugged Clare and said 'don't worry about Daniel, sure, I won't let anything happen to him while you are away'.

When they arrived at the cottage the door was open and went inside. Looking around they could see it was clean and a fire had been set in the hearth with the peat stacked in a pile outside the door. They carried the luggage into the bedroom. Finbar hadn't exaggerated the size. It contained a double bed and a small chest of drawers. There was just enough room to move around the bed. Clare and Bridget unpacked the clothes, food etc., while Declan lit the fire and filled a big kettle from the outside pump and hooked it over the fire to boil. Meanwhile, Finbar had gone to let Fr. Quinn know they had arrived and to discuss the schedule for the week.

'Sure it's good to see you again Finbar. I've managed to acquire two horses for your needs, but I think it would be wiser to leave them here in the field nearby. 'You and your companion can saddle them each morning'. 'Thank you, that's grand. I've brought my wife and brother-in-law and his wife with me this year'. 'I'll call to see them when you get settled' Fr. Quinn responded. Meanwhile, Bridget and Clare had organised the kitchen and prepared the evening meal of soup and soda bread and hot tea. Clare and Bridget said goodnight and left their husbands talking in the kitchen. Some time later, the men wrapped themselves in blankets and lay down on each side of the fire to sleep. They had an early start in the morning.

Clare and Bridget spent most of the following morning baking. They also prepared the evening meal. They had just sat down to drink a well earned cup of tea, when they heard a knock on the door. Bridget opened the door and Fr. Quinn stood there smiling at them. She greeted him in Gaelic and he was delighted. She invited him in and introduced him to Clare, and asked if he would like a cup of tea. 'Indeed, I'd love one, these old bones of mine protest sometimes and I'll be glad of a seat and a chat', he replied. Fr. Quinn was about sixty years of age, quite thin, with a slight stoop to his shoulders. As they chatted to him, the girls could see he was an intelligent and cultured man, he and told them he knew Dublin well. He had been educated in the Seminary there; his first Parish had also been in Dublin. 'Would you like to take a look at the village? he asked. 'The Agent is away on business at the moment, so it is quite safe'. 'That would be lovely', they answered. They reached the first cottage, the door was open. Fr. Quinn knocked, nevertheless, and walked inside. A young woman stood there, a baby in her arms and another child clutching her skirt and smiled when she saw them. Bridget spoke to her in Gaelic and she told her that her husband was working in the fields. Bridget translated the conversation for Clare, her Gaelic was not that good. After giving her a parcel of clothing and some food they then said goodbye. When they were out of earshot, Clare suddenly burst out angrily. 'Sure I've never seen such poverty and suffering. That poor woman or girl, I should say, had no boots on her feet, the children were half naked and all of them looked half starved. Sure the slums of Dublin are palaces compared to that hovel, something has to change. These landlords cannot be allowed to continue to get rich on the backs of these suffering people. Indeed, I'm so angry I could cut cold iron!. When I return to Dublin I'm going to work very hard for 'The Cause' in any way I can. I want my son to grow up and live in a free Ireland!'. 'Don't be too distressed'. Fr. Quinn said. 'It will take time to change the laws we have to live under. I believe the time will come when we will have our land back again, I know the situation is tragic, I live here, and I have never got used to the poverty and suffering of the villagers, we do what we can, which isn't enough'.

'Charles Stuart Parnell has done a great deal for Ireland and its people. He worked very hard to get the 'Home Rule' Bill passed in the Westminster Parliament. Even though it wasn't passed, people became aware of the cruel laws inflicted on the Irish people, so some good came of it. He has also encouraged tenants-at-will to refuse to pay exorbitant rent increases which will make them even poorer, if that is possible, and the landlords richer. He gave them the courage to resist and the money to support themselves and their families from donations received from immigrants in Australia and America when they are evicted from their cottages and watch them burnt to the ground'. 'Parnell has also made it quite clear, that any man who takes over a tenancy of an evicted tenant's farm, at the increased rent, will be shunned completely by the rest of the people in the village. This creates a real problem for the landlords. We have ways and means of letting the Irish National League know when we need their help. They move very quickly to come to the assistance of those who need them. Parnell is a truly great patriot, God bless him!. By the way, Finbar knew the Agent was away reporting to his master, that is why he chose this week to come here, he added. We must pray that the violence and bloodshed, which is inevitable, will achieve its goal and not too many young lives will be lost. Now!, what do you think of Connemara?' he asked as he changed the subject. 'I think it has a stark beauty, there is something haunting about it, Clare answered. It is very different from our farm, it is soft, green and bountiful'. 'I'm longing to see a Connemara sunset' Bridget remarked. 'Sure you won't be disappointed, sunrise, sunset here are truly magnificent and they are free thank God', Fr. Quinn answered. He left them at the door of their cottage and promised to call some evening when Finbar and Declan were home.

One afternoon a few days later, Clare and Bridget decided to take a walk, on the way they met Fr. Quinn, he was delighted to see them and asked if they would like to meet his sister Frances who kept house for him and promised to drive them home in his donkey cart. Frances was a pleasant middle aged woman, she was surprised to see them but welcomed them warmly. She set the table with a lovely hand embroidered cloth and used her best tea service. They chatted over a cup of tea about Dublin and discovered she had only lived in Connemara for a couple of years. Her parents had died and her brother Fr. Quinn took ill, so she came out to nurse him and stayed to keep house for him and visited Dublin occasionally. After discussing books, music and their favourite composers it was time to leave, they had an enjoyable visit. Fr. Quinn brought the donkey cart to the door. As they said goodbye Bridget invited Frances and Fr. Quinn for dinner later in the week.

As they neared the cottage, they could see a group of men and children sitting on the ground near the door. Fr. Quinn tethered the donkey and helped Clare and Bridget down and asked them to stay where they were and then walked quickly over to the group and spoke to them in Gaelic. Fr. Quinn explained to Clare and Bridget that they were from a village further north. 'There is a potato blight and some of the people took ill, so they decided to walk away from the village. They heard we were here and wondered if we had any food to spare. I must talk to your both Fr. Quinn said and followed them into the cottage. You must be very careful, some of the sickness they talked about is very contagious, give me what you have for them and I'll tell them to go back to the village and wait until I make arrangements to have them looked after'. Clare and Bridget collected food and also a little medicine and gave it to Fr. Quinn 'Don't go near the village. I'll go out now and speak to them'. Finbar and Declan arrived shortly after the group of people had left. Bridget explained what had happened. They were all very subdued for the rest of the evening. 'Ireland's troubles seemed to be encapsulated in this group of wandering, ill, and starving people' Clare said.. 'Did you manage to send the letters to the family?' Bridget asked Finbar. 'Yes, I also mailed Clare's letter'.

Everyone was tired and worried. Bridget and Clare left the kitchen to the men and went to bed. Declan heard it first, a knock at the door of the cottage, and opened it, one of the villagers stood there. He spoke to Declan but he couldn't understand him. He shook Finbar awake and he spoke to the man in Gaelic. 'He asked if we have any medicine to spare, he says his wife is very sick', Finbar explained and collected as much medicine as he could spare and handed it to the man. 'I'll go with you, perhaps I can help' Declan said. 'Do you think that's wise?' Finbar asked, Fr. Quinn advised us not to go near the village'. 'I'll be very careful, will you explain to the man that I will come with him to see what I can do to help'. 'God Bless you' the man said and hurried off as Declan followed him.

The following morning, the men explained to Bridget and Clare what had happened during the night. 'I've decided we should return to Dublin at once' Finbar said.. I'll make arrangements with Fr. Quinn to leave as soon as possible. I suggest while I'm away, you pack all your belongings'. 'Ah! to be sure it's no-one's fault, but I'll be glad to get back to Dublin', Bridget remarked. 'I'm longing to see Daniel, I've missed him so much', Clare replied. Most of the day was spent as Finbar had suggested. They also cleaned the cottage and parcelled the remaining food to give to Fr. Quinn, for the villagers. After a makeshift dinner, they all went to bed. Declan and Finbar slept fitfully, they were upset and disappointed at the way things had worked out and were anxious to get away. During the night Finbar awoke, he wrapped his blanket around him and put more peat on the fire and noticed Declan tossing and turning in his sleep and went over to him. He realised something was wrong and lit a candle so he could take a closer look.

'Holy Mother of God! he exclaimed and blessed himself. He knocked on the bedroom door and Clare opened it, still half asleep. 'Declan's sick, he's delirious', he said. She ran over to where he lay on the floor and looked at him in horror. 'Get me some water and some towels Finbar'. They watched over him all day, but there was no change in his condition. 'I' think I'll ask Fr. Quinn to say some prayers for him' Finbar said. Clare and Bridget nodded their heads in agreement. Declan died the following morning. Clare looked at him and cried and immediately thought of Daniel, who no longer had a father. Finbar wrapped Declan's body in a sheet and carried it outside, he gathered all the bed clothes and set fire to them. Finbar stood between Bridget and Clare, his arms around them both as they silently watched as Declan's body was placed in the shallow grave. They wept silently.

Finbar left to make alternative arrangements for their departure to Dublin. Clare and Bridget were exhausted and sat outside the cottage in the afternoon sun in silence. When Finbar returned, no-one had any appetite for food. They watched the sun slip below the horizon, the sky blazed with glorious colours crimson ,vermillion, rose, purple and gold. For one special moment in time, heaven and earth seemed united by the fiery rays of the setting sun. No one spoke, eventually they all went inside to bed. Finbar couldn't sleep, he had too much on his mind. Wrapping the blanket around him he sat and stared into the fire. He thought about Declan, then Bridget and Clare and John and Mary, then baby Daniel and finally Kate. His mind raced. Bridget couldn't sleep either, she slipped out of bed quietly and went into the kitchen. Seeing Finbar was awake, she ran to him, they fell asleep in each other's arms. When they awoke, they realised they had overslept. 'I'll wake Clare while you make a pot of tea', she said.

Finbar heard a piercing scream. Holy Mother of God! he exclaimed and ran into the bedroom. Bridget stood transfixed. He looked and gasped, all the signs were there. Clare was flushed and had vomited during the night. Pulling himself together he brought Bridget some cold water to bathe her. Between them they stripped Clare down to her shift and removed all the bedclothes then collected all the clothes in the bedroom, except those in their cases and took them outside. He lit a fire and burnt them at once. Bridget carried the case outside and took out the clean clothes. She dressed outside as quickly as possible and prayed while tears streamed down her face. 'Please God, not Clare' she begged. Fr. Quinn arrived and administered the Last Rites. They managed to get some medicine down her throat, but it was difficult, Clare seemed to choke. It was no use Clare took her last breath. Bridget was nearly demented. Bridget and Finbar watched as they lowered Clare's body into the shallow grave where Declan was buried. She wept bitterly and was beyond consolation. A cold shiver ran through her body, she knew her life would never be the same again. A lot of innocent pleasure and happiness had been buried with Clare. Finbar and Bridget sat in silence as the cab carried them on the last leg of their journey home. Finbar prayed silently that Bridget wouldn't catch 'the sickness'. He knew it was 50/50, however, for some reason everyone did not contract the sickness/fever. No one knew why.

Finbar thought about Kate and Daniel then his thoughts turned to Michael. He had dealt effectively with Declan's homosexuality and kept the secret. No one would ever know the truth. He wondered how he and Bridget would tell her parents of Declan and Clare's death. Then he remembered Tom. He would be left with a full Practice and would have to decide what to do about it. Finbar thought his head would burst. Taking hold of Bridget's hand he thought how much he loved her. Bridget looked out of the cab, they were home. While the cab driver lifted their cases and placed it on the pavement Finbar helped Bridget alight from the cab. Bridget followed Finbar up the steps leading to the front door and prayed silently to God and His Holy Mother to help her choose the right words when she told her Mammy and Da., that both Declan and Clare were dead and buried in Connemara. Stepping inside, Bridget listened for the sound of voices. The kitchen door was closed so she led the way down, no-one was there. She heaved a sigh of relief and turned to face Finbar. 'Thank God! Mammy and Da. aren't home. We have a little more time, we can freshen up before they get back. Bridget changed her clothes quickly and washed her hands and face. When she had tidied her hair she went downstairs to make a pot of tea, as Finbar walked in he put down his cup and saucer he said 'sure there's no easy way to tell them their son and daughter-in-law are dead. Whatever we say and however we say it, their grief will cut deep into their hearts. We will have to wait until they are both together.' 'Holy Mother of God! how am I to tell them Finbar?' she asked as she wiped the tears from her eyes. 'I'll tell them if you want to', he answered. 'No darlin' it will be easier coming from me' she said. Sometime later they heard the front door open and the sound of voices. Bridget sat up straight and braced herself for the coming ordeal.

Mary and John were delighted to see them. 'It's good to have you home' Mary said. Bridget made some fresh tea and as she sipped her tea her mammy asked 'tell me now, how was your visit to Connemara?' Bridget decided the time had come to break the news. Taking hold of both of her mammy's hands in her own and said. 'Mammy, Da, something terrible happened, I've some terrible news'. Her parents looked at her rather bewildered and waited for her to continue. 'Declan and Clare caught 'The Fever', they are not coming home. They are dead and buried'. Her mammy let out an agonising scream as she slumped in her chair sobbing. With Finbar and John's help the two men managed to get her upstairs. She could hardly put one foot in front of the other, Bridget put her to bed. Her da returned to the bedroom and sat in a chair beside his wife holding her hand in his. As Bridget and Finbar sat together on the sofa, Bridget said, 'If I hadn't asked them to come with us to Connemara, they would be alive today'. 'It's no ones fault Bridget', Finbar answered, as he put his arm around her shoulders. The following morning Bridget's Da said 'We will have to go to the farm and tell Kate and Michael, she will be expecting Declan and Clare to drive over and collect Daniel'. 'I'll go with you Da.' Bridget said. The cab moved off as they both sat in silence, what was there to talk about?

As the cab turned into the road which led to the farm, Bridget said 'Da.. 'I'd like to tell Mrs. O'Hara the sad news'. The cab stopped outside Kate's door and as Bridget and her Da alighted Kate stood on the doorstep ready to welcome them. Kate ushered them inside 'I thought you were Clare and Declan coming to take Daniel home?' Kate drew Bridget and her Da over to where Daniel was sleeping, Bridget knelt down by the cradle and looked at Daniel 'poor darlin' she thought as she touched his cheek with her fingers, struggling to hold back the tears. Kate made a pot of tea and sliced and buttered some freshly baked soda bread and offered it to John and Bridget. Bridget watched her da stand up and ask where Michael is, he couldn't tell the terrible news to Kate without him with her and decided to take a stroll to find Michael. Before too long, Michael and her Da. walked into the kitchen. By the look on Michael's face she knew her Da. had told him about Declan and Clare's death. Both men walked over to where Daniel was sleeping and looked down at him for a short time. As they sat down Bridget reached over and took hold of Mrs. O'Hara's hand and said. 'I've terrible news, terrible news'. Michael walked over to his Ma's chair and stood beside her. 'Clare and Declan caught 'The Fever' they died. They are buried in Connemara', Bridget said. Kate put up her hands and covered her face as her tears ran down her cheeks. She rocked herself to and fro and said 'Not Clare! No, No, No. 'I can't bear it' and Declan dead as well'. Michael put his arms around his mother and tried to comfort her. Bridget knelt down and put her head in her lap and sobbed. Kate lowered her hands and gently stroked Bridget's hair. Michael and John looked on in silent sorrow as the two women shared their grief. Sometime later Kate asked. 'What happened John?' after he explained, Kate sat in silence for some time still gently stroking Bridget's hair. Then she shouted 'The cruel and callous laws we live under caused this tragedy. My life has been shadowed by misery, starvation and death sometimes I wonder will it ever stop?'

'It's going to stop Ma', Michael said angrily. 'I'll see Ireland free of the oppressors and they will pay the price of their greed, it will happen, God is just'.

My mother, God rest her soul, used to chant these lines when the situation seemed desperate' Kate said:

'Ireland was Ireland when England was a pup! and Ireland will be Ireland when England's Empire is bu......... Up!'

Daniel began to cry, Kate kissed Bridget on the forehead and said 'Daniel needs me now darlin'. Three pairs of eyes watched her as she walked over to Daniel's cradle. As soon as he saw her he stopped crying and his little arms and legs punched the air in time to a tune only he could hear. She picked him up and sat down on the old rocking chair. Cradling him in her arms she gently rocked backwards and forwards until he fell asleep again.

When Mary had recovered, to a degree, from the shock of her son Declan and Clare's death, the two families met to discuss what should be done in the circumstances they found themselves in. Declan's partner Tom was included. Tom told them he couldn't continue to run the practice alone and he had also decided to emigrate to America, and had already told Declan. His cousin, who lived in Montana, had offered him a job on his ranch and he had accepted. The two families agreed to send a sum of money to Fr. Quinn for Masses for Clare and Declan and what was left would be used to erect a headstone. Discussion arose as to who would look after Daniel and it was agreed that Daniel should be brought up by his grandmother Kate O'Hara and his Uncle Michael on the farm. Gradually,

Kate's life took on a new rhythm. Daniel was a delight. Life has to go on!.

Daniel grew into a very healthy boy. By the time he was one year old, he could walk – at least 'toddle'. His grandparents O'Reilly, Aunt Bridget and uncle Finbar came over to celebrate his 1st birthday. Scooping him up she kissed him. Six months had passed since the death of his parents and the family felt a great sadness that Clare and Declan could not see their beautiful son. Daniel resembled his mother in looks Kate thought and had inherited his mother's large green eyes, he was very tall for his age and had nut brown hair like his grandfather O'Reilly. Everyone loved him. Michael always made time to spend with him each day. 'If you wrap Daniel up well, Kate, I'd like to take him down to the fields' his grandfather said. Carrying him down to the chicken pen, he put him down on the ground to watch him feed the chickens. Daniel threw a handful of grain and laughed heartily as they scrambled for it and then ran off. He showed him the pigs, the cows and then walked down to where Michael, Sean and Paddy were working in the fields. Michael came over for a chat. 'Hop up on the cart John' he said 'I'll take you and Daniel back to the house'. After lifting Daniel down into his grandfather's arms, Michael said 'I think you'll be gone by the time I'm finished, I'll see you next time you visit'. He shook John's hand turned the cart and drove back to the fields. Kate had the meal prepared and Bridget had set the table when John walked into the kitchen. Bridget removed Daniel's outside clothes and sat him on her mother's knee as Molly came into the kitchen and Kate asked her to take Daniel upstairs for his nap. 'The meal was absolutely delicious Kate' Mary said. When it was time to leave Bridget hugged Mrs. O'Hara and promised she and Finbar would be over again soon. Kate wrapped her shawl tightly around her as she stood at the door and waved them all goodbye. She shivered slightly and hurried inside, it was a cold January day. Removing her shawl, she thought how different Mary is since Declan's death. Bridget had confided in her that she was very worried about her Mammy. Perhaps time would be the healer?.

Michael walked into the kitchen one Sunday morning after Mass and sat with his mam 'I need to talk to you about the farm' he said and waited until his mother was ready to talk. Watching his mother as she bustled about the kitchen he thought how proud he was of her. She was a remarkable woman. She had taken looking after Daniel in her stride, she loved him very much and was getting on in years and young children could be very tiring. Yet, she never complained and seemed to thrive on the fact that there was more work to do. Kate poured herself a cup of tea and sat down next to her son. 'Well son, what is it you want to talk about?' she asked. 'As you know mam, the leasehold runs out next year. We need to decide what to do about it. What do you think will happen, do you think the Landlord will renew the leasehold?' 'I honestly don't know son?' his Ma. replied. 'I think we should make an appointment to see the Landlord's Solicitor as soon as possible and discuss the matter with him. We can't leave it until the lease runs out. If he refuses to renew it we will have to leave the farm and find somewhere else to live. I'll ride into Dublin later this week and make an appointment to see the Solicitor. If the Leasehold isn't renewed , what would happen to us, where would we go?' 'We'll worry about that when the time comes, we have another year on the farm anyway and we have some money saved, we are not penniless' said Kate.

Michael was a little early for his appointment and sat down to wait. He didn't have to wait too long. 'Mr. O'Hara, you can go in now' the secretary said with a smile. The two men shook hands and the Solicitor asked him to sit down. 'I'm Seamus Brennan, what I can do for you?' he asked. 'I hold the leasehold on a farm a few miles outside of Dublin. I inherited it on the death of my father, Martin O'Hara. The Leasehold runs out next year in fact. I would like to renew it in my own name' he explained. Michael handed him the document and waited until he had read it, watching as he noted the details and file number, then handed it back. 'There might be a problem, Mr. O'Hara, he said . The original owner, The Duke of Lancaster, is now dead'. The present Duke lives in London and does not visit Ireland. I have no dealings with him at all, so I cannot give you an opinion on the matter. I will write to the London office and explain the situation. When I hear from them, I will offer you an appointment. That is all I can do at the moment'. Michael stood up, thanked him and left the office.

It was approximately three months later when Michael received a letter from the Solicitor offering him an appointment after he had seen the farm and would call at their home the following Monday. 'I've a letter here Ma from the solicitor, he is coming to inspect the farm next Monday'. 'Well son he'll find it in excellent condition, but that could be a problem?' 'You mean because of the condition, he may not wish to renew the Leasehold?' 'Sure that's on the cards, but that's not what I meant. The rent may be too high on the farm as it is today for us to be able to pay it', she explained. 'Ah well!, sure we'll just have to pray that God's on our side' he said.

The following Monday morning Kate and Mrs. Kelly had been up early to make sure that the house was in perfect order. Michael would check the farm.. Hearing the sound of horse's hooves outside Kate waited until she heard the knock on the door, a middle-aged man stood there. He lifted his hat and said. 'I'm Mr. Brennan', Mrs. O'Hara, I'll just ask the cabbie to wait for me'. Kate showed him into the kitchen and asked him if he would like to sit down. He finished his cup of tea and asked to see the rest of the house. Kate showed him the parlour and then the bedrooms. When he saw Daniel's cot he asked did she have a grandchild. I do, his name is Daniel. Molly, a young girl who helps me has taken him to feed the chickens. Daniel is my daughter's child. She and her husband died over a year ago, he now lives with me, I take care of him'. 'I'm very sorry to hear about your daughter Mrs.O'Hara' he said. They went downstairs and walked towards the half open door, which led into the farm. Mr. Brennan was just about to step outside when Kate said. 'Would you be good enough to change into these boots, I don't like mud on my clean floor and there's lots of mud on the farm' 'I understand' he said as he took the boots from her and put them on'. Molly and Daniel were still feeding the chickens when Kate and Mr. Brennan reached them, he watched as Molly showed Daniel how to place the eggs in the basket without breaking them. They moved on towards the pigs, and when they reached the field he watched the cows as they munched on the lush grass. Michael came over to them. Kate sat down on the old seat while Michael showed him the rest of the farm and then returned to sit beside Kate.

'It's a very well kept farm. I wish you well' he said as he shook Michael's hand. As he and Kate walked back to the house he said. 'Forty Five years is a long time Mrs. O'Hara, sure you and your husband must have worked very hard in the early years'. 'Yes! life was very, very hard' she replied. After returning to the house and changing into his boots he picked up his hat and held out his hand and said goodbye 'I'll send my report to London as soon as possible. You will hear from me'. Ah well! she thought, we will soon find out if we have to leave the farm.

Michael received a letter about two months later asking him to call into the office in Dublin on Friday. He arrived in time and Mr. Brennan was waiting for him. They shook hands and Michael sat down to hear what he had to say. 'I have received an answer from London. The Duke of Lancaster has advised me, through his solicitor, that he has read my report on the condition of his land and property and is very pleased to hear that your family has made such a success of the farm. The Duke is a member of the Westminster Parliament and has no intention of returning to Ireland at the present time and is fully aware of the difficulties many Absentee Landlords experience regarding their land and indeed the tenants also. For 45 years the conditions of the Leasehold have been met and it is his opinion that you have earned the right to renew the Leasehold in your own name, there will of course be an adjustment to the ground rent, but it is also very reasonable. As you have no son, he will renew the Leasehold for your lifetime. The same conditions apply as before, the ground rent must be paid regularly and the condition of the land must be maintained. I have the Leasehold Contract prepared for you, please read it and sign it'.

Michael read the document very carefully and then signed it. Mr Brennan then handed him a copy of the document that he had just signed and asked him to sign this also. The copy was handed to Michael. 'The new agreement begins in January 1893.'Thank you' Michael replied and left the office. Michael felt absolutely wonderful, Thanks be to God!. Now Ma, wouldn't have to leave the farm, the only home she had ever known. As he walked towards the stables he felt as if a heavy load had been lifted off his shoulders, then saw his Ma and Molly with Daniel sitting on the old seat. When he reached them he picked Daniel up and swung him high in the air Daniel as screamed with delight. Handing him to Molly he turned to his Ma and said 'I need to talk to you Ma'. When they were out of earshot, he said. 'The Duke of Lancaster renewed the leasehold for the duration of my lifetime. Isn't it wonderful! I never thought that I, an Irishman would ever say anything good about an Absentee Landlord, but I have to say the new Duke is a 'fair man'. 'That's grand news Michael, I'm delighted for you she said. 'You won't have to leave your home Ma. I can hardly believe it?'. Back in the kitchen Michael handed the copy of the Leasehold to his Ma to read. She read it very carefully then handed it back to him. 'The Duke of Lancaster is definitely a different breed from the other Absentee Landlords' 'He is to be sure, a fair minded man. Let's have a toast'. Michael filled his Ma's glass with wine and his own glass with whiskey as he raised his glass he said 'Slainte!'.

Life went on at the farm with only minor changes. Michael signed contracts with two restaurants to supply fresh vegetables and he, Sean and Paddy travelled more often to Dublin. Daniel was now three years of age and Kate suggested to Michael that he take him into Dublin and drop him off at his O'Reilly grandparents for a few days. The 18th January, 1895 was Daniel's 4th birthday and Kate decided he was old enough to enjoy a proper birthday party. Michael brought toys and sweets home from Dublin and Kate went to great trouble to make it very special for him. A few of the village children were also invited, as well of course, his grandparents and aunt Bridget and uncle Finbar. Kate and Michael had a big surprise for him. When the children and adults had eaten enough the children were all playing with Daniel's toys and they became rather noisy so Michael thought it was time for them to run outside. Besides, he wanted Daniel to see his special present. 'Put on your outdoor clothes boys and boots and we'll go down to the field to play'. The children were out of the door like a shot. Michael carried Daniel on his shoulders and the family followed. When they reached the barn, Michael told the children to wait outside, Sean and Paddy made sure they did just that. Michael went inside the barn and after a few minutes led out a beautiful little pony. The children jumped up and down with excitement as Sean and Paddy led them over towards the pony so they could pat it's nose. Michael lifted Daniel onto the pony's back and showed him how to hold the reins then led him around in a wide circle. Daniel was not afraid and loved every minute of it. He lifted Daniel down and Bridget took hold of his hand as he watched his friends ride the pony. Some were better at staying seated than others, but it all added to the fun. As the sky became leaden, Kate thought it was too cold for the children and decided they should all go back into the house. Michael led the pony with Daniel on it's back into the stall. Lifting Daniel on to his shoulders, and said 'now Danny boy, your pony needs a name, what do you want to call him?' 'He's my friend' Daniel answered 'to be sure he is, but what name shall we give him?' 'He's my friend' Daniel insisted. 'Well now, that's a grand name, 'My Friend' it is. The children left for home sometime later and shortly afterwards, John, Mary, Bridget and Finbar left for home. Molly played with Daniel and his new toys while Kate prepared the evening meal and Michael, Sean and Paddy sat by the fire enjoying a rest from work.

It's time for your bed Daniel', Kate said. Daniel lifted his fingers and said '2 more minutes Granny' in a pleading voice. 'Just 2 more minutes then' Kate replied and smiled at him. Molly helped Daniel get ready for bed, it was warmer in the kitchen and Kate always saw that he was kept warm. He kissed everyone goodnight and tucked his favourite toy under his arm and holding his grandmother's hand, climbed the stairs to bed. Kate covered him with his blanket and tucked him in. Sleep came easy to him and soon she left the bedroom closing the door behind her. They all sat down at the table and ate a hearty meal. Molly helped wash and dry the pots and pans etc., then Sean and Paddy walked her home. Michael left to attend to a cow whose udder was infected. Kate was alone. She loved the silence and drew great strength and courage from her own thoughts. Tonight was no different. She thought how lucky the two families were to be united in their love for Daniel. She remembered how blissfully happy Clare had been on that spring day when she told her she was with child. How Kate wished Clare had lived to see her son growing up. It was times like these when she missed Martin too, he would have been so proud of Daniel. Sitting quiet awhile with her own thoughts she still thought she was blessed. Picking up a lamp Kate climbed the stairs to bed. It had been a very busy day, but a joyous one. Thanks be to God!.

Kate lingered at the door for a few minutes and watched Daniel as he joined his friends. He turned his head once to look at her as she and smiled at him and left the classroom. As she walked home, she wondered if he would like school. It made it easier for everyone if they did. She and Michael thought he was a clever little boy, but they didn't really know. She missed him already and would be glad when it was time to go back to school to collect him. Daniel would probably tell her everything that had happened, good and bad. It doesn't seem five years since he was born she thought, how quickly the years have passed.

Kate waited outside the school. A few mothers were there but most of the children found their own way home. The door opened and the children spilled out, Daniel among them with two friends, as soon as he saw her he flung himself at her as she hugged him. He ran on in front of her on the way to the farm with his two friends. Kate gave them all a drink of fresh milk and some thickly buttered slices of fresh soda bread. They finished the food very quickly and were ready for 'off', so to speak. They all put their boots on and Kate opened the door for them and they ran off to where Michael waited for them. They always had to wait until Michael took them across the fields to a safe spot where they could play without disturbing the cattle. That was the rule they were not allowed to break. The boys usually had a ride on 'My Friend' first, then ran off to play their own exciting games. When the boys had left for home, Kate asked Daniel what he had done at school. 'Played' he answered. 'I'm sure that was grand, but what else did you do?' she asked. 'We drew things on a slate, I liked that. Paddy was a bad boy and was smacked by the teacher, I didn't like that' he said rather sadly. 'Well now! That was a grand day, I'm sure tomorrow will be just as nice' Kate said.

Life on the farm continued it's seasonal cycles; planting, harvesting and finally selling the produce. Daniel grew very tall for his age and Kate saw his grandfather O'Hara in him, in lots of ways. He had his toughness to do what had to be done, but he also had his gentleness. She watched him one day as he fed a baby calf holding the bottle of milk confidently in his large bony hands, but he also held the calf's head firmly in his arms when it struggled to get free and stayed with it until the milk was finished, then stroking the calf's head said. 'Sure you won't grow big and strong if you don't drink your milk'. She smiled broadly when she heard her own words repeated by Daniel. How happy and peaceful she thought it is here on the farm.

However, in Ireland itself, there was a lot of unrest. There was lots of trouble between the tenants – at – will and the Agents for the absentee landlords. The Irish National League was much more in evidence in order to help tenants who had been evicted from their cottages. By the time Daniel was seven years old he was able to read and write and do simple sums. The teacher told Kate he was a very bright little boy. She was proud of him and she and Michael encouraged him to read, by providing him with suitable books. Daniel could ride his pony very well and looked after 'My Friend' himself, he brushed his coat, fed and watered him and cleaned out his stall. Michael always helped to put the pony back in his stall and secure the gate.

Daniel idolised Michael, he thought his uncle was wonderful. Michael spent as much time as he could with him, encouraging Daniel to do things little boys should do. He taught him to fish for tiddlers and sometimes in the summer months, the water in the stream, at certain points it was so clear and showed Daniel how to catch tiddlers with his bare hands. Michael also showed him how to milk a cow and eventually he managed to fill a mug with fresh milk, Daniel laughed with the sheer magic of it. He also helped on the farm in small ways, Kate and Michael wanted him to have a happy childhood and encouraged his friends from school to come and play with him. Daniel was growing up into a real boy, loving and kind but full of mischief. Kate kept him on a 'long rope', he had plenty of freedom but she hauled it in when necessary. She had no intention of allowing him to be spoiled, in any way.

Bridget and Finbar brought Daniel home one weekend after a visit. They said they would stay overnight and Kate was delighted. She was very fond of Bridget and Finbar, they were a lovely couple. It was Friday night and Michael and his friends had gone into Dublin for their weekly visit to 'Doyle's. When the meal was ready, everyone sat down at the table. Kate had prepared thick slices of juicy ham with a favourite recipe of spiced apple sauce, jacket potatoes nearly bursting out of their crisp skins and young buttered carrots, not to mention some delicious cabbage. It looked very appetising! mid-way through the meal Daniel suddenly said. 'Granny what happened to Ma and Da? Tommy Ryan asked me why I didn't have a Ma. and Da.? I told them they were dead. They all turned to look at him. Bridget put down her knife and fork and looked at Kate. Finbar looked at his wife. Kate rummaged through her thoughts to find the right words, she was surprised by the question but knew it would be asked sooner than later.

'Sure it was very, very sad darlin. One summer, your Da and Ma went to Connemara for a week to help the little boys and girls who lived there to read and write'.' I can read and write' he said proudly. 'Yes darlin, I know you can, you're a clever boy. Some of the people who live in Connemara are very, very, poor they don't have enough to eat and they get sick'. 'Where's Connemara?' he asked. 'It's a long, long way across Ireland, she replied. While your Ma. and Da. were there, they met some people who were sick and because they talked to them and stood near to them, they got sick themselves. That's how your Ma. and Da. died, they are buried in Connemara. Your Ma, left you with me and uncle Michael, so you would be safe until she got back she loved you very much. That's why you live with me and your uncle Michael'. 'Granny', he asked 'did you cry when Ma. and Da. Died?' 'Yes darlin' we did, we still miss them very much, but we have you, you are their legacy to us and you are very precious, we love you very much'. Daniel looked satisfied with the answer and finished his dinner. The others finished theirs but they had lost their appetites. After Daniel was in bed asleep, Bridget, Finbar and Kate sat together around the fire having a drink, wine of course for the ladies and whiskey for Finbar.

'Mrs. O'Hara', Bridget said 'I'm worried about Mammy, in fact we are all worried about her. She seems so low spirited, she was always so fond of company, now she won't visit her friends, she says he is too tired, indeed, she won't come down from her room when they call. Da is out of his mind with worry over her, I don't know what to-do. The doctor doesn't seem to help her much. She's never been the same since my brother Declan and Clare died'. 'I suppose it was a terrible shock for her?' 'Their death was a shock to all of us Bridget I lost my daughter whom I adored and your mam lost her son. It was very hard for me also, but having had a very hard life from a very early age, misery and death was part of my childhood. Having the farm has kept me going because I had the help of Michael. I had to keep the farm going too when Martin died, even though I thought my heart would break, it was all we had. I had to keep going because of Michael and Clare. Then there was the loss of Michael's future wife, Moira, he was devastated and he hasn't got over it to this day. When Clare and Declan died, I really believed I had suffered too much, I just wanted to give in to my grief – but again there was Daniel and my promise to Clare to look after him until she came back from Connemara, he needed me. It was different for your Mammy, she had her whole family around her. Clare was already a member of the family before she married Declan, everything was going so well. Your mam just wasn't prepared for the sudden death of them both, it was a terrible shock to her and me. Sure time is a great healer, she is a fine woman and with your support she will eventually heal, but she will never forget and some days will be better than others. Do you think a few days at the seaside with your Da. would help, sometimes a change does help' 'I'll speak to Da. when I get home, God knows he needs a change' Bridget said. They chatted long into the night, mostly about old times. Bridget told funny stories of incidents that had happened to her and Clare which made Kate and Finbar laugh. It was late when they all went to bed. Kate handed Finbar a lamp for their bedroom. Kate followed soon after, and as she undressed she thought about Mary O'Reilly. She felt her pain, it was the first real sorrow in her life and it took time to cope with it. If only Bridget and Finbar had a child, maybe that would help to heal her spirits. As she pulled the bedclothes around her she thought, sure life isn't easy at all.

'Da', Bridget said one evening, 'I think you and mammy need a holiday. Why don't you both go off for a few weeks? it would do the both of you good, sure, the seaside would be just beautiful now, it's lovely weather'. 'I don't think she would go Bridget' her da answered,. Bridget looked at Finbar for help and he said 'maybe you could persuade her Bridget? it would be grand to see the sea, her da said. Bridget, hugged her Da, 'I'll try Da'. Bridget persuaded her mother to go away for a few weeks by suggesting to her that her Da. didn't look very well and needed a change. She told her she had suggested he have a holiday by the seaside, but he wouldn't go without her. She considered a little licence where the truth was concerned and was warranted in the circumstances. Her Mammy agreed to go because of her Da. A few weeks later Bridget and Finbar saw them off for their holiday. As the cab disappeared out of sight, Finbar said 'Sure it's grand that they have got away at all. I thought your Ma was going to change her mind.' 'I had to remind her that Da needed a break, she would do anything for him. I hope it works?' she said.

Finbar brought Daniel home from his usual visit to his grandparents O'Reilly's home himself. As soon as Daniel saw his granny he ran straight into her arms. She hugged and kissed him and he ran off to find his uncle Michael so he could ride 'My Friend'. Finbar sat down in a chair by the fire and Kate handed him a cup of tea. She poured herself a cup and sat down.. 'Tell me Finbar, how is everyone?' she asked. Finbar took a drink of his tea and said 'not too good, Bridget is still very worried about her mam, that's why she didn't come with me today she didn't want to leave her, she sends her love to you'. 'What's the matter with Mary?' she asked. 'It looks like she has pneumonia, the doctor says she has lost the will to live. I don't think she has ever recovered from the shock of Declan's death. The spirit seems to have been knocked out of her' he said. 'Holy Mother of God! Kate exclaimed, that's terrible news, how is John, poor man, and Bridget?' 'Bridget hasn't really been the same since Clare and Declan's death either, when Clare and Declan died it was as though a light inside her dimmed'. 'Finbar, Kate said 'you never really get over the death of someone you love. Time heals the hurt, but not the loss. Sure I still miss Martin after all these years and Clare's death seems only to have happened yesterday. Somehow we do move forward the best we can, especially for the living, but that doesn't mean we don't have very sad days on reflecting on 'what might have been. Will you tell John and Bridget that I'll ask Michael to take me into Dublin this week to visit Mary?'

Shortly after they had finished eating, they walked down to the fields, Finbar wanted to say goodbye to Daniel. As they neared the fields, they could see Daniel riding 'My Friend' in the distance. 'Sure, Daniel's a grand little lad, he's growing fast', Finbar said and Michael agreed. 'I can't see any likeness to his Da. in him at all', he has his mammy's beautiful eyes and looks, I can also see John in him sometimes and Kate says he is like your father Martin, in so many ways'. Daniel saw them and waved. Finbar returned to the house and said goodbye to Kate and left the house to return to Dublin. When Kate saw Mary she got a shock, she realised she was very ill indeed. She sat beside her bed holding her hand. Mary recognised her and Kate was thankful for that. She held a one-sided conversation until Mary fell asleep. After kissing Mary on the forehead she went downstairs, Bridget had tea and cake waiting for her. As Kate sat down at the table she prepared herself for the questions she knew would be asked. 'How did you think Mammy looked?' she asked Kate 'she seemed brighter today don't you think, maybe she has turned the corner at last?'. 'Your mammy knew me, I think that's a very good sign, I left her sleeping peacefully'. Mary O'Reilly died two days later. Finbar brought the sad news to Kate who was very upset, she and Mary had become much closer to each other since Clare and Declan's death and of course their love of Daniel. 'How shall we tell Daniel?' she asked. Finbar thought he was too young to attend a funeral and asked Kate to tell him of his grandmothers' death in her own way. 'I'll do that and tell Bridget that I'll be over tomorrow to help with her mammy's funeral. Michael will be here to keep an eye on things, tell John I'm really sorry for his loss'. 'I'll not stay Mrs. O'Hara, Bridget needs me. I'll tell her you will be over tomorrow, I know she will be glad of your help'. Later, Kate told Michael the sad news that Mary had died. 'God rest her soul' he said. 'How are Bridget and her Da. Taking it?' 'I'm going to Dublin tomorrow, Bridget needs a woman to help her. Mrs. Kelly and Molly and you can keep an eye on Daniel until I get back. John thinks Daniel is too young to see his grandmother buried'. After dinner Kate put her arms around Daniel 'I have some news that will make you feel very sad darlin' he looked at her but said nothing. 'You know your Ma. and Da. are with Jesus in Heaven, well, your grandmother has also gone to be with Jesus too'. Michael and Kate both waited for him to say something. 'Jesus is nice, will granny see Ma. and Da.?' he asked. 'I'm sure she will' Kate said. As Daniel started to cry he said 'I won't see her again will I?' Kate held him closely to her.

It was a beautiful Spring day when they laid Mary to rest. Kate and Michael stood with John, Bridget and Finbar at the graveside as the Priest said prayers for the dead. Kate's heart went out to Bridget as she watched the slight figure dressed in black, hold on to her husband's and Da's arms as she wept for her dead mammy. She remembered the high-spirited girl she had known as Clare's best friend. They had laughed a lot in those days, now it seemed such a long time ago. After the Wake, Michael hugged Bridget and said goodbye to Finbar and John, then left for home. Kate stayed another night in case Bridget needed her. As Kate was leaving for home she reminded Bridget that she will come and see her again. 'I'll miss your mammy very much and you know if I can help you in way, sure you only have to ask'. As the cab moved off, Bridget waved as Finbar put his arms around his wife's shoulders and gently lead her inside.

One evening shortly before Daniel's 9th birthday, Kate and Michael were alone. Daniel was in Dublin visiting Bridget and Finbar. Michael washed and changed his clothes and hurried downstairs into the kitchen, he was ravenous, work on the farm gave him an appetite, so he said. 'What's for dinner ma?' he asked as he sat down at the table. 'Chicken soup and dumplings' she answered. Carrying a dish of steaming hot soup with delicious dumplings bobbing up and down she set it down beside a dish of mixed vegetables. She gave her son a large helping and then served herself. When the meal was nearly finished, Kate said 'Son, we need to talk about Daniel'. Michael looked sharply at his mother and asked 'What about Daniel?' 'His future' she answered. Daniel can't inherit the farm so he needs another occupation. 'I think he should go to school in Dublin next year, he will be nine years of age, and needs a decent education, sure we've saved money enough for that'. 'He won't like leaving the farm' Michael said. 'Sure I know that son. I thought he could live with his grandfather during the week and come home every Friday afternoon. Bridget would take good care of him. What do you yourself think?' she asked. 'Ma, you're wonderful, I think it is a grand idea but I will miss him being here.' 'I'll speak to John when he comes over to the farm next week. When everything is settled, and not before mind, then we will tell Daniel'. 'Sure he's a grand lad, he'll see the sense of it'. Kate washed the few dishes and lifted the lamp off the table. 'I'm off to bed now son, God Bless'. 'Goodnight Ma' he answered. Kate slowly climbed the stairs, as usual it had been a long day. One hand held up her long skirt, the other the lamp. I'm getting old she thought as she reached her bedroom, but I've got a good few years left in me yet!

It was settled, Daniel was to live with grandfather during the week and Michael would bring him home every Friday. He was to start in the New year. Bridget was very pleased, she loved Daniel for himself, but also because of Clare and she had been a little lonely since her mammy died. Finbar knew Bridget wanted children of her own, it was a great sadness for both of them that they had no children. 'Come over here Daniel and sit by me. I have some good news for you' Kate said as she and Michael sat beside the fire. 'The family has decided that you need an education that means you will have to go to school in Dublin. You will live with your grandfather during the week and Michael will bring you home every Friday after school. All your holidays will be spent here on the farm'. Daniel looked at his granny and then at his uncle in surprise. He didn't like the idea very much at all. 'Danny boy, now you know we love to have you here with us all the time but I'll explain the situation to you. We don't own this farm, I can't leave it to you when I die. The owner will take possession of it. Irish people can't own land in Ireland, only the English can do so. It's this bad law which has caused so much trouble for the Irish people. So we decided that one day, you have to earn your own living, and should be given every opportunity to do so. Times are changing and one day you might be able to own a piece of land yourself, but meanwhile you will have to find something else to do. Do you understand what I say Daniel?' Michael asked. 'Yes, I think so, but I'll miss the farm and 'My Friend'. Will you promise me that you will bring me home every Friday uncle Michael?' he asked. Michael put his arms around him and gave him a big hug and said; 'I've never broken a promise in my life, I'll be at your grandfather's house every Friday to bring you home'. 'Did you go to school in Dublin?' he asked 'Yes I did'. I was a bit older than you but I enjoyed it, and I'm sure you will Danny Boy. You know your granny and I will miss you very much'. 'Well then, sure I'll go, as you say, I might like it' Daniel answered. 'Sure you're a grand lad, I knew you'd see the sense of it' Kate said as she hugged him. 'Your Ma and Da would be proud of you'. Michael added.

The first week of Daniel's absence, Kate and Michael missed him so much. Michael set off early for Dublin on Friday morning, he had business to attend to and he wanted to be at Daniel's grandfather's house when he arrived home from school. When Bridget and Daniel arrived from school, he ran around the back of the house to see if the horse and cart was there 'Yes' he shouted and raced inside following the sound of voices to the kitchen. Michael sat there with Finbar and his grandfather. His eyes lit up and he grinned happily at his uncle Michael. 'Well now! Danny Boy, how was your first week at your new school?. Sure you look happy enough' Michael said with a smile. 'Well it's a lot harder than the other school; the boys seem to know a lot more than I do. I've made friends with Timothy O'Shea, sure he knows everything'. 'Indeed, isn't that a bit of luck? We'll have to leave as soon as you are ready'. While Daniel raced upstairs to collect something, Michael asked Bridget if he had settled down. 'Sure he's fine Michael, he's a very bright boy and Finbar can help him if he needs it'. Daniel walked into the kitchen carrying his case. Michael said his goodbyes and they walked to the back of the house, untethered the horse and moved off at quick trot. Daniel chatted to Michael all the way home and had a fair idea of how his first week at school in Dublin had been spent. Kate heard the crunch of wheels on the road outside, Daniel ran into the kitchen and gave Kate a big hug. Over his head she looked quizzically at her son and he answered her unspoken question with a big smile. Thank God! She thought. 'It's grand to have you home again, go upstairs and get changed. 'Yes granny', he replied taking two stairs at a time.

'Bridget says he's a very bright boy and we don't have to worry about him. He's made friends with Timothy O'Shea, evidently, according to Daniel, he knows everything', Michael said. Daniel came downstairs shouting 'I'm off to see 'My Friend' granny' Kate asked 'aren't you hungry?' 'I must see 'My Friend' first, I'll be back later'. Daniel was very tall for his age and could handle himself in the rough and tumble of school life and could fight when necessary. The school bully soon learned to leave him alone. His friendship with Timothy grew stronger so Kate wrote to his parents and invited him for a couple of weeks visit to the farm. Michael brought the pair of them home one Friday at the beginning of the summer holidays. After introducing Timothy to his granny the pair of them ran upstairs to change. As they left the house to go down to the fields Kate reminded Daniel to be careful, 'remember Timothy lives in the city'. 'I'll go down with them' Michael said, we can give Timothy a ride on 'My Friend'. The weeks passed and soon Timothy would have to return to Dublin. Daniel missed him, but there was lots of work for him on the farm and he soon slipped into his regular routine.

The following year, Daniel's pony 'My Friend' died. Fortunately, Daniel was home for the weekend and found him lying in his stall and couldn't get him to stand up and ran outside yelling to Sean and Paddy waving his arms wildly. They came over as quick as they could and Michael joined them. Paddy set off to get the Vet. When he arrived he gave Michael some pills and told him the pony wouldn't last much longer. Michael stayed with Daniel through the night, neither of them slept a wink. In the early hours, 'My Friend' just stopped breathing. Daniel couldn't believe his pony was dead, he tightened his grip on the pony's neck and sobbed loudly. Michael let him cry for sometime, then he gently lifted him up and put his arms around him. 'I'll miss him so much'. Daniel blubbered. 'Sure I know you will, you would be a 'poor sort' of a boy if you didn't'. 'You know 'My Friend' had a grand life on the farm' he knew you loved him and you took good care of him always, he just grew old, he didn't suffer and he knew you were with him. Indeed, that was a blessing' Michael said, trying to comfort the boy.

'Sit here beside me Daniel, you know we never really lose the people or animals we love, we keep them in our thoughts, close to us always. You will never forget the happy times you shared together, so you see, he will always be with you, his body grew tired, come now, be brave and say goodbye to 'My Friend'. Daniel whispered in the pony's ear. Uncle and nephew walked back to the house where Kate was waiting for him. Sadly, she thought, that's his first experience of death, he didn't remember his grandmother O'Reilly at all.

Daniel's school years passed uneventfully. He had grown very tall and sometimes when Kate looked at him, her heart turned over, he reminded her so much of Martin, he had his big hands and big frame. Not much flesh on it yet, but he would be a big man one day, God willing! Bridget heard the front door slam shut and the sound of voices. Looking over the banister rail she saw Daniel and Timothy sitting on the stairs. They looked at one another then laughed out loud. Bridget knew something had happened. Timothy always went straight home and decided she had to find out what they had been up to. 'You closed the door with a bang' she said looking at Daniel. What made you boys run into the house?' 'We threw stones at the English soldiers, we didn't hit them, but a man saw us and tried to run after us yelling for us to come back, so we ran as fast as we could and finally outran him. We were glad to get inside the house' he exclaimed. Bridget wanted to laugh, most of the boys played the same game. It was their way of showing resentment. However, she knew she could not condone it, if they had been caught they could have been in serious trouble. 'Daniel, you know you have been warned not to do that, indeed, I'm quite sure Timothy has also been warned by his parents. It is very dangerous, if you had been caught you would be in serious trouble now. You must both promise me that you will not do so again. Do you understand me?' 'Yes' they said. 'Well now! by the look of you both you could do with a drink of lemonade'. She led the way down the hall as the two boys trailed behind her. Later that evening Bridget went into the parlour to play the piano, Daniel followed her and she asked him would he like her to teach him how to play. 'Yes' he replied as he sat down beside Bridget. Gradually Daniel improved and eventually after some time he could play 'set' pieces competently. He enjoyed playing duets with his aunt and Bridget was delighted that someone in the family was interested in music.

Kate adjusted the hook on the iron bar which hung over the fire and left the large pot of vegetable soup to simmer. It was a beautiful day, Daniel and two of his friends were out playing in the fields and she needed to know what they were doing. Changing into her boots she opened the lower half of the door and stepped outside into the warm sunshine. The sun was warm on her face as she walked along. When she reached Sean he stopped working to chat with her. 'Sean, I need more vegetables, could you fill a basket for me' she asked. 'I'll do that' he replied. Kate sat down on an upturned box and looked around her. She could see Michael and Paddy in the distance but there was no sign of Daniel and the other boys. Then she heard the sound of laughter, obviously it could only be the three boys. As she walked to where she thought the sound came from she reached the stream and she saw the boys swimming and splashing each other. How on earth had they managed that? she thought, as the stream wasn't that deep. She drew closer, but still out of sight of the boys. They had dammed the stream at a bend in the bank with stones and mud and were stark naked. She watched them for a few minutes and then moved away, they hadn't a care in the world and she knew Daniel would not like to know his granny had seen him naked. Walking back towards Sean she knew that Daniel was truly happy. She had tried to give him the love and security she knew Clare would have given him. Michael had proven himself to be a grand uncle and held Daniel in a gentle grip, encouraging him in the good things, and persuading him from the bad; he loved him as if he were his own son. She blessed herself and said a prayer to Our Lady to protect him and help him when she was no longer there to do so.

The summer afternoon slipped away from the three boys, they decided they had had enough. They cleared the mud and stones from the stream and let it run freely again. When they were dressed they raced each other barefoot to the house and burst into the kitchen like a breath of fresh air. Kate knew of course, that they had been swimming, but rules were rules. 'Did you all wash your hands before you came inside?' Kate asked 'Yes! they chorused. 'Well now you can sit down at the table'. She had already placed a large plate of freshly baked soda bread lavishly spread with fresh butter on the table and a large apple pie with a jug of fresh cream beside it. 'Granny! you made my favourite pie' Daniel exclaimed. When the children had finished eating Daniel said goodbye to them, he couldn't be sure when he would see any of them soon. 'Mind now! go straight home' Kate admonished them'. Daniel ran out again to play, he always found lots to occupy himself with the freedom he had on the farm. Kate sat down gratefully in the old rocking chair and picked up a basket full of darning. She picked out one of Michael's socks and wondered, not for the first time, how he managed to make such a large hole in the toe. She loved this time of day. It was peaceful and she felt content with the present and the past she had shared with her beloved Martin.

It was the middle of December. As usual, the routine of the farm was dictated by the season. Business had grown over the years. Michael, Sean and Paddy worked hard to fulfil the orders for their produce on time. The years had brought many changes, some were physical. Michael's once raven black hair was now grey and the boisterous twins had mellowed, even their humour had been tempered by age and the routine in the farmhouse had altered dramatically. Mrs. Kelly came earlier and left later. Molly, who was now a very pretty young woman, helped in the house as well as her work on the farm. Kate was no longer the first person downstairs each morning, in fact, she did not get up until Mrs. Kelly brought her a cup of tea in bed. She still did light work around the house and most of the cooking, but Mrs. Kelly and Molly did the bulk of the housework. They too, were busy preparing for Christmas. Kate's pride and joy, the parlour, had been cleaned and all the furniture polished. She had placed a sprig of holly with lots of scarlet berries behind every one of the pictures that hung on the wall. The whole family looked forward to Christmas, it was a family feast and celebration. Kate wondered if Daniel would be able to come home next year as he will be studying so much. Although farming was Daniel's first choice, he had accepted the inevitable and had decided to study Law, Politics and Law, especially the bad land laws which were a constant topic of conversation in most Irish homes. He reasoned that if he understood the Law better, he might be able to grasp the logic of the bad land laws. Daniel was now 6'2' tall, well built and very handsome. His large green eyes reminded the family of his dead mother, Clare. They were proud of him, Daniel was a fine young man. Tears ran down her face as she thought about Clare, she was so young when she died, Daniel had missed so much. She raised her glass and said 'Slainte!. She looked with pleasure at her son and grandson as they stood side by side, they were both so handsome, Martin she thought, would be so proud of them both. Christmas morning was spent opening and giving presents. Michael only had a minimal amount of work to do, he had planned it that way. The men strolled down to the fields after breakfast. The women were glad they weren't under their feet, they had a lot to do in the kitchen. The dinner was delicious, it really was a feast and a family celebration of life. Afterwards, as usual, Mrs. Murphy and Molly carried baskets full of food and presents for their family. Everyone was asleep as soon as their heads touched the pillow. The food and wine had done its work.

A couple of days later, after the visitors had left, Kate, Michael and Daniel chatted after dinner about the day's events and business matters. Eventually, Kate stood up and said: 'Sure I'm off to my bed, I'm tired'. Michael kissed her on the cheek and said 'Goodnight Ma', 'Goodnight son', she answered. 'I'll carry the lamp for you granny', Daniel said as he lifted the lamp and helped her upstairs. Kate sat on the edge of the bed thankfully, she really did feel tired. Daniel placed the lamp on the table beside the bed and on impulse sat down beside her and gave her a hug. 'Goodnight granny I'll see you in the morning, sleep well' he said as he kissed her on the cheek. 'Goodnight darlin, God be with you always' she answered with a smile. Daniel left the bedroom and ran downstairs to continue his chat with his uncle Michael. The talked late into the night, but eventually, they both decided they needed to sleep and went upstairs to bed. When Michael reached his mother's door he opened it quietly to see if she had blown out the lamp, she had done so and he could see she was sleeping like a baby. The following morning Mrs. Murphy poured a cup of tea and carried it upstairs to Kate's bedroom. She opened the door and saw that Kate was still sleeping so she put the cup and saucer down on the table and crossed over to draw the curtains. Mrs. Murphy knew better than to let Mrs O'Hara sleep longer than her allotted time so she gently shook her by the shoulder and said. 'Wake up now Mrs. O'Hara ,sure your tea will be cold'. There was no response, so she shook her again. When she still didn't respond she turned her face towards, her face was cold to her touch. 'Holy Mother of God!' she exclaimed as she blessed herself. She ran out of the room and hurried downstairs and out of the house. She could see Michael and Daniel standing on a cart, in the distance. Shouting loudly and waving her arms above her head she tried to attract their attention. Finally, as she drew nearer to them, Michael heard her and handed the reins to Daniel. He hurried over to meet Mrs. Murphy wondering what was the matter? 'It's your Ma. Michael, sure I can't wake her', she said as he caught up with her. 'Daniel' Michael shouted as he tethered the horse and ran after them. Michael was first through the door and they followed him upstairs. Michael entered the bedroom and looked at his mother, she seemed to be sound asleep. He touched her on the cheek and said 'Ma, wake up, wake up!' There was no response so he put his head on her chest and listened for a heartbeat, there was none. His Ma. was dead, she was gone!. Daniel heard Michael's voice but it seemed to come from a long distance. He ran upstairs and saw him fall to his knees beside his Ma's bed and bless himself and gently smooth away a few strands of hair from her forehead then kissed her on her cheek. Turning to Daniel, with tears streaming down his cheeks he said

'Ma's dead'. Daniel moved very slowly towards the head of the bed, his legs didn't seem to work very well. Looking down at the face of his granny, she looked somehow younger, at peace. Kneeling down beside her bed, he blessed himself then put his head on the pillow beside her and sobbed.

Fr. O'Conner arrived just after Sean and Paddy came into the room. Mrs. Kelly knelt by the bed with a very distressed Molly, who struggled to understand what had happened. Fr. O'Connor led the prayers for the repose of the soul of Kate, a most remarkable woman. Kate O'Hara's funeral was held a few days later. Besides the family and close friends some villagers took time off from their work, which they could ill afford to attend. Business associates, some second generation. It had been their father's who had done business with Martin and Kate O'Hara. Michael, Daniel and the O'Reilly family stood together at the graveside as the coffin of Kate O'Hara was slowly lowered into the grave beside her beloved husband Martin. The burial service was dignified and simple, just the way Kate O'Hara had lived her life.

Life went on but Michael was very worried about Daniel, he seemed too quiet. He knew he was grieving for his granny and tried to distract him, or talk to him about it as he wished. Daniel didn't seem to want to talk about anything. Suddenly during dinner he blurted out. 'Sure I can't stay here any longer, I don't want to live and work in Dublin. I'm going to have to get away from Ireland'. Michael dropped his fork, he was shocked, he could see Daniel was distressed and spoke very calmly to him. 'I know you are upset and miss your granny, I miss her too. It's a great loss for both of us, but she wouldn't want you to grieve too much. You are young and she would want you to carry on with your law studies in Dublin She was very proud of you, her death hasn't changed that. I'll always help you in any way I can, you know that. I think of you more like a son than a nephew'. 'I just feel I have to get away, Daniel said, America is too far so England will do. I'll find work over there' he replied. Michael was stunned, he had not expected this reaction. 'Are you sure about this Daniel? life is not easy, especially in a strange land. The Irish are not always welcome'. 'Indeed, I know that, but I can take care of myself, you showed me how'. You know, I never really wanted to live in Dublin and study law, I only did it to make granny happy, I love the farm' he explained. 'Well Danny boy, if that's what you want to do, then all I can do is to help you in any way I can but I will miss you' said Michael. Daniel stood up, hugged his uncle and said. 'Sure I'll miss you, the farm and Ireland. I know I'll be lonely but I've got to go' he said. 'Well now! let's talk about how you will get to England' Michael said as he lit a cigarette. He felt such a sense of loss, Ma and now Daniel. Holy Mother of God he prayed silently, please look after him. The family were at the dockside to see him off and to wish him well. Bridget, wiped the tears from her eyes as she hugged and kissed him. His grandfather O'Reilly patted his shoulder and wished him 'God Speed!' Finbar shook his hand and made him promise to come and visit them. Michael was the last to say goodbye, they embraced and Daniel fought hard to stop the tears from falling. 'Danny boy', don't you forget to write now' Michael said as the bell rang on the steamer warning all passengers to board. As he carried his bag up the gangway, Daniel felt a sadness creep over him as he left the family who had shown him nothing but love. When he reached the deck, he put down his bag and stood by the rail and waved. The Steamer began to move and gradually their figures disappeared into the distance. He knew he would miss them, but he also knew he had to leave. He would not return until he had 'found his feet'. It was a warm Spring day so he decided not to go down below and found a sheltered spot from the wind. He wondered what he would find when he reached Liverpool. He knew it was a big port and a lot of Irish people had crossed the Irish Sea. He had an address of a Mrs. O'Flaherty where he could lodge, she was expecting him. Michael had given him a sum of money, with strict instructions to let him know if he needed more. However, Daniel knew he would never ask for more, he was determined to support himself.

PART 11

As the Steamer docked in Liverpool, Daniel saw a huge Cunard Liner being loaded ready for its next sailing date to America. I suppose I could always get a job on a Liner if all else fails, he thought to himself but deep down he knew he didn't want to go so far away from Ireland. As he left the Steamer, he walked behind other passengers carrying their bags, all going in the dame direction, so he reasoned they must know where they were going? There was a great deal of activity going on in the dock area. Fish stalls with fishwives loudly calling out the price of their fish, children running around, in and out of the various stalls. It was all hustle and bustle. Eventually the crowd of people he was following reached a Tram Station and heaved a sigh of relief, he was 'on the right track', he sat down and pulled out the envelope containing the address of Mrs. O' Flaherty and the number of the tram he needed to get there. Slipping the letter back in his back pocket he waited until the tram arrived.

Daniel boarded the tram and asked the driver to let him know when they reached Rodney Street. A short time later the driver of the tram called out 'Who wanted Rodney Street? it's the next stop'. As Daniel left the tram he thanked the driver and looked around him for the street sign. He was at the wrong end of the street, so he walked along and looked at the houses as he did so. They were three storeys high, each with steps leading down to a basement. Brass number plates and door knobs were highly polished. Reaching number 10 he lifted the brass door knocker and rapped loudly. It was opened by a young girl wearing a white apron over her dress. She looked at him enquiringly and he responded. 'My name is Daniel O'Reilly, Mrs. O' Flaherty is expecting me'. 'Come in and wait there please', she indicated a long bench against the wall. 'I'll tell Mrs. O' Flaherty you're here'.

A few minutes later a tall, grey haired woman dressed severely in black, walked down the hall towards him. As she drew near Daniel realised he was being scrutinised. When she reached him she held out her hand and said. 'Mr. O'Reilly, I'm Mrs. O' Flaherty'. Daniel shook her outstretched hand and smiled. 'I hope the crossing wasn't too rough for you, if you will follow me, I'll show you to your room'. She led the way up two flights of stairs until they reached a large landing. Taking her key from the pocket in her dress and opened the door. Daniel followed her inside and looked around. It was spotless and contained a single bed, a tall-boy, wash stand and of course a jug and basin set. There was also an easy chair. She walked over to the sash window and opened it. 'I hope you will be comfortable here, Mr. O'Reilly, lunch is over and supper is at 7.00 pm sharp. However, as you have had a long journey, when you have unpacked your clothes, come downstairs to the kitchen, Sarah will make you a sandwich and a pot of tea'. 'Thank you, sure you're very kind' he said. 'This is the key to your room; Sarah will give you a key to the front door, please remember to keep it on your person when you go out, we have quite a few guests and cannot be opening the door every five minutes' she added. After she had left the room, Daniel sat down on the edge of the bed and put his head in his hands and wondered what he was doing here in this strange room, in a strange house, in a strange country? As he ate his sandwiches he watched as she opened a cupboard door and selected a key from a huge bunch hanging on a hook on the inside of the door. Sarah handed him the key and said. 'this is your front door key, Mr. O'Reilly make sure you always carry it with you. Mrs. O' Flaherty gets very angry if I have to leave my work to open the door to the guests'. Daniel stretched out his hand and took the key from her and put it in his pocket and said. 'Thank you, sure I'll do that'.

After reaching his room he took off his boots ,picked up his book and lay down on the bed and immediately fell asleep. Hearing voices outside the door, he awoke with a start. Looking at his watch he realised it was time for supper and scrambled off the bed to put on his boots, splashed water on his face and combed his hair. He looked at his reflection in the mirror above the tallboy and decided he looked tidy enough. Locking the door behind him he went downstairs. The sound of voices further down the hall drew him along to the dining room and he could see about ten men seated at a long table in the middle of the floor. At the other end of the room a fire blazed in a large open fireplace, two men stood in front of it, warming their backsides. 'Ah! there you are, Mr. O'Reilly, come in and I'll introduce you to the other guests'. Daniel turned at the sound of her voice and followed her into the dining room. 'This is Mr. Daniel O'Reilly, all eyes turned to look at Daniel, with one voice they all said. 'Welcome'. Daniel smiled and said 'Hello' and sat down on the nearest empty chair. As he looked around at the men, he noticed there no women 'guests' and also realised there was no-one anywhere near his own age. The youngest of them would be over thirty years of age.

Supper was served by Sarah and Mrs. O' Flaherty. There was plenty of it and was very tasty. When the table was cleared most of the men left the house to sample the delights of Liverpool's nightlife. One chap left his chair and sat down next to Daniel. 'I'm Pat Clancy, what part of Ireland are you from?' he asked in an Irish accent. Daniel's heart leapt at the sound of it. 'I'm from Dublin, where are you from, I know it's not Dublin by your accent,' he replied. 'No! I'm from Galway, although I've been in England nearly ten years now and I've only been in Liverpool about six months. I have to go where the work is' he explained. 'You're obviously not from 'the bog' as they say, what do you do for a living?' 'I was to training in Law but something happened and I changed my mind and decided to try my luck over here' Daniel answered. 'Well now, and educated Irishman, sure there aren't many of them around here, I wish you luck. You might try The Custom House, it's near the Pier Head. Daniel decided to have an early night and would leave after breakfast the next morning to look for a job. A week had passed and Daniel had still not found work. He was either too young or too inexperienced. At one of the Companies in the Corn Exchange, it was subtly imparted to him that 'No Catholics need apply'. One thing he had noticed that was different from Dublin, was the absence of soldiers. Dublin was full of them. He walked towards Lime Street and passed The Adelphi Hotel, it looked very imposing and decided to join a group of people who were climbing the steps to the entrance. The uniformed doorman opened the door to allow them to pass through. He found himself in a very large carpeted foyer, liveried porters scurried around carrying guests luggage, and groups of very well dressed people stood chatting to each other, he couldn't help comparing these guests with the poorly clad people he had seen roaming the streets of Liverpool. He walked towards Lime Street and entered the railway station where passengers bustled about on each platform then decided he would buy a rail ticket one day and explore the countryside outside of Liverpool but for the moment, he had to find a job, his money would not last forever and he had to pay next week's board and lodging. As Liverpool was a port, he would see if he could find work on the docks, there were always plenty of ships entering or leaving ports.

He was beginning to realise that without money life was very difficult, he had taken so much for granted while living with his granny. Walking back to the next tram stop he boarded a tram back to Mrs. O' Flaherty's. The following morning he left his lodgings about 4.00 am but when he reached the dockside, a queue of men were already lined up outside the Loading Dock Office waiting for the manager to open it and hire them. He was nearly at the top of the queue when the boss came outside and shouted 'No more today'.

Daniel watched the older men walk away, dejection in their every step. They had wasted a whole morning waiting to be hired and would have to do the same next day if they wanted work. Daniel realised it was a terrible system, he thought the men should join together and demand some sort of contract so that they would have some security, even if it was only for a month or so, he wondered why they didn't tell the boss that he needed them as much as they needed him. The ships couldn't sail before all provisions etc., had been loaded. Daniel knew he was not prepared to work under those circumstances and would have to try something else. He also realised 'life was a harsh task master'.

'How was your day Daniel?' Tom Clancy asked. 'Did you find a job?.' 'I stood in line all morning waiting for a job on the docks, there were a lot of men in front of me, I never even reached the head of the queue. I'll not be doing that again, I promise you' he replied. 'Do you mind what sort of job you're looking for?' Clancy asked. 'That I don't, to be sure I need a job and soon', he said. 'You can work with me if you like, I'm a navvy, it's hard work but the money is good'. 'We have a big job at the moment laying pipe lines. You're a lad but you're tall and I'm sure you can handle a pick and shovel, there's a gang of ten. We all meet in the morning and travel to the site by horse and cart and travel the same way home to drop the fellas off as near to their lodgings as is possible'. Daniel couldn't believe his ears, someone was actually offering him a job. 'Sure that would be grand' he said, his face beaming with pleasure. 'We leave at 5.00 am, meet me in the hall, don't be late because I can't wait for you' Clancy said.

Clancy was right, after a day's work Daniel felt as if every bone in his body ached and also had blisters on his hands. Clancy had given him some mentholated spirits to rub on his hands to harden them, and advised him to buy himself a pair of good leather gloves. Gradually the gang left Liverpool behind as they moved along with the pipes. When it was too far to come home each night, they stayed in a small pub during the week and returned to their lodgings at the weekend. Six months later they reached the end of the pipe line. The job was finished in good time. They had by now, left Liverpool far behind and were on the outskirts of Westmoreland, farming country. Daniel loved the fresh air and the sight of horses and cows in the fields. He missed the farm and Ireland so much. It was beautiful countryside, green fields and distant hills where sheep were grazed and made up his mind to leave Liverpool and find a job in this district, probably helping on a farm. After supper that same evening Daniel spoke to Mr. Clancy.

'I've decided to take a train further North and try to find a job there. I know quite a bit about farming, my family have a farm outside of Dublin. I'm grateful to you Mr. Clancy, thanks to you I've learned quite a lot and I've money in my pocket I've earned myself, I'll be leaving in the morning' Daniel said as he held out his hand. 'I wish you 'God Speed Daniel' Clancy said taking his outstretched hand. 'You're a grand lad, Good Luck to you'. Daniel left his lodgings early the next morning and boarded a tram to Lime Street Station. It was a cold, damp, miserable October morning and the houses and streets looked grey and dismal. He went inside the station looking for some information regarding the cost of a single ticket to his destination, whatever that might be? and decided to ask the advice of the man behind the ticket window. Explaining as best he could, the area he wanted, the man told him in a strong accent to buy a ticket to Lancaster and move on from there saying 'EE it's a grand town, and tha'll really like it lad'.

Daniel took his advice and bought a single ticket. He crossed to the correct platform and sat down on a bench to wait for the train. As it pulled into the station belching large clouds of smoke, he boarded and sat down in a seat by the window. The train chugged out of the station and gradually gathered speed as it rattled along. From the window he saw houses, factories and farms pass by until a few hours later the train pulled into Lancaster Station. Daniel looked around as he left the train and noticed that it was a much smaller station than Lime Street. He passed through the barrier and handed the ticket collector his ticket. When he reached the pavement outside he realised he didn't know which way to go. Walking back inside he asked the ticket collector the way to the town centre. 'It's only a 15 minute walk and to turn left as he left the station' he said. Daniel thanked him and set off. As he walked along he could see in the distance a large Castle, it was built of grey stone. In fact he realised all the walls, houses and buildings were all built of grey stone. Although it was October and the wind was cold, Daniel loved it, the air was fresh and in the distance he could see hills with sheep grazing in the nearby fields, horses and cows also grazed. He felt happy and walked more quickly towards the town centre and found a nice looking pub and went in. There weren't many customers in the bar, it was just 'opening time'. Crossing to the bar he ordered a glass of beer and sat down at a nearby table hoping some of the locals could give him the information he needed. He had gained quite a lot of experience working as a navvy in Liverpool. The manager came over and said 'you're a stranger in these parts' Daniel said 'Yes I am, I've been working for six months in Liverpool and I'm hoping to find work. I need a change of scenery, sure it's beautiful here'. 'You're Irish aren't you, I can tell by your accent' 'Yes! I'm from Dublin' Daniel answered. 'Where are you staying, and what sort of work are you looking for?' the manager asked. 'I was hoping I could get a room around here somewhere and work on a local farm, I'm used to farm work, my family have a farm outside of Dublin'. 'I have a room vacant at the moment, you can have it if you like?' the manager offered. 'That would be grand, sure I'll take it' Daniel replied. 'Right then, when you have finished your drink I'll show you upstairs to the room'.

The room was small but clean and the furniture adequate, but that was all Daniel needed. The cost was well within his ability to pay and he settled down to enjoy this new chapter in his life and decided to take a week off and just explore the surroundings. He discovered that the local people were not eager to accept strangers, they seemed to be a bit wary of him. However, he knew it would take time and it didn't worry him. They were certainly different from the Liverpudlians, who were generally outgoing, very friendly and witty people. It seemed hard at times to realise that although Liverpool was not that long away by train but the difference in the scenery and the people was enormous. After having finished his supper he decided to go down into the pub for a chat and a drink. The locals were getting used to him and he felt comfortable with them. There was an old man who came into the pub most evenings and sat in a corner near the open fireplace. Daniel decided he would buy him a drink and get to know him. He always felt at ease with older people, probably because he was brought up by his granny. He told him about the farm in Ireland and his family, the old man listened as he smoked his old pipe and told Daniel he had lived in the district all his life and hadn't been away from it for a number of years. Daniel told him he had worked on a pipe line, as a navvy and it had finished some weeks ago and was hoping to get some work on a local farm. The old man looked at Daniel intently and said 'I'll ask around for you lad'. Daniel thanked him and bought himself and 'Bob' another drink and listened as the old man told him lots of stories, some funny, some sad, about himself. The evening passed very pleasantly and soon the old man said goodnight and left the pub. Daniel finished his drink and went upstairs to his room. As he undressed he knew he had made the right decision to come North. As soon as he found work he would write to his family in Ireland and tell them how well he was doing.

After Mass on Sunday, Daniel introduced himself to the Parish Priest, Father Devlin. The Priest invited him into the Presbytery for a chat and a cup of tea and asked about his family because of Daniel's age and decided to keep and eye on the lad. They chatted about anything and everything and Fr. Devlin invited him to call in and see him anytime he wanted to. Daniel thanked him and left for 'home'. Later that evening while eating supper, Tom the manager of the pub, came into the dining room and sat down at the table next to Daniel. The girl who helped with the cooking brought in fresh soup and mashed potatoes for him. He tucked in and when he had nearly finished, he asked Daniel if he had found work. Daniel told him no, but knew something would turn up soon. 'I need someone to help with the cellar work, I know you are young and it's obvious you have no experience, but you're a big lad and sensible, would you like the job?' he asked. Daniel's face lit up 'sure I'd love to do it, when do I start?' 'This afternoon, I'll take you down to the cellar and show you how everything works. The brewery will deliver barrels of beer and crates of bottled beer tomorrow morning, I will need your help. I'll show you how to 'tap' a barrel and when to do it'. Daniel finished his meal and ran upstairs to write a letter to his family, he would tell them he now had a good job and give them his address.

After two months, Tom decided he would train Daniel to serve and mix drinks and explained to him that if a man asked for a certain brand of whiskey that was what he wanted. It was no good trying to sell him another brand, he would know the difference. He also showed him how some of the regular customers wanted their drinks to be served. 'A gentleman usually calls in about 11.00 am each morning, he is a local Solicitor, he drinks Jamaica Rum and likes it served like this'. Tom poured a large Jamaica Rum into a heavy glass and placed it on a small tray covered with a paper doily. Taking a small 'Toby' jug down from the shelf he filled it with very hot water and placed it on the tray with a small plate containing slices of fresh lemon, 'he will just ask for a large Jamaica Rum, but you must serve it like this, so remember his face'. Gradually, Daniel recognised the regular customers and things went very smoothly.

One evening, Daniel had finished his cellar work and wandered into the lounge. A large room, it contained amongst other things a rather nice piano, he sat down and began to play the tunes he knew. Tom was filling the empty shelves in the bar with bottles and glasses when he heard the music and wondered who was playing and walked into the lounge to find out. To his great surprise it was Daniel.

'Daniel!' he exclaimed. 'You never told me you could play the piano'. Daniel smiled 'sure, I'll never make a Concert Pianist'. A few regulars wandered in, drinks in hand to listen to him play. The customers enjoyed the music and joined in some of the songs until Tom called 'Time, Gentlemen Please'. From then on, whenever Daniel had some time to spare he played the piano. He learned to play more popular tunes and often wondered what his aunt Bridget would think of him now, if she knew he was playing a piano in a pub?

It was early December and already the few shops in the town displayed Christmas items, holly, Christmas trees and more. It was nine months since Daniel had left home and he was homesick. One day after he had finished the cellar work, he went to look for Tom and found him wiping the tables in the Bar. 'Tom, could I take two weeks off work for Christmas? I would love to spend the holiday with my family in Ireland.. Sure I know it's short notice' he added, when he saw the expression on Tom's face. Tom looked at Daniel closely and saw a teenage youth in a strange country away from his family waiting anxiously for an answer. 'That's alright lad, I know a fella who used to work for me, he'll be glad of a few weeks work. 'You go home and see your family'. 'Thanks Tom, I'm grateful to you'. Sitting down at a table Daniel wrote a letter to his uncle Michael and told him he would be home for Christmas and would let him know his time of arrival. After he posted the letter he felt much better.

The following Friday, while Michael and his friends were on their way to Dublin for their usual night out at 'Doyle's', they called in to see the O'Reilly's. They were delighted to see them and even more delighted when he told them Daniel was coming home for Christmas. Bridget clapped her hands and said 'Ah! that's grand news, it will be lovely to see him again, don't you agree?' she asked her Da and Finbar. 'Indeed it is' they replied. Michael suggested that they spend Christmas at the farm, so that the can all be together as a family. 'I'll expect you early on Christmas Eve, can you come?' Michael asked. 'Of course, they all replied. 'Thank you Michael' 'right you are then', Michael said as he prepared to leave. Sean and Paddy stood up also. They said their 'goodbyes' and left for 'Doyle's'. For the first time in months, Michael felt happy. He worried about Daniel and now he would see for himself how he really was. A load seemed to have been lifted off his shoulders. I must make sure Molly and Mrs. Kelly polish all the furniture, especially the parlour, he thought to himself.

When Daniel entered the farm kitchen, he stood quite still for a few minutes then looked around. Everything was the same, but not the same, it felt empty, his granny was not there. Michael watched him, he could see he was upset and knew why. It had taken him some time to even walk into the kitchen where his granny had seemed to spend most of her life, and the fact that he would never see her again. 'It's not the same without Granny, is it?' he said. 'No Daniel, it isn't' Michael replied. After he had unpacked his bag, he walked across the landing to his granny's room. He opened the door and closed it quietly behind him. Crossing the floor, he sat down on the bed and looked around. It looked just the same, everything was in it's special place, even her black Rosary Beads were still hanging from the bedpost. Walking over to the dressing table he picked up a photograph. A beautiful old lady smiled back at him. Wiping the tears from his eyes he replaced it and thought, she never seemed old to me.

After Midnight Mass on Christmas Eve, Fr. O'Connor spoke to Daniel and welcomed him home. The church seemed so much smaller than Daniel had remembered it. He loved Midnight Mass, his granny took him with her when he was seven years old for the first time. He loved the darkness of the night outside, and the brightness of the flickering candles inside. To him, it was the Spirit of Christmas.Mrs. Kelly and Molly excelled themselves, everything was perfect on Christmas Day, the meal, decorations. Daniel answered all their questions. He explained the difference between Liverpool and Lancaster. Especially the difference in the people, telling them the Liverpudlians were very friendly, witty and bright. The people who lived in Lancaster and the surrounding district took time to accept strangers. He also explained the strange feeling he had experienced when he first arrived in Liverpool, and felt as though something was missing, then realised there were no soldiers on patrol in the streets as they did in Dublin. As the family listened to him they saw quite a few changes. Daniel the youth, was giving way to Daniel the man. When the meal was finished the ladies washed the dishes and tidied the Kitchen. Mrs. Kelly and Molly left for home, laden with Christmas gifts and a special gift for each of them from Michael.

'Let's all go into the parlour and have a drink' Michael suggested, leading the way.

When they were seated around the fire, he handed each a drink and offered a toast.' To Daniel, may he have lots of happiness and very little heartache in his future life. To the O'Hara and O'Reilly families may we all share many a Christmas together'. Michael and Bridget made them all laugh with witty and humorous anecdotes. The warmth of the fire, good food and wine and pleasant company had the effect of making everyone, except Daniel sleepy. Daniel helped his grandfather upstairs for a short rest and Finbar and Bridget decided to take a nap. Daniel put on his overcoat and wrapped a scarf around his neck and went downstairs. Looking into the parlour he could see Michael asleep in his chair. He closed the door and left him to enjoy his well earned rest. When he stepped outside the house the cold air bit into his face. He huddled down in the collar on his coat and walked on briskly. He reached his grandmother's and grandfather's grave and looked down at it for a few minutes, then knelt down and placed a white flower, which had always been his granny's favourite at the base of the headstone. After blessing himself he closed his eyes and prayed for the soul of the woman who meant the whole world to him, and the soul of the grandfather he had never known. He remained at the graveside for some time remembering the years he had spent with her. He knew she had been a remarkable woman, who loved him dearly, she had been the most important person in his life. He suddenly felt cold and got up from his knees. Running his hand slowly over the granite headstone he whispered, more to himself than to anyone else. 'I'll love you for ever and will never forget you granny. God Bless!' Brushing the tears from his eyes he turned and walked quickly back to the farm. The family were still asleep, he ran upstairs and flung his coat on the bed, then went downstairs to see if his uncle Michael was awake.

The family tried to persuade Daniel to stay and spend his 17th birthday with the family. He explained that Tom, the manager of the pub was expecting him back after Christmas. He had given his word and did not want to break it. They understood and Bridget organised a special birthday dinner for him, plus gifts, mostly useful ones. They were very upset when it was time for him to return to England but he promised he would always keep in touch. After hugging everyone he said goodbye. Daniel held his grandfather a little longer, he could see he was very frail.

Some months later, one Sunday morning after Mass, Fr. Devlin caught up with him and said. 'I never see you at the dances Daniel, don't you like dancing?' 'Sure but I've never done much dancing Father, my job keeps me away' he replied. 'Yes! I can understand that, but will you take a bit of advice from an old man, find some friends of your own age and live a little'. Daniel smiled and said. 'I'll take your advice Father, soon'. As he walked back to the pub he thought about what Fr. Devlin had said. He had never had the time since his arrival in England for any activity except work, he had to work to live, dancing and friends would have to wait a little longer. However, the seed had been sown and a few months later Daniel told Tom he was leaving. He had decided to move further North and try to get some work on a farm as he had heard that the Furness Peninsula was good farming land and would wait until Tom had found a replacement for him. They parted good friends.

Daniel bought a train ticket to a small town called Ulverston. As he watched the landscape slip by, he noticed the red soil and the fields lush and green and was happy with what he saw. Booking into a bed and breakfast place for a couple of nights, he decided to have a look around the district. He enjoyed walking around the countryside and stumbled on the ruins of an old Abbey and discovered it was Furness Abbey. As he walked among the ruins he marvelled at the skill of the monks who had built the beautiful Abbey with their own hands and wondered if the skill needed still existed? He heard in the local pub that there was a Shipbuilding Yard and also an Iron Works a few miles further down the coast and decided to have a look as he needed some work and as farmers hired workers on a pre-determined period, they were no jobs on offer.

Daniel found the town, it was Barrow-in-Furness a bustling industrial town noted primarily for its Ship building yard and Iron works. He knew he would never get a job in the shipyard, so decided to try the Iron works. After walking a short distance to the Iron Works he went through the gate, a man was sitting near the open window of an office so he went up to him and asked about a job. 'How old are you lad' the man asked. 'I'm, seventeen' Daniel replied. 'What kind of job are you looking for?' 'any job, I need a job'. 'Well! you're big for seventeen, so I'll give you this card, take it to the employment office, it's on the 2nd floor of the building further down, good luck! 'You'll be sweeping the floor and carrying pails of water all day, do you think you want that job?' the foreman asked. 'Indeed I do' Daniel replied. 'Report to this office at 5.00 a.m. tomorrow and I'll show you where you will be working. What's your name lad?' 'Daniel O'Reilly' he replied. 'address?'. 'I haven't got one yet, I'll find somewhere to lodge tonight and I'll give you the address tomorrow when I report for work' he explained.

Walking around the area, he found it rather grimy, streets of houses joined together, some looked cleaner than others. Spotting a sign in one of the windows 'Room to Let', he knocked on the door and waited for someone to answer. The door opened and a middle aged woman stood there. 'I saw the sign in the window and wondered if the room is let?' 'No lad', come on in, she replied. The room was small but clean and that was all he was hoping for. The rent was reasonable and he paid a weeks rent to Mrs. Jones and gave his name and told her he had a job at the Iron Works. The following morning he presented himself to the foreman who took him down to where the big furnaces were. Daniel thought for a moment that he was in Hell. The giant furnace looked like a huge red mouth, wide open asking for food. It was fed with shovelfuls of coal. The men worked stripped to their waists as sweat constantly dripped off their bodies glistening in the light from the furnace as they worked the Pig Iron. He hated the place on sight but he knew that 'beggars can't be choosers'. The foreman showed him where the large sweeping brush was and explained that he was to keep the floor clean and carry buckets of clean drinking water over to the men, they would help themselves to it.

Daniel worked at the Iron Works for a few months and had saved quite a bit of money. Sometimes he went to the local pub for a drink, but people didn't seem to be very friendly so he kept to himself. Daniel finished his shift and decided to take a short cut back to his lodgings. Cutting through some backstreets he turned the corner, three youths stood there and barred his path. He pretended to ignore them and tried to push past them. Daniel knew if he turned and ran they would never leave him alone. The three youths stood firm then one of them let fly with a punch to the jaw. Returning the favour Michael had made sure he could defend himself. However, he was no match for three of them and they rained blows and taunts such as 'Irish Pig! Go back to the bogs. You come over here and take our jobs!'

The last thing he remembered was a blow to his head which seemed as though it had split wide open, he sank down on his knees on the pavement, semiconscious. He thought he heard a man's voice shouting, perhaps it's reinforcements, he wondered. 'Stop it, I say stop it you hooligans, you blasted cowards!' The three youths turned around and saw a man running towards them shouting at the top of his voice and waving a black rolled umbrella wildly in the air. They ran away as fast as they could, leaving Daniel lying on the ground. Daniel heard the man ask if he was alright? but as he reached Daniel he could see his face and head was covered in blood and was nearly too frightened to look closely. However, he pulled a clean handkerchief from his pocket and wiped away some of the blood, and could see a great gash on Daniel's head. Dragging him to the wall he sat him up. 'My name is Fearon , I don't live far from here'. For a moment he was undecided what he should do, he couldn't leave him lying on the ground, but he obviously needed a doctor. 'If I help you lad, can you stand up?' he asked. After a struggle he managed to get Daniel on his feet and half carried half dragged him to his home, which fortunately was not far away. After reaching his house he knocked loudly on the front door, he couldn't use his key because he had his hands full with the 'lad'. His wife opened it and nearly fainted when she saw Daniel. 'My God!, what happened to him?' she exclaimed. Helping her husband she took a clean towel and wrapped it around Daniel's head. 'I'll fetch Doctor Scott', Mr. Fearon said as he left the bedroom. By this time Grace, their daughter had come upstairs to see what was happening. The two women managed to get Daniel to drink a glass of water which they held in their hands. They took off his shoes and socks and covered him with a blanket and sat beside him until the Doctor arrived.

Mr. Fearon and Dr. Scott asked the two women to leave the room so that he could examine Daniel. He cleaned the wound and bandaged it but decided not to stitch it. Looking at Daniel's body which was already bruised, especially around the ribs, bandaged them tightly then took two pills out of his bag and lifted Daniel's head and helped him to swallow them. 'He should sleep through the night' Dr. Scott said. 'He is very badly bruised and also a couple of broken ribs, he has taken a terrible beating'. 'Will he be alright?' Mrs. Fearon asked anxiously. 'Well, it will take some time, but he is a very strong looking lad. Do you know who he is?' he asked . 'I don't think he is a local lad?. I only found him lying in the street, the three youths were punching and kicking him when I arrived on the scene. We'll look after him until he improves. When we know his name and where he lives, then we will let his family know he is being looked after', he added. 'It's down right disgraceful to think a person can't walk the streets going about his own business without being set upon by three hooligans'. 'I'll call again in the morning to see how the lad is'. Dr. Scott said.

The following morning Mr. & Mrs Fearon stood at the end of Daniel's bed looking at him. The bandage was reasonably free of blood and Daniel was still asleep, so they left the room. The following day Dr. Scott called in and after examining the wound rebandaged it, he was reasonably pleased with Daniel's progress. 'I'll call again tomorrow' Dr. Scott said as he left the room. Mrs. Fearon set about cleaning the house with the help of Grace, she looked in on Daniel and heard him mutter something as she reached his bedside and noticed his eyes were still closed. 'Can you tell me your name and where you live?' she asked. Daniel's mouth was so swollen he was struggling but managed to mutter 'Daniel O'Reilly'. 'Your name is Daniel O'Reilly, is that what you are trying to say?' he gave a slight nod of his head. 'Can you tell me where you live?' she asked. 'Mrs. Jones, 10 Clyde Street', he muttered. 'I'll let Mrs. Jones know where you are and I'll bring you up some soup, just rest'.

'Grace, his name is Daniel O'Reilly and he is lodging with Mrs. Jones, I want you to keep an eye on him until I get back, I'll let her know what's happened to him. I won't be long'. Sometime later Mrs. Fearon and Mrs. Jones returned to the house, she gasped when she saw Daniel, he looked dreadful..

'Daniel it's me, Mrs. Jones. Now don't worry, you are in good hands' she said as she patted his hand gently before the two women went downstairs. Over a cup of tea Mrs. Fearon said 'he seems very young to be on his own, do you know much about him? 'I do know his family live in Ireland, they have a farm there, he told me he couldn't settle down after his grandmother died, evidently his mother died shortly after he was born and his grandmother and uncle brought him up. He has been very well educated and is a very nice young man, no trouble at all. Why would anyone want to nearly beat him nearly to death?' Mrs. Fearon mused. 'He's Irish and Catholic, that's more than enough for some people. I'll bring a change of clothes over tomorrow' .

Ten days later Daniel rallied and actually opened his eyes. The joy and relief he felt nearly overwhelmed him, he had wondered if he would ever see again. Struggling to sit up he swung his legs over the side of the bed and looked around the room. Spotting a dressing table with a large mirror and with some difficulty he reached for it and looked at himself, he couldn't decide whether to laugh or cry, he didn't recognise himself. The face in the mirror was a great round blob!, a swollen mass of bruises and a kaleidoscope of colours. His eyes, even though the lids had opened were still puffy and swollen he looked terrible, disgusting, he thought!. Lifting his nightshirt to examine the bruises, he touched his ribs, Oh! boy did they hurt! Walking slowly back to bed he was so angry. Had they beaten him simply because he was Irish? It's funny, he thought, Ireland belonged to England but obviously some English people don't like the Irish and wondered what it was going to take to make people see the senselessness of trying to hold on to Ireland.

Hearing Mrs.Fearon moving about, he hoped she would come in as he wanted to see what she looked like and to thank her for looking after him so well. Hearing the knock on the door he turned to look at her. Daniel saw a pleasant, plump middle aged woman with her hair pulled back from her face and pinned in a chignon on the top of her head. He watched her as she came closer then saw the expression of surprise on her face when she saw his eyes were open. 'Daniel! you can open your eyes? thank God for that' she exclaimed. 'I can see you now Mrs. Fearon and you look just wonderful' Daniel said. A short time later Mr.Fearon entered the bedroom. 'Well Daniel, my wife tells me you can open your eyes. Daniel looked at him and saw a tall, slim bald headed man, dressed in a black suit. His tie fastened with a gold tie pin and across his waist he wore a gold watch chain. He looked what he was, a successful Solicitor, 'Now that you can see and find your way around, why don't you come downstairs and spend the day with my wife and daughter' he asked Daniel. 'I'll do that' Daniel answered. Mr. Fearon turned to leave the room and then stopped and took a yellow envelope out of his pocket and handed it to Daniel. 'I took it upon myself to call at the Iron Works to let them know what had happened to you. They were very pleasant and have paid you the money due to you'. Daniel thanked him for the kindness shown by his family, and with some difficulty, dressed himself and went downstairs.

As he reached the kitchen Mrs. Fearon pulled out a chair and helped him sit down, he felt exhausted, but was glad to be out of bed at last. Grace came into the kitchen and sat down at the table 'when you are feeling stronger you can come out into the garden with me, the fresh air will do you good'. 'Indeed, I'd like that' he answered. While she was talking he had time to look at her, she was a very pretty girl. Grace had dark hair, blue eyes and a wonderful smile and wasn't a bit like he had imagined her.

Over the next few weeks Daniel and Grace got know each other very well. They were about the same age and could talk to each other easily, a firm friendship grew between them. Daniel thought not only is she pretty but intelligent too and liked her very much. One evening after dinner the family were sitting in the garden enjoying the Summer evening when Mr. Fearon asked 'have you thought about what you will do when you are completely better Daniel? you know you can come and work in my office'. 'Thank you for your offer I'm truly grateful to you for so much but I was thinking I would like to work for myself,

I suppose it's because I was brought up on the family farm. It has made a difference to the way I think, but the question is what?, I'm grateful to you for so much'. 'If you change your mind just let me know', he said. Another two week passed and Daniel's face was beginning to look 'normal' again, the swelling and bruising had completely disappeared. The gash on his head had healed and although he had lost weight, he looked very well and his old handsome self.

'Daniel!' Mrs. Fearon said one afternoon, 'I can't believe you are the same lad we brought home a month ago. If I hadn't seen it, the difference I mean, I would never have recognised you'. 'Sure I agree, when I saw myself in the mirror, I could hardly believe it was myself, I was a disgusting sight, sure I was'. Grace burst out laughing and said, 'I like the new Daniel better', they all laughed. There was a knock on the door and Mrs. Fearon opened it. Mrs. Jones stood there. The two women walked through the house into the garden to join Grace and Daniel. 'Well Daniel, you look very well, and handsome too' Mrs.Jones said with a smile. Here is a letter for you' she said as she handed it to him. Daniel recognised the handwriting, it was from his uncle Michael. 'Will you excuse me, I'd like to read the letter', Daniel said as he returned to his room.

Daniel read one line in the letter again – *'your grandfather has not been too well lately, he is getting rather frail'*. Daniel remembered how grief stricken he had felt when his granny died in her sleep, he hadn't been able to say goodbye. Replacing the letter in the envelope he put in his pocket. There was no question what to do and decided he would go back to Dublin and spend some time with his grandfather. 'The letter is from my uncle Michael', Daniel told Mrs. Fearon and Mrs. Jones, he is quite well, everything is fine on the farm but my grandfather is not very well, indeed rather frail. I have decided that I have to go home to Dublin, possibly tomorrow, if I can get a train to Liverpool to catch the boat?' 'Will you come back here Daniel?' Mrs. Fearon asked. 'I'm not sure, but I will write to you from Ireland. Sure I'll never be able to repay you for all you have done for me, but would like to visit you, if I may, sometime in the future?' 'Daniel, you are welcome to come and visit whenever you like, drop us a line when you are coming'. 'Indeed, I'll do that, thank you'. Daniel was up early the following morning, he had to find out about the train to Liverpool and he also wanted to see Mr. Fearon before he left for the office. As he went downstairs he caught him just as he was putting on his hat. As they walked together on the way to the railway station chatting, Daniel promised to let them know where he was and what he was doing. They shook hands and said goodbye.

A train was leaving for Liverpool at 12.00am, he bought a ticket and as he had a few hours to spare he went in search of a suitable gift for the family. He bought a tie for Mr. Fearon and two bunches of flowers for Grace and Mrs. Fearon. Both Grace and her mother were in the kitchen when he returned, he handed them a bunch of flowers. 'They are beautiful Daniel, thank you' they both said. He handed Mrs. Fearon the small parcel which contained the tie for Mr. Fearon, 'will you be giving that to Mr. Fearon for me'. 'What time does your train leave Daniel?' she asked 'it leaves around 12.00, I'll just run upstairs and pack my bag' he replied. 'I'll have your breakfast cooked, you can't travel on an empty stomach', she said. They wished him well 'Sure they're grand people' he thought.

The train arrived at Lime Street Station in time for him to catch the next boat to Dublin. It was a rough crossing but it didn't upset him too much, although he was glad when the boat docked in Dublin. He hired a cab and went straight to the O'Reilly's house. As Daniel climbed the steps, the door opened and his uncle Finbar stood there. His mouth dropped open as he saw the difference in Daniel then he smiled and put his arms around his shoulders and drew him into the hall. Taking his bag, he said 'It's grand to see you again Daniel, so it is'. They walked down the hall to the kitchen to where his Aunt Bridget was pouring hot milk into a mug 'I've a surprise for you Bridget'. She finished what she was doing and turned to face her husband. She flew her arms up in the air as she exclaimed! 'Mother of God' and blessed herself. Daniel walked towards her and she hugged him. 'Let me look at you, sure you look as if a few good meals wouldn't come amiss'. Daniel just smiled and said. 'It's grand to be home and you both look so well. How is grandfather?'. Ah! Well, the truth is. he isn't, he is getting very frail and spends most of the time in his bedroom, he doesn't seem to want to make the effort to come downstairs, but seeing you will cheer him up. I'll just take his milk up to him and tell him you're here, come upstairs in a few minutes'. Daniel went upstairs and stood at the door of his grandfather's bedroom just looking at him, he was shocked to see how frail he was. Walking over to him he put his arms around his shoulders and felt him pat him on his shoulders, as he had always done when he was a small boy. 'Daniel! sure you're looking well, it's grand to see you' he said looking sharply at Daniel. 'How long are you staying in Dublin?' 'Well granddad the truth is I've just finished one job, which I hated and I thought I would come over and see you before I start to look for another', he replied. 'Michael didn't tell us you were coming' Bridget said. 'He doesn't know I'm here. I decided to come on the spur of the moment and surprise you all. I'll set off for the farm tomorrow morning, but I'll come back and spend a week with you, that's if you'll have me?' he said with a big smile on his face.

The following morning, Daniel hired a horse and set off for the farm. On arrival he dismounted and led the horse down to the fields where Michael, Sean and Paddy were working. Molly spotted him first as she walked back to the house and nearly dropped the pigswill bucket in surprise at seeing him standing there. 'How are you Molly?' Daniel asked cheerfully as he smiled at her. 'Ah! Daniel, I'll tell mammy you're here' she replied. 'Tell her I'll be up at the house soon' he said as he walked away in search of Michael. Molly stood for a few minutes and watched him. Where had little Daniel gone, she wondered. Finally she turned and hurried back to the house to tell her mammy Daniel was home. Daniel unsaddled the horse and let it run free in the nearest field. Sean and Paddy were busy in the cow shed, milking. Sticking his head inside the doorway Daniel shouted 'are you not finished yet, sure you've been here long enough?' Both men looked towards the door and stopped milking for a few seconds at the sound of the voice. They both laughed when they saw Daniel. Paddy said, 'sure if you can do it any better or quicker, you're very welcome to try'. Daniel left them to their milking and went in search of his uncle Michael, he could see him a short distance away. Michael's back was turned away from him as he reached him. 'Top of the morning to you' Michael turned around to see who was speaking, his face lit up in a warm smile when he saw Daniel. 'Top of the morning to yourself' he answered as he stood up and gave him a big hug 'This is a grand surprise, indeed it is' he said.

Daniel sat down on the grass and waited for Michael to finish his work. Mrs. Kelly was delighted to see Daniel and set about frying slices of ham and eggs for both of them. When they had finished eating, Michael asked Mrs. Kelly if she could cook a grand meal for everyone then he and Daniel went back to work in the fields. She cooked a grand meal and they all sat round the table talking and laughing, asking Daniel all about England. Sean asked him, with a twinkle in his eye 'how do you like working for the enemy?' After the meal they sat around the fire laughing and joking while Mrs. Kelly and Molly cleared the table then joined the men around the fire. Michael stood up and brought out a bottle of whiskey, and a bottle of wine, after he had poured each one a drink of their choice proposed a toast.

'To the family and Ireland, Slainte!. Eventually Michael and Daniel were left alone.

'I wished you had let me know you were coming Daniel'. 'After I read your last letter uncle Michael telling me grandfather wasn't well, I felt I should come home and spend some time with him before it's too late'. 'Indeed, I got a shock myself last time I saw him. Tell me Daniel, what do you really want to do in England, you seem to have had quite a few jobs?'. 'I don't know yet? I have tried many jobs and saved as much money as I could from my wages, but I would like to work for myself? I think it's because you and granny worked without a boss looking over your shoulder. I often think about it and hope that one day I'll be my own boss', he explained. Daniel told Michael what he had been doing and also about the Fearon family. However, he did not mention he had also been attacked, he knew his uncle would be very angry and upset, it was all over now anyway. They talked well into the night. Michael was not only Daniel's uncle, he was also his very wise friend.

Daniel returned to Dublin the following day to spend a week with his relatives, especially with his grandfather, who had never been out of Ireland and was very interested in the verbal picture Daniel painted, highlighting the extreme differences in culture between the two countries and naturally made light of any problems he had experienced in England. The time came for Daniel to leave Dublin, so he sat down on the chair beside the bed of his grandfather. 'I've got to go back to the farm grandfather, but I'll be over again to see you soon. I have to go back to England in a couple of days'. His grandfather stretched out his hand and clasped both in his. 'Daniel, I know you are doing very well in England and indeed I'm proud of you, you're a grand boy but sometimes things go wrong and accidents happen to the best of people. I want you to do something for me so that I can rest easy, will you do that for me?' 'Indeed, I will, what is you want me to do for you? he asked. His grandfather withdrew his hand from Daniel's and slipped it under his pillow, pulling out an envelope and handed it to him. 'There's a bit of money in the envelope, sure it's not that much, if I had more I'd give it you. I want you to put it in a bank and use it when you really need it, it always helps to have a bit of money tucked away'. Daniel took the envelope from him and chocked back his pride. Putting his arms around his grandfather's shoulders he felt the familiar pat on his back response. 'Thank you, sure I'll keep it until I really need it' and put the envelope in his pocket. Bridget walked into the room carrying a tray with a hot drink for her Da. 'Sit up now Da' she said as she plumped up his pillows. Daniel stood up, it was time to go. 'I have to go now grandfather' he said as he hugged him once again and hurried out of the room and downstairs, he didn't want the old man to see he was upset.

Michael had arrived earlier and was drinking a cup of tea with Finbar, when Daniel walked into the kitchen, Bridget soon joined them and prepared a light lunch. It was now time for Daniel to leave. It was, as usual, an emotional goodbye. 'Don't' forget to write now Daniel' Finbar said. Bridget just hugged him. As he jumped up onto the cart standing outside the house, he heard her call out 'Let me know you're well and happy Daniel'. Michael lifted the reins and the horse trotted off as Daniel waved goodbye to his aunt and uncle as they stood in the doorway.

On the last day of his visit, Michael and Daniel walked to the cemetery and placed some flowers on the grave of parents and grandparents respectively. Daniel blessed himself and said a few special prayers for them. Although he knew his granny's body was buried in the ground beneath his feet, he also knew her spirit was always close to him, especially so, when things were not going so well for him. Michael was deep in his own thoughts. They left the cemetery and walked back home in the late afternoon at ease in each other's company.

Daniel caught the boat in good time. Standing on the deck he held on to the railings as he watched his beloved Ireland's shore slip away. During the crossing, he wondered what to do when he reached Liverpool?. He loved being out in the open air and the only way he could do that, as far as he was concerned, was to find a job working on a farm. He finally decided to go back to the small country town of Ulverston in the Furness Peninsula and would make that his base while looking for work. There were plenty of farms in the area and perhaps this time a farmer would hire him. As soon as he left the boat in Liverpool he walked to Lime Street Station to find out the times of trains to Ulverston. He bought a single ticket and checked his luggage into the left luggage office, then went in search of something to eat. Later, he walked around the shops and bought a few articles he needed, then strolled down to the Pier Head and watched the boats on the River Mersey. In the distance he could see a large P & O Liner on it's way to America. Looking at his watch Michael had given him he decided it was time to make a move, he had a train to catch.

On arrival at Ulverston station, he walked the short distance to a hotel he knew from his previous visit. It stood near the corner of the town square, it was called 'The Prince'. It was a Tudor style building, cream walls and black timber beams. Opening the door he went inside. The Proprietor approached him, Daniel explained he would like to book a room for a week. When all the necessary details had been completed a young man carried his luggage upstairs and unlocked the door to his room. He handed the key to Daniel and thanked him for the tip, When the door closed Daniel looked around the room. It was very nice indeed, fresh and clean. By the time he had unpacked his clothes, washed and generally tidied himself it was time to go downstairs to dinner. The following morning, he opened a bank account with Barclays Bank and deposited the sum of money his grandfather had given him, then strolled around the town taking in the sights. Daniel noticed a poster on a wall 'Cattle Auction, 10.00 – 4.00 pm Thursday. I'll be there to see that, he thought as he wandered on.

Daniel arrived at the Cattle Auction about 11.00 a.m. it was in 'full swing'. The horses had already been auctioned and the sheep were being herded into the arena. Many farmers and on-lookers lounged against the barrier to watch the proceedings. Daniel didn't know much about sheep and wasn't particularly interested in them. As he was about to leave the auctioneer announced that the cows would be auctioned next. He knew something about cows, then was surprised to hear someone ask him in a very strange dialect. 'What dos' tha think of yon cows?' Daniel turned to see who was speaking and saw a young man about 20 years of age and said 'Sure they are as good as I've seen' Daniel replied. 'My boss is o'er yon buying more cows' the young man said. Daniel looked over to where he pointed and saw a burly man dressed in tweeds on the other side of the arena. 'Does he have a farm near here?' Daniel asked. 'Nay! It's miles away, near Windermere. I'm leaving soon as I've loaded yon new cows and delivered them to the farm', he explained. 'Don't you like the work?' Daniel asked. 'Nay!, it's not that, I've worked on farm since I was a young'un. He's a good boss mind. I'm courting a young lady and she don't like me living so far away, we can only see each other on Saturday. I've got a job on a farm near here' he explained. Daniel's mind began to race, should he ask him about a job, or perhaps someone else has already been hired? Nothing to lose he thought. 'Who's doing your job when you leave?' 'T' boss has hired another hand, but he still needs another, he's bought more cows'. 'Do you think he would hire me?' Daniel asked. The young man looked at him sharply and said. 'Tha'don't look like a farm hand?'. 'I've lived on a farm all my life' Daniel replied. 'What's tha' name? he asked. 'Daniel O'Reilly, what's yours?' 'Harry Smith'. 'Stay here lad, I'll go o'er yon and ask the boss'. Daniel waited for some time, then he saw Harry and his boss walk towards him, he felt very nervous; he wanted the job so badly.

When they reached him the man looked him up and down and asked; 'What farm did'st tha work on lad?' 'A farm in Ireland' he replied. The man just looked at him for a few minutes and said nothing. 'Reet, tha can work for a week, at the end of the week, if tha's no good, tha must leave. I'll pay what I owe tha, he said. Tha can help Harry load yon cows and travel back t' farm this afternoon'. Turning to Harry he said 'Get a bite to eat lad, load the cows about 3.00 o'clock, my business will be finished by then. Tha can explain to yon lad what he has to do, where to sleep and what t' wages are T missus and myself are staying t' meet with friends. I'll be back at t' farm tomorrow afternoon. Don't leave till I get there' he added. With that subtle message, he walked away. 'What's the boss's name?' Daniel asked. 'Sampson, Tom Sampson' Harry answered. Daniel offered his hand to Harry. 'Thanks Harry, sure I'm very grateful to you for getting me the job'. Taking Daniel's outstretched hand 'Tha's alreet lad, I can see that, be back here at 3.00 O'clock sharp'.

Daniel watched him walk away and couldn't believe his luck. Walking back to the hotel he settled his account, then went upstairs and packed his clothes. He looked at his watch, it was only 1.00 p.m. Time for lunch he thought, as he locked the door of the room behind him and went downstairs to the bar. He ordered a drink and a couple of sandwiches, food had never tasted so good! When he had finished his lunch, he went upstairs to collect his bags and handed the manager the key to his room and left the hotel. Harry was waiting for him when he reached the Auction Market. He put his bag down nearby and helped Harry to harness the two horses to the wagon. They drove the cows up the ramp into it and locked the tailboard, Harry climbed up and took hold of the reins. Daniel collected his bag and jumped up beside him. With a slap of the reins they set off at a trot.

As the countryside unfolded before him the horses clip-clopped their way along winding lanes, sometimes so narrow it was nearly possible to touch the hedgerows as they passed. Eventually they climbed a steep hill and before them lay the farm. Daniel jumped down from the wagon and opened the gate for Harry to drive in, closing it after him and jumped back on the wagon. It was quite a drive to the farm house and outlying buildings so Daniel had time to look around him. He realised it was a big farm. As they reached the outlying buildings four farm hands came out to meet them. They untethered the horses and led them off to graze in a nearby field. The others helped Harry and Daniel to unload the cows. With a lot swearing and pushing and an occasional slap with a stick on the rump, they managed to get them into their allotted cowsheds. Harry introduced Daniel to the men, they nodded and left to get on with their work and Harry took Daniel to the large barn which had been converted into a dormitory. Pointing to the far corner of the room where a single bed and chest of drawers stood. 'O'er yon is tha bed, when tha have unpacked, cum o'er to the house for tha's supper' he said and left the barn. Daniel was used to sharing a room with a group of men when he worked as a navvy, so lack of privacy didn't bother him too much. It's clean enough he thought as he unpacked his clothes. When he reached the open door of the house, he could see Harry and the other farm hands seated at a large table. A middle aged woman was dishing up the meal. When Harry saw him, he said 'cum o'er her Daniel, this he'r lad is Daniel, the new farm hand Mrs. Dodds', the woman nodded her head and said 'eat tha supper lad' and walked away. He did so and enjoyed it. When the others had left the room Harry said 'Cum o'er here Daniel and I'll tell tha what tha needs to know about your job. By the end of the conversation Daniel was a lot wiser about the farm hands and what his job entailed. It wasn't much different from the work on his own farm in Ireland, except there was more of it. Mr. & Mrs. Sampson arrived home the following afternoon and Daniel watched Harry go into the house, no doubt to talk about the new cows. Shortly afterwards, Mr. Sampson and Harry came over to the cow sheds were Daniel and the other farm hands were working and inspected the stalls. Harry winked at Daniel, which made him feel a lot better. Mr. Sampson checked each new cow to make sure it had not been injured during the journey home from the auction.

'Take yon cows in calf o'er to yon fields, then take the rest down to the far fields to join the others, there's plenty of pasture' he ordered, as he walked away. When it was time for Harry to leave, he shook hands with his old friends and said goodbye. There was a great deal of repartee and they wished him well. At the end of the week Mr. Sampson spoke to Daniel and told him he was happy with the way he worked and he could stay until Christmas. Daniel was delighted, he had a few months of secure work. About a month later Daniel was given a day off. He had heard of Lake Windermere and wanted to see it for himself. It was a beautiful Autumn day as he set off to walk over the fells. Eventually he reached the top of a fell and looked around him. The fell sloped down to the edge of a deep blue lake. On the other side of the lake the water lapped a sandy strip of beach. To his right he could see a large building, it looked like a hotel, to his left a couple of rowing boats were moored to a small jetty bobbing up and down on the surface of the water. Looking around him again, taking in the ground cover of the surrounding fells, green, mauve, yellow and the blue of the lake, he watched as a bird hovered overhead for a short time then swoop down into the lake and surface with a fish hanging from it's beak. Taking a deep breath and for the first time since he had left his beloved Ireland, felt at peace with himself. This is where I'm going to live he thought, and one day I'll have a hotel of my own on the edge of this lake. He lay back on the bracken and put his hands behind his head and dreamed his dream.

The time passed quickly for Daniel, he knew his job and did it well. He got on well with the other farm hands and even managed a few Saturday nights at the local pub with them. Once he even managed to get to a dance and had a grand time. In early December he wrote to Michael and his family in Dublin and told them he would be leaving 'Top End Farm' at Christmas and would write again soon when he was settled in another place. He also wrote to Mr. & Mrs. Fearon. Any time he had off from his work he would walk around Windermere and the outlying villages for some place to live. The rent had to be cheap though. About a week before Christmas he spotted an old cottage. It was built of grey stone and stood in a fairly large walled garden. The windows were boarded up and it looked derelict. Climbing the wall he took a closer look at the place and tried to see inside, but it was impossible. Walking around the back of the cottage among the grass and weeds he spotted the handle of a pump. Daniel tried to pump the water but it was very stiff, so he tried again and suddenly water gushed out drenching his boots and trousers, he was delighted, it was all he needed.

Daniel set off to walk to the nearest pub to find out who owned the cottage. No one seemed to know, all they knew was that it had been empty for years. Suddenly an old man sitting in the corner drinking a glass of cider beckoned to Daniel so he walked over to him and sat down. The old man told him it belonged to the chap who owned the timber yard further down the road, Daniel bought him another glass of cider, thanked him and left the pub. It wasn't long before he spotted a man loading a cart with bundles of firewood. When he reached the yard he spoke to the man and explained he wanted to speak to the owner. I' own it' the man said. Daniel explained that he would like to rent the old cottage. The man stopped what he was doing and asked in surprise, 'You mean 'Rose Cottage?'. 'If that's the name, indeed I do' Daniel answered. The man couldn't believe his luck, someone wanted to rent the old place and said 'come into the office lad'. Daniel followed him into a small room which served as the office and sat down. The owner sat down behind a desk and stretched out his hand to Daniel. 'My name is Thompson, what's yours?'. Daniel shook his hand 'Daniel O'Reilly' he replied. 'Where do you work?' Mr. Thompson asked. 'Top End Farm but I'm leaving after Christmas I want to work for myself, so I want a place to live in'. 'If you don't have a job, how will you be able to pay the rent?' Mr. Thompson asked. Daniel told him he had saved his wages and had money in the bank, 'you will always get your rent on time'. 'Does your family live around here?' Mr. Thompson asked. 'No, sure they all live in Ireland' he replied. Mr. Thompson thought quickly, the place was a dump, no-one had lived in it for years. He had nothing to lose if he let it to the lad and he seemed to know what he was doing. 'Right lad, you can rent it' he said. They agreed on the rent and Daniel signed a short contract. After giving Daniel a copy he asked 'when do you want to live in the cottage?' 'After Christmas, but I'll pay the rent from today' he replied. Handing Mr. Thompson a month's rent Daniel waited until he had a receipt for it. Mr. Thompson couldn't believe his luck and handed Daniel an old key and said 'The lock will be a bit rusty'. They shook hands and Daniel walked away. Mr. Thompson watched him until he was out of sight and wondered why the lad lived so far away from his family.

The lock was very rusty and it took Daniel a few minutes to open the door. Walking inside he gasped for air, the place was covered in a thick layer of dust, a little light filtered through the broken panes. There were two rooms, one was a kitchen and the other a bedroom, he supposed. A table and two chairs stood in the middle of the floor of the kitchen, they were covered in dust, brushing some of the dust away he examined them. They were quite sound. Good! he thought, at least I will have somewhere to sit and a table. The floor of the cottage was dark blue slate, a bit chipped, but very solid. He walked over to the fireplace and wondered how long it would take him to clear the chimney before he could light a fire. The walls were whitewashed. Looking up at the roof, light was filtering through a gap. Being quite satisfied that there was nothing he couldn't repair, he locked the door behind him and walked around the back and pumped some water and was surprised that the water was quite clear, he pocketed the key and made his way back to 'Top End Farm'.

At supper on the evening before Christmas Eve, Mrs. Dodd said The postman had left parcels and letters in Mr. Sampson's office and some were for Daniel. After supper all the farm hands hurried over to the office to see if any of the letters etc., were for them. Daniel had two parcels and three letters. He recognised Michael's handwriting and Finbar's but did not recognise the handwriting on the other letter. Hurrying over to the barn Daniel sat down on his bed to read the letters moving the lamp nearer, it was quite dark in the barn.

Michael's letter was full of information about the farm and everyone was well, he missed him but understood why he couldn't come home to Ireland for Christmas. Then Daniel opened the parcel. There was a lovely thick woollen scarf and a pair of gloves, also a new wallet. Putting the scarf around his neck, it felt warm, then he tried the gloves on, they fitted him perfectly. Opening the wallet he noticed there was a note from Michael. Danny boy, the money enclosed is a Christmas present, enjoy yourself. There was quite lot money, so he replaced it safely back in the wallet and thought, now I can buy a few things for the cottage. The letter from Finbar wished him well and gave him the good news that his grandfather was a lot better and Bridget wished him a Happy Christmas and hoped he liked his present. Tucking the letters away in his pocket he opened her parcel. It was a huge box of his favourite sweets and chocolates bought from an exclusive shop in Dublin. Daniel felt very happy, he knew his family were thinking of him. He opened the last letter from Mr. Fearon, he was invited to spend Christmas with the family. Daniel's first reaction to the invitation was to refuse, he wanted to clean the cottage and repair the roof etc., After thinking about the invitation he decided he would like to see them and a few days wouldn't make that much difference, as he would no longer be working on the farm and decided to accept.

Early on Christmas Eve Daniel milked the last cow and made his way to Mr. Sampson's office to join the other farm hands. Mr. Sampson strode into his office and sat down at his desk. Shaking hands with each man he handed each the wages due and an extra week's money as a bonus for Christmas. He wished Daniel 'good luck' and said goodbye. Daniel hurried over to the barn to change his clothes and pack his belongings. One of the farm hands, Fred, had offered to give him a lift in the milk cart to Ulverston. Wrapping his new scarf around his neck and pulling on his gloves, he felt very thankful for them, it was a very cold December day. Fred dropped him off on the outskirts of the town. Daniel thanked him and wished him a Happy Christmas then set off for the 'The Prince Hotel'. When he reached the hotel he opened the door and went inside. The proprietor recognised him and greeted him cordially. Daniel ordered a drink and a bowl of nettle soup, which his wife Mairead makes herself and sat down at a nearby table. The proprietor brought the drink and the bowl of hot nettle soup over to Daniel, which was his favourite and tasted as good as his granny used to make then sat down at the table for a chat. They knew quite a lot about each other's backgrounds from previous conversations. Daniel knew he was born in Scotland and his parents came from Donegal in Ireland, his wife's parents also came from Ireland. His Scottish accent was still very broad, even though he had lived in England for a number of years, He was a very interesting man and had travelled all over Scotland and England. Daniel discovered something new about him and learned that he had played soccer beginning as a teenager for Hibs, and had his caps and medals hanging on the wall in the bar, but a knee injury had ended his career. They discussed the pros and cons of hurling until it was time for Daniel to make a move, he bought a bottle of good sherry for Mr. & Mrs. Fearon then wished the proprietor and his wife a Happy Christmas and would return to see them again and how he loved her nettle soup, then set off to walk to the railway station.

Daniel caught a train to Barrow-in-Furness and arrived at Mr. & Mrs. Fearon's house early in the afternoon and knocked on the door, Mrs. Fearon opened it. When she saw Daniel she smiled with pleasure and ushered him inside. Grace heard voices in the hall and wondered who it was? Daniel walked into the kitchen where Grace was busy preparing vegetables 'Sure it's grand to see you again Grace, you're looking well' he said. Grace blushed a little when she saw him and smiled. She thought, I had forgotten how handsome he is. 'It's nice to see you again Daniel, I can see you have not been in any fights lately' she said as she smiled at him. As Daniel climbed the stairs to take his luggage up he felt quite at home.

Mrs. Fearon had made sandwiches and placed a home baked cake on the table in the kitchen. He sat down with Mrs. Fearon and Grace and started to tell them about Rose Cottage. Soon after, Mr.Fearon walked in and was delighted to see Daniel and shook his hand warmly. Daniel thanked them for inviting him to spend Christmas with them and retold the story of Rose Cottage and his plans for the future and gave them the address. After Midnight Mass with the Fearon's, Daniel once again felt the magic, he couldn't explain it. Somehow as he knelt and prayed for his dead parents, his family in Ireland and his beloved granny, he realised Christmas 1908 was a landmark in his life. He was away from home but was really glad he had decided to spend it with the Fearon's, they were a very special family.

Daniel moved into Rose Cottage on a permanent basis in January. By the end of a couple of weeks the leak in the roof had been repaired, the boards taken down from the windows and the broken panes of glass replaced. The inside walls had also been whitewashed. The cottage was now quite comfortable to live in. One night as he wrapped his blanket around him and lay down to sleep on the slate floor he decided it was time he had a bed to sleep on, his back ached every morning.

Early the following morning he walked down to the village to the second hand shop hoping to find a bed and mattress plus a few bits and pieces he needed. Daniel only had a small amount of money to spend on the bed etc., he needed the money for other things he had in mind. When he reached the shop he looked in the window, it was full of furniture, pictures, brass ornaments, fire-irons and clocks etc., Daniel stood beside the counter and looked around the room. It was stacked to the ceiling with sacks of second hand clothes bursting out of them. There was just enough space to walk through into the adjoining room and decided he would go through, perhaps, he thought, the owner would be there.

The room was in the same state as the other one, stacked to the ceiling with second hand goods. 'Hello! I'm Percy' he heard a voice say and wondered where the voice came from? there was no-one else in the room except himself. Out of the corner of his eye he caught a slight movement and looked up into the face of a brightly coloured parrot perched on a rod chained to it's cage. Daniel laughed and said 'Hello Percy'. He heard the door open and turned to see who had come into the room. The old man closed the door behind him and said' 'Hello! I'm Percy'.

Daniel bought a bed and mattress, two blankets, a chest of drawers, some pots and pans and to his delight he spotted a toasting fork. The articles were very cheap and he had the distinct impression that the owner was grateful to get rid of them. After paying for them he arranged to have them delivered later in the day. As he walked out of the room, he turned to the parrot and said 'Goodbye Percy' with a smile on his face, and walked further down the road to the timber yard. Mr. Thompson was at work in his office so he went inside and sat down. 'Morning Daniel, what brings you here today?' he asked. 'I'm here to buy timber to build a large shed in the back garden' he replied. 'A shed, why on earth would you need a shed?' Mr. Thompson asked in surprise. 'To shelter a horse' Daniel said. Mr. Thompson sat back in his chair and looked at him in total disbelief, it certainly was not the answer he had expected. 'I intend to buy a horse and cart and start a delivery service', he explained. 'Daniel, you never cease to surprise me, sometimes I don't know what to make of you at all', he said. 'Sure, I've got to find the goods to deliver first', Daniel responded.. I'll ask the shopkeepers when I have the shed built. Part of it I will use as a stall for the horse and the rest for storage'. They discussed the amount of timber, tools etc., and agreed on the cost. Later, Mr. Thompson delivered the goods. As the two men unloaded the cart, Mr. Thompson asked. 'Would you like me to give you a hand to build the shed, Daniel?' Daniel looked at him in surprise and said 'Indeed that would be grand'. 'You help me and I'll help you, so it is agreed'. By the end of the week the shed was built. They both stood back to admire their handy work. As Daniel slotted the bar across the door he said 'It's a grand shed, sure it is I'm grateful to you for your help. How about a drink and something to eat at the pub?' Later the same evening Daniel sat at the table and counted his money, leaving a small amount to put in his bank account. The horse and cart would have to be cheap, he thought. Daniel explained to every shopkeeper who would listen, that he intended to start a delivery service. The cost of delivery would depend on the length of the journey. He told them the rates would be reasonable and he guaranteed delivery on time. By the end of the day he had three contracts and a promise of work in the future. One of the shopkeepers was Mr. Hart, the owner of the second-hand shop. Sure it's enough to keep body and soul together, he thought as he walked back home, it's a start, so it is.

Daniel had heard that a farm in the next village would be auctioned. The farm was a long way away, but he guessed that quite a few farmers would go to the auction, even if only out of curiosity and hoped he could get a lift. He was halfway there when a local farmer gave him a ride to the farm. Already groups of men stood about waiting for the auction to begin. Daniel was only interested in a horse and cart. Two horses stood tethered nearby. Looking closely at them, he thought only one was worth bothering about. After examining the horse he was interested in he decided what he could afford to pay for it. An old cart stood to one side of the ploughs etc., the shafts and wheels were sound but half of the floor of the cart was missing and decided that was not a problem and would bid for the horse and cart. The auctioneer strode into the field and climbed up onto a box. The auction had begun.

It was after lunch when the horse was put up for auction.

Fortunately, most of the farmers had drifted away. However, one man wanted the horse as well. He made a bid so Daniel made a higher bid. The price was rising but the horse was still worth the price. Soon Daniel reached the limit he could afford and decided he would make one last bid, he couldn't go any higher. The other man dropped out, the horse was his. The cart was the last item to go under the hammer. No one bid except Daniel. The auctioneer accepted his bid and threw in a couple of bales of hay and a bag of feed. Daniel was delighted, he couldn't believe his luck. After settling the account he harnessed the horse to the cart and drove home to Rose Cottage. He led the horse into it's stall and after he had made sure the horse was settled closed the stall door and leaned over and patted it then slipped the bar into place and went inside. After he had eaten he sat own at the table and wrote letters, one to his uncle Michael, one to his grandfather, his uncle Finbar and his aunt Bridget telling them he had a decent place to live and had bought a horse and cart and intended to start a delivery business of his own. He also invited them all to come over to England for a visit. Sealing the envelopes he placed them in front of the teapot then undressed and climbed into bed. I'll post the letters tomorrow or the next day, after I have repaired the cart, he thought as he drifted off to sleep.

It was now early May. Daniel had kept his promise to deliver on time and the shopkeepers were very happy with the arrangement. However, Daniel was not. The amount of money he earned was barely enough to pay for his expenses. Sitting in front of the fire one night, toasting thick slices of bread, he realised where the problem lay. He returned from delivery of the goods with an empty cart! Somehow he had to return with a full cart. As he munched on his buttered toast he thought about it and stopped eating, he had an idea. He would buy second-hand clothes and anything anyone offered for sale. Once he had delivered the goods he was paid to deliver the day was his own, so he decided he would travel to the more outlying villages as well and would try out the idea when he made the next delivery.

As he passed through a village he called out: 'Any old wares, any old clothes, old pots and pans, any old wares?' Some children heard and saw him first, they ran up to the cart to inspect the bells on the horse's harness. Soon doors opened and mothers came out to see what the noise was all about. One women said, 'Do'st tha'buy anything lad?' 'Indeed I do, I'll give you a fair price' he replied. 'Wait here lad, I'll be reet back', she said as she disappeared inside. Daniel talked to the children warning them not to come too near. 'What's t' horse called?' one boy asked him. Daniel hadn't given the horse a name, so on the spur of the moment he answered 'Darkie'. The woman returned with a basket full of odds and ends. However, as he examined what she brought he knew any woollen garment brought a good price. He opened the money pouch he kept strapped around his waist and gave the woman her money. She looked at the money in her hand in disbelief, they were only rags, she thought. 'Wilt tha' be coming again? she asked. 'Indeed I will, I'll be around in a month's time', he replied. He waited until the children had moved away from the cart and it was safe to move off. Daniel could hear the children as they ran behind the cart, he couldn't help but laugh as he remembered the time he had hitched a lift on the back of a cart. Sure children are the same the world over, I suppose, he thought.

Gradually over the following months he arranged to be in a certain village on a certain day each month. The children were always the first to spot him, they heard Darkie's bells jingling and ran inside to tell their mothers or fathers, as the case may be, that Daniel had arrived. Daniel always carried a tin of sweets in the cart and gave each child a few. He realised that sometimes women sold articles they really did not want to part with, he could tell by the look on their faces. However, he always gave them a fair price. He sorted everything out into separate piles and stored them in the space provided in the shed. When he had collected enough, they were sold to the wholesale dealer. One morning, after he had sold his goods, he walked to the bank and deposited some money. It wasn't much, but it was the first time he had managed to save a penny.

Daniel finished his round and was on his way to 'Rose Cottage. It was a warm summer afternoon in late August. As Darkie meandered along the winding lanes, he savoured the sights, sounds and scents of summer. Wild flowers grew in profusion in the hedgerows, blackberry bushes promised luscious fruit. A bee buzzed overhead and settled finally on a pink and white wild rose. A farmer somewhere was making hay and the sweet scent of it lingered in the air. He felt happy, young and glad to be alive. Turning the cart into the lane that led to 'Rose Cottage' he let his thoughts drift. I might sit in the garden after I've eaten something and read a book, he thought. Or maybe I'll answer Aunt Bridget's letter, but sure there's no rush! In the distance he saw something in the ditch. As he drew nearer he dropped the reins and let Darkie graze. ' Perhaps it's a bundle of clothes he thought as he walked across the lane to get a better look'. In the ditch lay an unconscious man. 'Holy Mother of God! he exclaimed and blessed himself.

All he could see was the deathly pale face of a man; most of his face was covered by a thick beard, his clothes were ripped and he wore no boots. Daniel felt quite scared, but had to find out if the man was dead or alive. Putting his hand on the man's heart, he felt a heartbeat. 'Thank God! he thought! Clasping his arms under the man's shoulders Daniel dragged him over to the ground while he lowered the tailgate on the cart. Making a bed of sorts from the rags and clothes, he dragged him headfirst into his cart, lifted the reins and set off at quick trot. When he reached 'Rose Cottage' he manoeuvred the cart so that he could take the man into the house. Removing the man's outer clothes he struggled to lift him into the bed, he was a big man and wondered what he should do next? Covering him with blankets he sat down thankfully on the floor to recover his breath. He got up from the floor and filled the kettle with water from the outside pump, filled a basin with water and a clean towel, then cleaned the man's hands and face and returned to the kitchen to light the fire, he waited until it was hot enough and put the kettle of water on to boil. Then he remembered the small bottle of brandy Mr. Fearon had given him, he poured a small amount in a cup and went back into the bedroom. The man was still unconscious. Lifting the man's head he managed to get some brandy down his throat, some spilled, but enough went down his throat.

Daniel looked at the man and wondered if he should get a Doctor. What if he dies while I'm out of the house he thought? but he decided to be on the safe side and fetch the doctor. Climbing into the cart he set off. The Doctor came back with him and Daniel watched as he examined the man who was still unconscious. There were no broken bones but knew there had to be some reason why he was in this 'state' then he found a large lump, the size of an orange on the back of his head. 'You said you found him lying in a ditch? Have you looked through his pockets, there may be a name or an address or something?' the Doctor asked. 'No!' he answered and handed him the man's clothes. Searching through the pockets, they were empty. 'Well! the Doctor said. 'There's nothing there to help us, we must just wait until he regains consciousness just keep his head cool, that's all you can do at this stage, except watch over him, I'll call again tomorrow morning to see how he is progressing'. Daniel wondered what had happened to him and why were his clothes ripped? perhaps he was a tramp? Or maybe he was drunk and fell, or had he been attacked and left in the ditch? He went outside to settle Darkie in his stall for the night, and closed the door behind him. Feeling very tired he wrapped a blanked around himself and lay down on the floor to sleep. Dear God! he prayed, please don't let the man die during the night and fell into a troubled sleep. When Daniel awoke the next morning, the first thing he did was to go into the bedroom and take a look at the unknown man in his bed. He hadn't moved at all during the night. Dipping the towel in the water Daniel wrapped it around the man's head. Later the following morning the Doctor examined the man and said 'If he doesn't regain consciousness by tomorrow, I will have to send him to the hospital, can you stay with him?' 'I deliver goods for the shopkeepers, I have deliveries today but I can't leave him here alone. Would you mind calling to them and explain the situation and that I'll be back at work as soon as I possibly can'. 'I'll do that and I'll call again tomorrow' the Doctor said as he left the house. Daniel returned to the bedroom and sat down on the chair looking closely at the man. He looked about fifty five, probably tall as myself, he thought and well built. He noticed the man's hands as they lay on the blanket. There certainly were not the hands of a working man, there were no calluses or healed cuts and his nails were well looked after, even if they were rather dirty. I wonder who he is? he asked himself for the hundredth time. He picked up the man's jacket and examined it. It was made from expensive cloth. Sewn into the lining of an inside pocket was a tailor's label, Smythe-Jones, London.

Daniel awoke with a start, for a moment he didn't know where he was and soon realised he had fallen asleep in the chair. Looking at the unknown man in the bed he could see that his eyes were now open. 'Thank God, you're awake!, now don't distress yourself, sure you're in good hands, you're quite safe', he said. 'Where am I?', the man asked. 'My name is Daniel, 'I found you lying unconscious in a ditch and brought you here, to my home', he explained. 'Thank you!' the man said in a weary voice and closed his eyes again. Daniel heaved a sigh of relief, he's alive, Thank God! he thought, and left the bedroom and went outside to take Darkie out of his stall. He patted him on the nose and gave him an apple and got on with his chores. Later on the Doctor arrived and Daniel explained what had happened. The Doctor examined the man and seemed quite satisfied and handed Daniel a box of pills with instructions when to give them. I'll call again tomorrow', he said.

It was late afternoon when Daniel returned to the bedroom. The man was awake, so he sat down on the chair next to the bed and removed the damp cloth from the man's head, then dipped it again in the cold water and replaced it on the man's head. 'Are you feeling any better?' Daniel asked. The man shook his head lightly, from side to side. Daniel gently lifted him up and managed to get him swallow the pills with a little water. 'How long have I been here? the man asked. 'Nearly three days, can you tell me your name and where I can reach your family?'

Daniel asked. 'James, my family is away', he said as he drifted off to sleep again.

The following morning when the Doctor arrived, James was awake but complained of a violent headache. 'I'm not surprised, you have a lump the size of an orange on your head, do you remember anything about what happened to you? 'Yes, two men attacked me, they stole my money and wallet' he replied. 'You're a very lucky man. If this young man hadn't brought you home and cared for you, I believe you would have died. I will call to see you again in a couple of days'. Daniel made James as comfortable as possible and made a pan of soup he'd seen his granny make many times, and besides, he thought, I don't have anything else. Gradually, James improved. The Doctor no longer called and most afternoons, Daniel and James sat outside in the garden, weather permitting, and talked. One evening, as they sat in front of the fire, Daniel said. 'Sure you never told me your surname? and I have noticed you speak with a cultured English accent. While you were unconscious I searched your pockets for anything that would identify you. I found nothing, however, I did notice a tailor's label stitched inside your jacket, it was a London tailor's label'. 'My full name is James Smith, and yes, my young detective, I do live in London with my family. I have one son and work for the Government. My position takes me away from home very often. I used to climb around the Lake District when I was younger, now I am content just to hike. Now dear boy!, you know all about me, tell me about yourself. For instance, why did you leave Ireland at such a young age?' he enquired. 'Ah! Sure it's a very long story James. Indeed my family's background is a 'triumph over tremendous odds, mostly none of their making. I don't think you would like my story very much at all', he declared. James looked at him very sharply, then said. 'Daniel, I know enough about you to know you are honest, hardworking and kind. I am not a stupid man, I am fully aware of the problems between England and Ireland. Nothing you could say would offend me, I have a great regard for you and look upon you as a friend. I would be delighted to hear all of it, if you wish to tell me'.

It was very late when Daniel finished speaking. He told James the story exactly as his granny had told it to him. How she had been a very young girl during the 1845/6 Famine, and left nothing out and explained the effect of the savage Land Laws imposed on the Irish people. The greedy Absentee Landlords, the dishonest Agents who worked for them, that led to abject poverty, starvation, misery and death of millions of women, men and children. The 'coffin ships' which took dying people to America. He also explained how his granny and grandfather had been granted a very long leasehold on a practically derelict farm, by the owner, the Duke of Lancaster, provided they paid the 'ground rent' on time and improved the land. A nearly impossible task, but they had accepted, they had no choice. The leasehold was long because it was impossible for the tenant to improve the land and pay the rent at the same time on a short lease. They took the view that it would be stupid to pay the Landlord to starve. He also explained that his uncle Michael, had been granted a lifetime Leasehold when the original lease ran out, by the present Duke of Lancaster. The farm made money, he was a good farmer and businessman. Michael was not married so there is no son to inherit the Leasehold on his death, I am his nephew. Daniel also explained that after his granny's death, he felt very unsettled and decided to leave Ireland for many reasons, but primarily because there was no future for him on the farm as he couldn't inherit it. James was silent for some time and then said, 'Thank you Daniel, you have painted a very vivid picture, I'm sure it wasn't easy for you. I do feel rather tired, I'll wish you goodnight'. 'Goodnight James', Daniel said as he handed him a candle. A few days later, Daniel asked James if he felt well enough to be left alone for a few hours, explaining he had some deliveries to make but wouldn't be away too long. 'Off you go, my dear boy! 'I shall be perfectly safe until you return'. When Daniel returned, he unharnessed Darkie and left her to graze on the grass. Opening the door he expected to see James, there was no sign of him. Then he noticed an envelope addressed to him and sat down, it was a letter from James.

My dear friend,

I feel I have abused your kindness and your hospitality long enough. I have left to return to my family in London. I hope you won't mind, but I have borrowed one of your jackets (my trousers are not too bad) and a pair of your boots, perhaps a little tight, but one cannot have everything, can one? I shall return your clothes to you as soon as I possibly can Daniel. To say 'thank you' for saving my life would be inadequate. I shall be indebted to you for the rest of my life. If I can ever help you, in any way at all, I should be delighted to do so. Pursue your Dreams Daniel. I do hope we meet again some day..

Yours Most Gratefully, James Smith

Daniel folded the letter and slipped it into the envelope and placed it in the small drawer in the table among other 'odds and ends' and wondered if they really would meet again.

Daniel worked very hard during the months leading up to Christmas. He made extra deliveries for the shop keepers and during his rounds and realised many people were willing to sell all kinds of articles to make extra money for Christmas, so he bought everything offered to him. On Christmas morning Daniel opened his parcels from Ireland. There was a hand knitted pullover and scarf from his aunt Bridget and uncle Finbar, a small card from his grandfather and from his uncle Michael, a new book and a sum of money. He smiled when he saw the money. Daniel knew his uncle wasn't too sure how well he was doing. He slipped the new pullover over his head and admired himself in the small mirror on the wall, swallowing the lump in his throat, as he remembered Christmas in Ireland when his granny was alive. I still miss you granny he thought as he left the house and locked the door behind him. Harnessing Darkie to the cart he climbed up and set off to hear Mass at Coniston Water. There were not many people on the roads, sensible people he thought, at home with their families. Daniel stopped the cart to look at Coniston Water. The fells were dotted with huge drifts of snow, small ripples broke the surface of the water. On the other side he could see a church spire. When Mass had ended Daniel left the church and walked over to where he had tethered Darkie. 'Good morning young man, Happy Christmas', he heard a voice say. He turned around and recognised the old white haired priest who had just said Mass. 'A happy Christmas to you father', he replied warmly. 'I'm Father Kelly, I have a very small flock, you are a stranger here?' 'Indeed I am, my name is Daniel O'Reilly, this is my first visit to your church, it looks very old and is very beautiful', he said as he shook the Priest's hand. 'I'd like a bit of company this morning, would you like a cup of tea?' Father Kelly asked. 'Ah! Sure that would be grand', Daniel answered.

Father Kelly ushered Daniel inside his room. It was very small, books littered the place. There was very little furniture, only a table and a couple of chairs but a bright warm fire burned in the fireplace. 'Make yourself comfortable , warm yourself by the fire, I won't be long'. Daniel took off his outdoor clothes and warmed his hands in front of the fire. It was a very cold day. Later, Father Kelly returned with a tray. There was a large fruit cake, cups and saucers, milk and sugar. He poured a cup of tea for Daniel and said, 'help yourself to the cake'. By the time the tea pot was empty and a large slice of the cake had been eaten, Father Kelly knew a great deal more about Daniel and how he earned his living. 'Daniel, I have a lot of articles stored here from the Christmas Fair. The ladies of the Parish run one each year and we have a party for the children, would you be interested in seeing them?' he asked. 'Indeed I would', Daniel replied. 'Come along then' he said. leading the way to a room at the back of the house and opening the door for Daniel to step inside. The room was stacked with boxes of all sizes. Daniel took a closer look and realised they had been there for a long time, dust was thick on them. He opened one nearest to him and looked inside. It was full of woollen hats, scarves and gloves. The next one contained books. 'Sure I'd like to buy the lot' Daniel said, Father Kelly's mouth dropped open and then a smile spread across his face. 'The lot?' he repeated. 'Indeed, I'll give you a good price for them'. They returned to Father Kelly's room to discuss details and Daniel arranged to pay for the goods when he collected them the following week. Putting on his outdoor clothes and accompanied by Father Kelly, left the house. 'Thanks for the tea and cake Father' Daniel said as he climbed into the cart. I'll call again next week.' 'You're very welcome Daniel, may God be with you'. Daniel flicked the reins and Darkie moved off. Father Kelly watched until the horse and cart was out of sight, then walked quickly to the church and knelt down before the altar and prayed. 'Thank you God, you have answered my prayer'. He blessed himself and then returned to his room. Warming himself in front of the fire he thought God works in mysterious ways, all I did was offer a stranger a cup of tea.

Meanwhile Daniel saw the sign 'Rose and Crown' as it swung in the wind. He liked what he saw and found stables at the back for Darkie. Inside the air was warm, a huge log fire burned in the fireplace. Large black beans crossed the whitewashed ceiling, copper and brass ornaments hung on the walls and the bottles and glasses sparkled behind the bar. Daniel ordered a meal and a drink then sat down at a nearby table. He noticed that most of the customers were in groups, only a couple of people, including himself were alone. After he had finished his meal, Daniel wandered over to the bar. He watched a large group of people celebrate Christmas in a very convivial fashion. One of the men began to sing and soon the others joined in. Another sat down at the piano and tried to pick out a tune with one finger. Daniel finished his drink and joined the group gathered around the piano. The man still struggled with the notes and constantly played a wrong one. Someone asked. 'For God's sake and mine, can anyone here play the piano?' 'I can' Daniel answered. 'Come on then, let's hear it, move over Fred and let the lad sit down'. Daniel played every tune he could think of and everyone joined in the sing-song. It was good fun. The afternoon slipped away and soon the customers drifted off home. Daniel decided it was time he did the same. As Darkie clipped-clopped along the lanes, he realised this Christmas had been very different.

Michael decided he would surprise Daniel and go over to England and visit him on his birthday, he was anxious to see for himself how he was getting on. He knew Sean and Paddy and Mrs. Kelly would look after the farm very well for a couple of days. January was a slow month in farming. He was a little nervous, he had never been out of Ireland, however, he looked forward to the experience and made arrangements.

Daniel awoke to a cold bleak January 17th, he shivered as he left his warm bed and dressed. He went into the kitchen and lit the fire. When it was glowing nicely, he popped the kettle on, still half full of water from the previous day on the fire to boil. He took a loaf of bread, some butter and jam from the cupboard and sat down at the table to wait for it to boil. I wonder why I didn't get a word from Ireland? he thought as he brewed a pot of tea and began to eat his breakfast. When he had finished, he tidied the place up and from a drawer in a nearby dresser took out a small cloth bag which contained his savings. He sat down and worked out his expenses and decided he would have to sell all the goods he had collected to the dealer. Wrapping his thick scarf around his neck he went outside to harness Darkie. When that was done he carried the sacks of goods to the cart and fastened a large tarpaulin over them. The sky was leaden and promised snow.

As Daniel was about to leave he heard a knock on the door. Hurrying to open it, he just stood there and stared. 'Aren't you going to ask me in, sure it's cold here on the doorstep' Michael said with a grin. 'Holy Mother of God' sure you're a sight for sore eyes, so you are', Daniel exclaimed., he felt so happy to see him and led the way to the kitchen and helped his uncle to take off his coat and carried his suitcase to the bedroom. 'Warm yourself before the fire, I'll build it up again' Daniel said. 'I'll make a pot of tea, you must be perished, it's a very bleak day'. When he had finished his tea Michael said. 'I have to get something out of my coat pocket, and went into the bedroom and returned with a few parcels. 'Happy birthday Daniel from all your family' Michael said as he handed him the parcels. 'This is from me, I know you are doing very well but an extra bit of money does no-one any harm' and handed him an envelope. Daniel opened it and found a large sum of money inside. 'Thanks uncle Michael, sure it's a great help he said and thank the rest of the family for me too, I'm really grateful' he said. The two men caught up with news of the farm and Daniel explained his business. 'Where you off somewhere when I arrived, you had your outdoor clothes on?' Michael asked. 'To the dealers, but to be sure that can wait', Daniel answered. 'Sure I would like to go with you, I could see some of the countryside on the way', Michael said. Daniel locked the door behind him and led the way to the cart. After climbing in, Daniel covered his uncle's knees with a heavy blanket, flicked the reins and Darkie moved off to the sound of jingling bells. Michael laughed heartily when he heard them, Daniel looked at him and said with a grin. 'The children in the villages hear the bells and they tell their parents I'm on my way. I give them sweets and sometimes I give them a ride on the cart'.

Daniel decided to show Michael Lake Windermere, they would pass it on the way to the dealer's. When they reached the lake, Daniel tethered Darkie to a nearby tree and the two men climbed down from the cart, they were glad to stretch their legs. As they reached the lake's edge, they stood together side by side and surveyed the scene before them.

Hardly a ripple disturbed the silver-grey surface of the water. The leafless trees were laden with soft white snow and in the distance the fells offered a perfect backdrop. Suddenly the grey clouds parted and a watery sun shone. For a few minutes the lake and the snow sparkled. 'I don't know why, but whenever I come here, sure, I feel at peace', Daniel said. 'It's a wonderful sight to be sure' Michael replied. 'Can the hills across the lake be reached by road?' 'Indeed they can. Top End Farm' is over there, it was while I worked there I discovered the lake. One day I'm going to own a hotel here, you can come over and help me run it' Daniel declared. Michael looked at him, thinking he was joking but by the expression on his face he realised he was serious. 'Good luck to you Daniel' he said. They returned to the cart and set off for the dealer's warehouse. Michael watched with interest as the men weighed and sorted the goods Daniel had brought to them. They quoted a price which Daniel accepted and the two men set off to find somewhere they could have a hot meal.

It was nearly dark when the two men arrived home. Michael helped Daniel unharness and stable Darkie. Daniel soon had a good fire burning in the fireplace and placed a large pot of soup on the hot coals. Michael moved his chair closer to the fire and held a screw of paper in the flames and lit a cigarette. He watched Daniel as he organised the meal and wondered if he ever felt lonely living here by himself, he thought he would feel the loneliness but would be too proud to ask for help if he needed it. The two men talked well into the night about the farm, Daniel's future plans and where they would go the following day. Daniel gave Michael a candle, 'the one thing I can guarantee is that my bed is soft and warm I'll sleep by the fire with a blanket'. Daniel built up the fire and lay down in front of it. Sleep soon found him.

All too soon the visit was over, it was time for Michael to return to Ireland. Both men stood on the railway platform and waited for the train. As the train entered the station and ground to a halt they spotted an empty carriage and walked towards it. Michael put his suitcase on the rack then stepped outside again. 'It was grand seeing you, give aunt Bridget and uncle Finbar my love and everyone on the farm. Tell them I'll be over as soon as I can', Daniel said. The guard blew his whistle, Daniel and Michael hugged each other then Michael got into the carriage and closed the door. The train moved off as Daniel walked alongside until it gathered speed.

It was a late summer afternoon, Daniel was nearly home when in the distance he saw someone seated on the wall at 'Rose Cottage'. As he drew nearer, he recognised James. 'Whoa!' Daniel said as brought the horse and cart to a standstill. James jumped down from the wall and walked towards Daniel, hand outstretched. 'My dear fellow, how are you?' I do hope I am not intruding?' James asked. Taking Daniel's outstretched hand 'Sure it's grand to see you again'. The two men emptied the cart and stacked the bags etc., in the back of the shed. As Daniel unlocked the front door he stood aside to allow James to enter the cottage first. 'Sit down James, make yourself at home, sure you're very welcome'. James sat down and looked around. It was clean and tidy, it hadn't changed from his previous visit, except the photographs on the mantel piece. James surmised they must be members of Daniel's family. Daniel set about preparing a meal. Later, when they had finished eating, James lit a pipe and puffed away contentedly while Daniel stabled Darkie and locked up for the night. 'Tell me Daniel, how is your business progressing? James asked. 'Ah!, sure it's a struggle, sometimes I manage to save a bit of money, but usually I only make enough to make ends meet. However, I do manage to support myself and that is very important to me', he explained. James asked if the photographs on the mantelpiece were members of his family? 'Indeed they are; my uncle Michael came over for a short visit in January and brought them with him. This is my granny', he said handing him the photograph. James took the photograph and looked at it intently. He saw an old white haired lady dressed in a high necked dress, she looked very serene. 'She was a very handsome lady', he said as he handed the photograph to Daniel. 'This is my uncle Michael' Daniel said as he passed the photograph to James. This is a photograph of my Ma and Da. on their wedding day. Indeed I never knew them, they died and my granny and uncle Michael reared me, I wish I had known them'. James saw a very beautiful young woman, he thought about eighteen years of age with large beautiful eyes and magnificent hair. The man seemed rather ordinary. 'You are an extremely handsome family. You were close to your grandmother, weren't you?' 'Indeed I was, when she died it was a great blow, he replied. She was old when I first remember her and yet, she never seemed old to me, she taught me to work hard, be honest and independent, she was a remarkable woman, God rest her soul'. The two men talked about several matters, until sleep finally defeated them. James gave in gracefully to Daniel's offer to sleep in his bed. 'Thank you Daniel, if it would not be too inconvenient, I would like to accompany you tomorrow?' 'Sure that's no trouble at all', 'Capital!, Goodnight'.

The following year, in early Spring, Daniel received a letter from the Fearon family inviting him to Grace's wedding. He was rather surprised but pleased for her and looked forward to seeing the family. It was a lovely wedding and Grace looked beautiful and happy. In late Summer, James turned up and asked if he could spend a couple of weeks at 'Rose Cottage'. As their friendship deepened, the difference in their ages did not seem to matter to either of them. Daniel was very comfortable in the company of older people, he had been brought up by his granny. A bond was forged between the two men, based on mutual respect.

It was during James' visit that Daniel was offered a lease on a second-hand shop. Daniel realised it was a wonderful opportunity, he could sell the decent articles he bought in the shop and not be at the mercy of the dealer. 'I've been offered the lease on a second-hand shop, the owner wants to retire. The lease is reasonable and I told him I would let him know tomorrow'. James listened then said 'Do I detect some hesitation in accepting the offer?' 'Ah! Sure, I never know from day to day whether business will be good or bad. Sure I'm tempted, but if I don't have enough money to rely on, it's no way to run a business', Daniel explained. 'My dear chap, you are very young, most things we want or perhaps think we want, out of life, usually come to us in time. We just have to be patient. I'm sure you will realise your dreams one day'. Daniel laughed and said 'Indeed, I hope you're right James'. Like all good things James' visit came to an end but he promised Daniel he would be back again the following summer.

A few days later, Daniel received a letter from Ireland. He sat down and read it immediately, he was anxious to hear all the news from home. It read.

Dear Daniel,

I have a bit of bad news for you. Your uncle Michael has had an accident and is in hospital in Dublin. He fell from a cart and hurt his back, but he is in good hands, thank God, and is improving. He didn't want me to tell you, but your grandfather insisted you had the right to know what has happened.

Now Daniel, we don't want you to be too upset, he is in good care. I'll write again soon to let you know how he is. Your grandfather and aunt Bridget send their love.

May God be with you.

Uncle Finbar.

'Holy Mother of God!' Daniel exclaimed as he blessed himself. I wonder if they are telling me the whole truth. I think it would be best if I go over myself and find out, he thought to himself. He left the cottage and soon reached the timber yard. Fortunately Mr. Thompson was still working in his office. When he saw Daniel, he said ' Hello lad, what brings you here so late in the day?' 'Sure I've had a bit of bad news from home, can I stable Darkie with you for a couple of weeks?' 'Of course, when will you go over?' Mr. Thompson asked. 'Tomorrow, I'll tell the shopkeepers before I leave in the morning. Here's my address in Ireland in case you need to get in touch with me' Daniel said and handed him a slip of paper. 'Thank you Mr. Thompson, sure I'm grateful to you'.

When Daniel arrived in Dublin he went directly to his grandfather's house. The family were surprised but delighted to see him. In the afternoon, Finbar and Daniel set off for the hospital. Finbar led the way to the ward where Michael lay and pushed open the swing door and approached a nurse on duty. She told him that Michael is still very ill and not to stay too long. When they reached Michael's bed his eyes were closed. Daniel got a terrible shock when he saw him, his dashing, young looking uncle had disappeared and in his place lay a pale, drawn old man. Daniel moved to the side of the bed and took hold of his uncle's hand. Michael opened his eyes and smiled wanly when he saw Daniel and squeezed his hand. 'Sure I'm glad you're here Daniel, but don't worry about me, I'll be up and about in no time at all, please God!' he said in a low voice. 'I'll be back tomorrow to see you, sleep well', Daniel said as he and Finbar left the ward. 'Holy Mother of God! he looks terrible, he looks like an old man'. Daniel exclaimed. 'Indeed, he doesn't look too well at all, but the medicine he takes may make him drowsy. In a few months he'll be fit, sure he's a very strong man' Finbar said.. 'Let's find out', Daniel said. The doctor was seated at his desk and looked up when they walked in. 'What can I do for you?' he asked. Daniel explained the situation and wanted to know the truth. 'Your uncle is a very lucky man, we thought he had broken his back, but fortunately we were wrong. However, it will be some time before he can be moved and when he returns home, he will only be able to do very light work for many months'. Daniel thanked him and he and Finbar left the hospital.

During dinner, Michael, the farm etc., were discussed at length. Bridget offered to go over and help Mrs. Kelly and Molly. Sean and Paddy agreed they would work their fingers to the bone for Michael, but they also knew it wasn't enough. 'Indeed, we all know that if Michael can't work the farm, the lease expires', Grandfather O'Reilly said. 'Your granny and Michael have worked long and hard, too long and too hard to lose the farm. Indeed, in six months probably he will be able to take the reins again'. 'What do you think should be done?' Daniel asked. His grandfather looked at Daniel for a few minutes then said. 'You've a good head on your shoulders Daniel, you take your uncle's place and run the farm. Sure you know enough about it for a start, the rest, you can learn as you go along'. Daniel sat silently for a few minutes thinking to himself. 'I'll do that' Daniel answered eventually. I'll have to write to Mr. Thompson and tell him I'm not coming back and to sell Darkie and the cart and what is left in Rose Cottage, he's a fair man, and there is no other alternative'.

It was January 17th, 1914, Daniel's 23rd birthday. Mrs. Kelly had prepared a special meal for him and also to celebrate Michael's return to the farm. When everyone was seated, Mrs. Kelly served Daniel's favourite meal, a large steaming hot chicken and vegetable pie, with lots of fluffy potatoes and fresh soda bread. When everyone had finished eating, Michael stood up, ' I'd like to wish Daniel a very happy birthday and thank him for his help on the farm, without his help, I doubt if we would be here tonight'. They lifted their glasses and Michael said 'Slainte,' 'Slainte', everyone responded.

The months went by and Michael grew stronger each day, soon he was able to take over the reins of the farm again. He had regained weight and looked more like his old self, however, he was a very worried man and worried about Daniels future. The longer he remained on the farm, the less time there was to start his business again and what about the farm he thought? he knew he would never be able to do the hard work necessary to run it properly. Daniel was doing his work and Sean and Paddy worked like Trojans, but they too were no longer young. Everyone had suddenly grown old, he thought. He knew he would have to make a decision soon whether to retire. I'll leave it for now, sure I'll know when the time is right. However, he made an appointment with his solicitor to discuss financial matters relating to the farm.Daniel himself often wondered about the future. Sure there is no use thinking about that at the moment, he told himself. Michael needs me here, everything else will have to wait. He could almost hear his granny's voice as she had admonished him 'Now Daniel, take your time, sure at your age you have plenty of that, sure you have'. Whenever he could be spared, Michael insisted Daniel spend the weekends in Dublin at grandfather O'Reilly's house. In this way he ensured that he had a reasonable social life with his friends. There was always something to do, Doyle's, a party or a dance.

One day in late June, Michael was in Dublin on business. He left the Connaught Hotel and set off to enjoy his day off. He heard a newspaper boy shout 'Read all about it'. Duke assassinated! After buying the newspaper and had digested the news, he thought, who the blazes is the Archduke Ferdinand? and dismissed it from his mind as unimportant.

On August 14th, 1914, Britain declared War on Germany!

Daniel and his friend Tim were in Doyle's, when the news broke. 'Sure I'll not lift a finger to help the British' Tim said vehemently. 'We may be conscripted into the British Army', Daniel suggested. 'I can't leave the farm at the moment, the leasehold expires on my uncle's death or retirement or if the farm gets-run-down, that's why I'm over here'. 'I'll fight and die if I must, for Ireland's Independence when the time comes'. 'I'll let you into a secret, it will happen sooner than later'. Tim declared. 'My God!' Daniel thought, he's with the 'Movement'. Daniel was worried he wasn't free, like Tim to do as he wished and discussed the situation with his Uncle Finbar, who confirmed his reasons for avoiding the army. 'Sure I'm certain there are ways and means of avoiding the 'call up'. Indeed, they will need farmers to grow more food, not less, to feed the soldiers. I'll make enquiries and could you ask Michael, when you get home, to meet me at Doyle's next Friday night'. As soon as Daniel reached home, Daniel explained that his grandfather was not well and they don't expect him to last much longer. Their conversation then turned to a discussion about the War and its implications especially for Daniel. He delivered his uncle Finbar's message and Michael agreed to be there.

Daniel never knew how it was arranged, but he worked all through the War on the farm. Admittedly, he kept a low profile. Some of his friends, including Tim, disappeared. No one seemed to know where they were, or what they were doing. A letter arrived from his old friend James. It read...

My dear friend,

I called to see you dear boy, at 'Rose Cottage' and instead of your friendly presence, I was greeted by a complete Stranger. I asked him if he knew of your whereabouts, he did not! However, he suggested Mr. Thompson might know. As you can see, he did indeed. I was very sorry to hear of your uncle's accident and do hope he is fully recovered. Because War has been declared on Germany, my job will entail a lot of travelling. I value our friendship too highly to lose contact with you Daniel.

I have instructed my solicitors, Smith, Jones and Roberts, 50 Windermere Road, Windermere, Westmorland, to act on my behalf. If you choose to write to me, as I hope you will, your letters will be forwarded to me. There may be some delay in the reply, but I most certainly will respond.

I trust our friendship will survive the War and that one day, I shall be able to visit you again.

My best wishes for the future Daniel and always, my gratitude.

I remain, Yours sincerely, James Smith

Daniel replied to the letter and some months later received a reply. So their friendship continued in this way. Some months later, he received a letter from Mr. & Mrs. Fearon, who told him, amongst other things that Grace's husband Michael was now serving in the Army. Grace herself, now worked as a volunteer for the Red Cross Society. As he folded the letter, he realised that the lives of people he knew, had already been changed by the War and wondered how long it would last. The British Government had claimed it would only last six months.

Christmas 1914 was no different from any other, but everyone was aware that many changes had occurred in their lives and no doubt, there would be many more. Life was different. The War still raged in Europe, lists of the dead, wounded and missing appeared regularly in the newspapers. However, people got on with their lives as best they could. Food was short; they could hardly keep up with the demand for fresh vegetables. That was a bit of luck! During the year Daniel heard from Mr. Fearon that Grace's husband had been killed in France and wrote to express his sorrow for her loss.

The year flew by, Christmas came and went, it was now Spring, 1916. Grandfather O'Reilly was dying. Daniel decided he would go up to Dublin and spend a bit of time with him, as he always felt regret that he had not been able to say goodbye to his beloved granny. On Easter Monday morning, Daniel helped his aunt with the chores then ran upstairs to sit with his grandfather. Finbar popped his head around the door to let him know he would not be long before he came up to sit with him and caught up with his wife in the hall, he gave her a kiss and said. 'Sure I'll not be long, I'll be back in time for lunch'. Finbar was correct, the meeting did not last long, a certain amount of confusion had arisen. He left the building and set off for home. As he reached the General Post Office, he noticed people were talking in small groups and felt uneasy and joined them. 'Is something happening inside the building?' he asked a man nearby. 'Do you not see the Republican Flag flying from the roof. Indeed there's been a 'Rising', he answered. 'Holy Mother of God', Finbar exclaimed. Then he noticed a placard placed near the door of the Post Office, walking over towards it, it read:

The Provisional Government
Of The Irish Republic
To The People Of Ireland

IRISH MEN AND IRISH WOMEN: In the name of God and of
the dead generations from which she receives her old tradition
of nationhood, Ireland, through us, summons her children to her
flag and strikes for her freedom.Having organised and trained
her manhood through her secret revolutionary organisation, the
Irish Republican Brotherhood, and through her open military
organisation, the Irish Volunteers and the Irish Citizen Army,
having patiently perfected her discipline, have resolutely waited
for the right moment to reveal itself, she now seizes that moment,
and supported by her exiled children in America and by gallant
allies in Europe, but relying in the first on her own strength, she
strikes in full confidence of victory.

We declare the right of the people of Ireland to the ownership
of Ireland and to the unfettered control of Irish destinies, to be
sovereign and indefeasible. The long usurpation of that right
by a foreign people and government has not extinguished the
right, nor can it ever be extinguished except by the destruction
of the Irish people. In every generation the Irish people have
asserted their right to national freedom and sovereignty; six
times during the past three hundred years they have asserted it
in arms. Standing on that fundamental right and again asserting
it in arms in the face of the world, we hereby proclaim the Irish
Republic as a Sovereign Independent State, and we pledge our
lives and the lives of our comrades in arms to the cause of its
freedom, of its welfare, and of its exaltation among the nations.
The Irish Republic is entitled to, and hereby claims, the allegiance
of every Irishman and Irishwoman. The Republic guarantees
religious and civil liberty, equal rights and equal opportunity to
all its citizens, and declares its resolve to pursue the happiness
and prosperity of the whole nation and of all its part, cherishing
all of the children of the nation equally, and oblivious of the
differences carefully fostered by an alien Government, which
have divided a minority from the majority in the past.

Until our arms have brought the opportune moment for the establishment of a permanent National Government, representative of the whole people of Ireland and elected by the suffrages of all her men and women, the Provisional Government, hereby constituted, will administer the civil and military affairs of the Republic in trust for the people.

We place the cause of the Irish Republic under the protection of the Most High God, Whose blessing we invoke upon our arms, and we pray that no one who serves that cause will dishonour it by cowardice, inhumanity, or rapine. In this supreme hour the Irish nation must, by its valour and discipline, and by the readiness of its children to sacrifice themselves for the common good, prove itself worthy of the august destiny to which it is called.

Signed on behalf of the Provisional Government 24 April 1916

Thomas J. Clarke

Sean MacDiarmada	*Thomas MacDonagh*
P.H. Pearse	*Eamonn Ceant*
James Connolly	*Joseph Plunkett*

Hurrying home Finbar wondered why there had been a change in the orders? And suspected that soon the British army would be swarming all over the G.P.O. and the surrounding streets. He walked away as quickly as he could. When Finbar reached home, he ran upstairs to John's bedroom and sat down on the edge of his bed. 'How are you feeling now, will you have some lunch?' he asked. 'Ah! Sure I feel a bit tired today Finbar, indeed I don't think I'll get up at all. I'll have a little rest and get up tomorrow', he answered. 'Good Man, I'll be up again after you've had a little nap'. When he saw John had closed his eyes, Finbar touched Daniel on the shoulder and mouthed the words, 'Come downstairs'. When they reached the kitchen Bridget had lunch ready and as they sat down at the table, Finbar said 'There has been a Rising at the G.P.0, Daniel dropped his fork and Bridget looked at her husband, food did not seem very important at that moment. They were both shocked. He described the incident and tied it to the arrest of

Sir Roger Casement and the sinking of the German ship 'Aud'.

'Holy Mother of God', Bridget said as she blessed herself, what will become of them?' Sure they will all be slaughtered. The British army will soon make a move, they can't have trouble in Ireland while fighting the Germans' Finbar declared. 'That's what Tim was trying to tell me, Daniel thought. 'Daniel, you will have to stay here in Dublin until we know more about what will happen. Indeed, I think it would be sensible to remain indoors, I'll get a word to Michael, he will agree with me'. Daniel nodded his head and wondered where Tim was at that moment.

In the afternoon a troop of British Cavalry galloped into Sackville Street. They expected to ride roughshod over rebels rioting in the surrounding streets. Unfortunately for them the rebels were all inside the G.P.O. and the surrounding buildings. Gunshots rang out from the G.P.O. windows, a few soldiers were killed and the British retreated. On Wednesday the British began their offensive with approximately 12,000 troops. The rebels knew they were out-numbered, they just waited. There began a crescendo of guns of all kinds continually firing at the strongholds of the 'Rebels'.

Shortly after midnight on Wednesday, Daniel was awakened by some noise, listening intently heard a stone hit the bedroom window. Pulling the curtain to one side, but it was too dark to see anything, he opened the window and looked out. 'Daniel, it's me' he recognised Tim's voice and raced downstairs to open the front door, as quickly as possible, he didn't want to wake his aunt and uncle. Tim was slumped on the top step, he helped him inside and closed the door quietly behind him.

'Come into the kitchen Tim' he whispered as he helped him into grandfather's big chair. 'Sit down man, I'll be back in a tick', Daniel said. Checking all the rooms downstairs to make sure all the curtains were drawn properly, Daniel then returned to the kitchen and lit a lamp. 'Mother of God! let me take a look at that hand of yours', he said. By the light of the lamp he could see that Tim's hand was covered with congealed blood. He helped him out of his jacket and could see that his shirt was also stained with blood. Gently he helped him out of his shirt and was shocked when he saw the wound. He poured a large glass of whisky and said. 'Drink this Tim, sure I don't have to ask what happened to you'. Daniel's aunt Bridget always left a large kettle of water on the hob, which burned slowly throughout the night. Thank God for aunt Bridget Daniel thought as he poured some hot water into a bowl. From a cupboard he took down a box containing ointment, antiseptic and bandages and poured some of the solution into the hot water and as gently as he could, wiped away the congealed blood, he could see a bullet had gone clean through Tim's arm. Daubing a large amount of ointment onto a bandage he wrapped it around Tim's arm. Tim was exhausted so he gave him another glass of whisky. 'I'll get a clean shirt for you, keep absolutely quiet, don't make a move until I come back' he admonished. Daniel helped Tim get changed 'Get some sleep now Tim, you can't leave until the morning, I'll sit with you and wake you up in plenty of time'.

While Tim slept, Daniel cleared away all traces of Tim's visit. He tore the blood stained shirt into pieces and burned them in the stove. I'd better get dressed he thought, in case I need to go outside. He reached his bedroom and dressed as quickly as he could then closed the bedroom door, raced downstairs and quickly blew out the lamp and waited for morning, he felt exhausted himself. Eventually, light filtered through the drawn curtains, he looked at his watch and decided it was a good time for Tim to make a move. Shaking him gently he covered his mouth with his hand in case he cried out. When he saw Tim was wide awake, he withdrew his hand. Daniel made a pot of tea and buttered some soda bread and waited until Tim had finished eating.

Have you a safe house to go to while your wounds heal?' Daniel asked. 'Indeed I have if I can reach it, sure I'll be safe', Tim answered. 'Good, sure you know Dublin like the back of your hand, take all the back streets and for God's sake man, don't draw attention to yourself. If you see any British Soldiers don't play the hero, stay out of sight until it's safe to move on. I'll just step outside and see if it's safe for you to leave, not a sound now.' Daniel opened the door as quietly as he could and stepped outside and lit a cigarette as he looked around. There were a few people walking to work, but no sign of trouble so he put out the cigarette and went inside. 'There are not many people around Tim, only a few walking to work. I think you will be safe? Get word to me as soon as you can', he whispered. 'Thanks Daniel, you're a grand friend, sure I'll get word to you as soon as I can 'Up the Rebels'. 'Up the Rebels', Daniel said.

Tim ran down the steps and quickly disappeared into the next street. Daniel closed the door and went back into the kitchen and checked that everything was in it's usual place. He knew his aunt would spot anything out of place. Satisfied that all was as it should be he ran upstairs into his bedroom and undressed and knelt by his bed and prayed for Tim and all the rebels. Daniel knew his aunt would be up and about very soon, he also knew she would have helped Tim, but what she didn't know couldn't hurt her. He climbed into bed and a few minutes later, he heard his aunt moving about in her bedroom. Thank God!, we made it. Daniel thought.

By Friday, all of Dublin was in flames. The rebels knew they were beaten. No matter how hard they fought the British sent in reinforcements. The loss of civilian lives was appalling. Padraic Pearse decided to surrender, most of the leaders of the Rising were arrested and many others who had taken part in it. On the 3rd May 1916, Padraic Pearse, Thomas MacDonagh, and Thomas J. Clarke were executed by a firing squad. Eamonn De Valera who was proclaimed The President of Ireland was also sentenced to death but because he had been born in America, his sentence was commuted to Life Imprisonment. On the 12th May, Sean Mac Diarmada and James Connolly were executed by firing squad. However, Connolly had been seriously injured in the Rising and no doubt his sojourn in prison did not improve his health. He was unable to walk because he was so ill. The British soldiers tied him to a chair and carried him to the place of execution. He was unable to hold his head upright, so a soldier tilted it in the correct position for the firing squad.

Details of arrests, solitary confinement and torture to obtain the names of their comrades were circulated by the families of the men concerned. Many of those arrested were very young, only youths, but the British had no mercy on them. They were treated the same as all the others they had arrested, imprisoned or executed. However, as young as they were, they never turned informer and their families were proud of that fact.

These acts only fuelled the anger in the hearts of the Irish population against the British. The guerrilla's were helped whenever and wherever possible. 'Safe houses' were provided for those 'on the run'. In the midst of all this chaos, grandfather O'Reilly died, he drifted peacefully out of this world into the next. Bridget of course was devastated she had never been separated from her Da and felt the loss deeply. Daniel tried to comfort her and he knew Finbar loved her and would take good care of her. Daniel was upset, he had loved and respected the only grandfather he had known. He had been a loving presence in his life and wept when the coffin was lowered into the grave praying that this grandfather would 'Rest in Peace'.

Meanwhile the acts of brutality happening in Ireland shocked and outraged most civilised people around the world. For the British Government it was a fatal mistake. The seed of rebellion which had lain dormant in the hearts of Irishmen and women flowered. The rebels were recognised as the heroes they were and the people vowed they would not have died in vain. A guerrilla war began against the British Army. The brutality of British actions, particularly the execution of the rebels after their capture led to a complete rejection of British rule by the Irish people.

The struggle for Ireland's Independence had begun!

Winter brought more problems. Michael developed Rheumatism in his back. At times he was unable to straighten up. Needless to say he was unable to do any physical work at all on the farm and knew the situation could not continue, he would have to surrender the leasehold on the farm. Daniel had a right to be free to pursue his own life. Daniel knew his uncle was finished as far as hard work was concerned and wondered how long it would be before he and his uncle left the farm. Christmas was the usual family affair. Bridget and Finbar were glad to be out of Dublin. Michael knew this would be the last Christmas they would all share at the farm and suspected they all knew it as well. Handing everyone a drink he said 'This Christmas I propose a toast to the memories we all share and to the loved ones no longer with us who made them possible. Slainte! 'Slainte!' the family answered.

It was Easter 1918. The War against Germany still dragged on, however, there did seem to be light at the end of the tunnel, so to speak! It was two years since the 'Rising' and the guerrilla war continued with even greater determination for Independence. Michael decided it was time to discuss the future with Daniel. 'I've decided to surrender the leasehold on the farm. I am no longer a young man, neither are Sean and Paddy, time has caught up with us. Ma had a good business head and saved money all her life. I continued to do so after her death. Sure it's not a fortune, and you will inherit your mother's share. We won't starve Daniel. Indeed, it is time you had a life of your own, we both know you can't inherit the farm. You are free to decide whatever you want to do. For myself, sure, I haven't decided yet'. 'Are you sure about this uncle Michael?' Daniel asked. 'Indeed I am', he replied. Daniel thought about the situation for some time and then said. 'It's hard to grasp the fact that soon the farm will be no longer our home.' Daniel was devastated but he knew the situation but it didn't make it any easier to leave. 'I think we should go away, go over to Windermere? If we have a bit of money, sure we can rent a shop and start a second-hand business. I know how to do it, and you could look after the money'. Michael looked at him in surprise then asked. 'Is this really what you want to do Daniel? you don't have to drag me over with you, unless you really want to start a business and think I would be able to help'. 'Indeed I am'. Daniel answered. 'Well then, if that's what you want to do, it's settled. Ma also left a little money for Mrs. Kelly, Molly, Sean and Paddy, she was afraid they would be left destitute. I'll tell them sometime this week' Michael explained. 'Granny was a truly remarkable woman, even after all this time, I miss her' Daniel said. 'Sure I miss her myself, let's have a drink' Michael replied. Michael completed all the details necessary to surrender the leasehold on the farm and concluded all the necessary financial matters regarding the family. Letters had been written to friends and posted. Only 'goodbye's' remained to be said. It was now time to tell his old friends he was leaving the farm. When he had finished speaking, Paddy said. 'sure I'm glad we are all leaving the farm together, we have all grown old. God knows we have been lucky to have worked for Mrs. O'Hara and yourself. Mrs O'Hara was always good to us, and it's good to know we have a bit of money of our own. Sure, she was a great lady, God rest her soul.' 'Well boyos, all we can do now is fulfil all our contracts until December'. Michael explained.

It was the 11th of November 1918 Germany had surrendered, the War was over. The Irish population were glad the War was over, but they wondered what further measures the British Government would take to restore order. The knew they would fight to the finish. Bridget and Finbar invited Michael and Daniel to spend Christmas with them in Dublin and accepted with gratitude. Michael arranged to store all the furniture etc., in Dublin until they knew where they would live.

The fateful day dawned during the last week of December. The Agent called and inspected the farm. He told Michael the owner had instructed him to buy all the cattle, chickens and pigs, farm implements, horses and carts and anything else he wished to sell at a good price. Michael negotiated a price and the Agent handed over the money. Michael handed him the keys to the farm and the removal van arrived. Michael and Daniel left the men to get on with their job of removing every stick of furniture and set off for the graveyard to say a final goodbye. Both men knelt down on the grass beside the grave and prayed silently alone with their own thoughts. They stood up and Daniel took one last look at the headstone and turned away. They walked briskly back to the farm for the last time. The Agent stood outside while Michael and Daniel went inside – it was empty! They took one last look at the farm then left the only home Michael had ever known and where Daniel had spent most of his life. They climbed into the removal van for a lift into Dublin. Neither looked back or said a word.

Daniel and Michael spent a very pleasant Christmas with Bridget and Finbar, in spite of the tensions in Dublin. Eventually, the time came for them to say goodbye and begin the second phase of their lives. Daniel promised his aunt he would write often and also promised to visit them when it was possible. After much embracing the two men left the house.

Passengers were being checked before being allowed on board. Michael and Daniel had no problem and walked up the gangway onto the deck. They stood together and watched emotionally as the coastline of Ireland disappeared from view. 'Let's go down to the bar for a drink?' Michael said. When they arrived at their destination they booked into a small hotel, unpacked their clothes then left the hotel to look around the town for shops to rent or buy. Daniel noticed that the second hand shop he had known years ago was now a bakery. A couple of shops stood empty, but there was nothing to suggest they were either for sale or rent. Nearby they found an Estate Agent's office and went inside. The receptionist smiled and asked if she could help them. 'Indeed, I hope you can?' Michael replied. 'We are looking for a shop to buy, but it must have living accommodation. We noticed two empty shops nearby, are either of them suitable?' 'Please sit down' she answered. One of the shops is suitable; would you like to inspect it?' 'Indeed we would', he replied. She disappeared into an inner office and returned in a short time accompanied by a young man. 'I'm Mr. Barker' he said as he introduced himself. 'I'll show you the premises'. The three men left the office and walked to the shop they had previously seen. Looking at the building for some time they thought it was very run down, but solid and decided they would look inside anyway. The room on the ground floor was quite large and there was a window on either side of the room. A small office led off the room into another room at the back and the yard was big enough. So far, Michael thought, it's not too bad. Upstairs there was a large living room, two bedrooms and a bathroom of sorts. The kitchen was big enough to eat in, but the whole place really needed renovating and painting.

'I'll wait downstairs for you, so you can discuss whether the property is suitable Mr. Barker said. Michael and Daniel discussed the property and decided that with a certain amount of work done on it, it would suit their purpose. However, the price had to be considered. 'Sure it needs quite a bit doing to it' said Michael, but the rooms are big enough for our purpose, how much do the owners want for it?' A price was named and Michael heaved a sigh of relief, it was a great deal less than he thought. 'Provided the surveyor's report is satisfactory, we will buy the property'. Mr. Barker looked pleased as the property had been vacant for some time.

By the end of a month, the shop had been renovated and repainted, Michael and Daniel would move in when their furniture arrived from Ireland. Meanwhile, Daniel was very busy; he attended lots of auctions and bought anything he thought he could sell. One of the lots he bought, contained books and comics. His first reaction was to sell them to a dealer, then realised he could use them himself. Shelves were built along one side of the shop and he displayed them. They were now open for business. The bell on the shop door jingled and a small boy of about seven or eight entered the shop. 'Hello! young man, can I help you?' The little boy looked up anxiously at Daniel and asked, 'How much are the comics Mister?' 'How much money do you have?' Daniel asked, 'a penny' he replied. 'Sure you have plenty of money to buy comics, pick the comics you want and then you can pay me'. The boy collected an armful of comics and walked over to Daniel, 'can I have all these Mister for a penny?' 'Indeed you can, and if you bring them back when you have read them, not any that have been torn or spoilt, you can have just as many for a halfpenny'. The little boy's face lit up.

'Thanks Mister' he said as he ran off home with his treasure.

Six months later, Michael and Daniel had settled in comfortably, their furniture had arrived safely and a local woman, Mrs. Davis, came in a few days a week to clean and prepare a meal for them. The business was running smoothly and Michael's rheumatism was not as bad, probably because he was indoors most of the time. Daniel thought it was time to invite Mr. and Mrs. Fearon and Grace and introduce Michael to them. 'Invite them for lunch on Easter Sunder, it's a holiday and the shop will be closed Michael suggested. I'm looking forward to meeting them'.

Daniel noticed changes in both Mr. & Ms. Fearon, they had grown much older. He hadn't seen them for many years, however, it was the change in Grace that was the most dramatic and couldn't keep his eyes off her. He knew if he had met her in the street he would not have recognised her. Gone was the young girl he had known and remembered. In her place stood a lovely modern woman. Her hair was cut short and she wore a smart small hat. Her beautiful suit showed off to perfection, her 'boyish' figure. The skirt reached just below her calves, revealing slim ankles and dainty shoes. A stranger stood before him until she smiled, then she became a 'familiar' stranger. Throughout the rest of the year Daniel saw as much of Grace as he possibly could. He realised the old Grace had gone. The death of her husband during the War had left it's mark on her, however, she was good company and he knew she was more than just a friend but he wasn't sure what Grace's feelings were. In December, Grace invited him to escort her to a Red Cross Ball. Daniel was delighted at the thought of it and looked forward to the evening with anticipation.

Perhaps it was the atmosphere, or the music, he didn't know but by the end of the evening he knew for sure he had crossed an imaginary line in his relationship with her. He was head over heels in love with Grace. The following day Michael was out with the friends he had made in the course of the business. Daniel was glad, he needed time to be alone with his thoughts.

He sat down on the sofa and lit a cigarette, he wanted to declare his love for Grace at once but something held him back. Perhaps it's too soon, he thought and stubbed out his cigarette and went to bed.

It was a December 1920 morning; Michael sorted through the letters and bills the postman had delivered, among them was a letter from Ireland. He opened it immediately, he was anxious to hear the news.

Dear Daniel and Michael,

It was grand news to hear your business is doing so well and that you, Michael, do not suffer so much pain from rheumatism. We are indeed, looking forward to coming over for a visit, Please God it will be very soon.

We wonder what the British newspapers are printing about the guerrilla war going on over here. Have they told their readers about a special 'Army', we call them The Black and Tans, because of their uniform. They have been recruited to terrorise the Irish population. They British also sent tanks into the GAA football match at Croke Park and murdered eleven spectators. We hope the world is watching and we can get some help? Ireland doesn't have the material and military experience but we will try and give them the reception they justly deserve. Take good care of yourselves now, Bridget sends her love to you both. May God be with you, and pray for Ireland. 'Up The Rebels' Finbar and Bridget.

After Michael had read the letter, he passed it over to Daniel to read.

During the summer, Michael heard the doorbell ring and a grey haired, bearded gentleman entered the shop. 'Good afternoon, can I help you?' Michael asked. 'I should like to see Mr. Daniel O'Reilly, if I may' the man answered in a cultured English voice.

Looking closely at the man, he noticed a haversack on his back and wearing hiking boots and wondered if this was Daniel's friend James? 'Daniel is out on business at the moment, but to be sure, he won't be long. I'm Michael O'Hara, Daniel's uncle'. James introduced himself 'I'm delighted to meet you' he said as he held out his hand. 'Sure, Daniel would be very sorry if he missed you, won't you wait for him?' 'I should be delighted' James replied. Michael brought two chairs from the back room and the two men sat down. Michael offered James a cigarette, but he preferred to smoke his pipe. The two men chatted and sometime later the doorbell jingled. Daniel entered the shop and his face lit up when he saw James. James left his chair and walked over to Daniel. 'You look absolutely splendid Daniel, I do believe you have grown, you seem to be a little taller than I'. Michael watched the two friends and said.' Daniel, I'll take care of the shop, why don't you and James go upstairs, I'm sure you have a lot to talk about'. James followed Daniel upstairs to the living room. 'Sit down James, I'll make us some tea' As James looked around the room, he thought it very pleasant, and the furniture was very good and well cared for. Settling himself in a large chair he puffed away on his pipe. The two friends caught up with all the changes in their lives. James was fully aware of the struggle in Ireland and gave his opinion that Ireland would be Independent sooner rather than later. Daniel and James hiked around the countryside for most of his visit. Mrs. Davies would prepare a cold lunch for them. When it was time for lunch, they chose the setting very carefully and more than often they sat by the side of a noisy beck watching the water tumble down rocks, over boulders and pebbles in it's headlong rush to the sea.

On one occasion they spent sometime in Grassmere, Wordsworth country. They even managed to visit his old home. James was delighted, Wordsworth was one of his favourite poets. When it was time for James to leave he thanked everyone he met, then putting his arm around Daniel's shoulder saying how delighted he was to see him and how good it felt to walk the lanes with him. After thanking Michael for his hospitality he said he would like to visit again next year. Daniel walked back into the shop and heard Michael shout 'Glory be to God!, I never thought these words would ever pass my lips. Sure James is a sensible, charming man, if all Englishmen were like him, sure we wouldn't have the problems we have in Ireland, they would soon be settled'. Daniel smiled, he had reached the same conclusion many, many, years ago.

Christmas had arrived. Michael and Daniel were invited to spend Christmas with Mr. & Mrs. Fearon and Grace. It seemed obvious to everyone that Daniel was in love with Grace. Michael was reasonably certain that Grace was very fond of him and perhaps her hesitation was because she had been married before. Life has a way of moving us forward, no matter how much we try to live in the past, he thought. Michael and Daniel were pleased with the way their lives were going. Their only regret was that they could not be amidst the turmoil in Ireland. However, each knew that for many reasons, it was impossible. They would continue to send as much money as they could, through the usual channels, to support the 'Rebels'.

One morning in early Spring, Daniel attended an auction. They needed more stock for the shop. As he had finished his business earlier than expected decided to take a walk before returning home. It was a beautiful day, he enjoyed the smell of the damp earth and the new mown grass, not to mention the perfume of the wild flowers. Daniel thought it would be a good idea to invite the Fearon family for lunch the following Sunday, he enjoyed their company. After lunch they talked about business, Ireland, and the imminent retirement of Mr. Fearon. Grace mentioned to Daniel that they passed a wood on the way and loved the bluebells and asked if it is far from where they are? 'Not too far, but over the fields, it's just a hop and a skip away', Daniel said. 'I would love to take some bluebells back home with me, would you take me?' 'Sure I'd love to' Daniel replied. Grace borrowed her mother's shoes, which were more suitable for tramping through fields. Daniel and Grace held hands as they walked down the lanes chatting amiably until they reached the field they were to cross. They closed the gate behind them and walked through the lush green grass and climbed over a couple of styles until they reached a small hill. Daniel helped Grace to climb it. When they reached the top, they stood on the edge of a wood.

The Spring sunshine filtered through the trees, it highlighted the new tender green leaves that sprouted from the branches. The ground below was a sea of thousands of bluebells. Daniel had seen it all before and watched Grace's face as she surveyed the scene before her. She was silent for some time, then turning towards him she said. 'Oh! Daniel, it's so beautiful, I want to cry'. She looked so vulnerable, he couldn't resist and took her in his arms and kissed her. Somewhere in his subconscious, he felt Grace's arms go around his neck as she returned his kiss. A few minutes later he released her, they smiled at each other and he took her into his arms again. 'Grace, I love you, I have for some time, I was a little afraid to tell you because of the loss of your husband'. 'Daniel, I love you too'. Suddenly everything was perfect in Daniel's world. 'Will you marry me Grace' he said kneeling down with a bunch of bluebells in his hand. 'Yes' she answered joyfully as she took the bluebells from him. When they arrived home Grace filled the kitchen sink with fresh water and placed the bluebells in it. She and Daniel sat side by side on the sofa . 'Daniel and I have some news, she said to her family and Michael, Daniel has asked me to marry him and I've said yes' Grace said with a smile. The news was greeted with surprise and delight, hugs and kisses.

The future bride and groom agreed there was no reason why they should not marry as soon as possible and with Michael's blessing they decided to live above the shop. They set the date for July 20th 1921 it would only be a small wedding, close friends and family. Michael was of course Daniel's best man and Grace asked her friend Nancy to be her matron of honour. The family from Ireland were unable to attend and James regretted because of the pressure of work at Government level , but sent a beautiful tea service as a wedding present.

Grace awoke early on her wedding day. She lay quietly in bed savouring her thoughts. Inevitably her thoughts turned to her first marriage. She had loved him as a naïve young girl and her safe world had been shattered when he was killed in France during the War. She had never expected to see Daniel again when he left to return to Ireland and couldn't believe how handsome he was when he came back and so different from the youth she had known. Today, she would marry him and become Mrs. Daniel O'Reilly. She slipped out of bed and opened her jewellery box and took out the engagement and wedding ring Michael, her first husband, had bought her and held them in her hands. Her memories of him were happy ones. She knelt down by her bed and prayed for the soul of her dead husband.

Meanwhile, Daniel also awoke early and climbed out of bed and into the kitchen to make a pot of tea. His thoughts turned to the incident in his youth when the Fearon family had befriended him and when he had met Grace for the first time, her first marriage, and yet today they will marry. Michael joined him in the kitchen and poured himself a cup of tea. As he sat down he asked 'are you nervous Daniel?' 'No, I have the strangest feeling that Grace and I were meant to marry. Our paths crossed many years ago, she married and I met lots of girls, but didn't marry. You and I decided sadly to leave Ireland and our paths crossed again. Today is our wedding day, do you not see some sort of pattern in all this?' 'Indeed Daniel, the future is always unknown. That's probably a very good thing. I doubt if we knew what was in store for us, it might all be too much to handle, all we have is now Daniel, thank God for the gift of love he has given to both of you, grasp the happiness tightly in both hands, don't question it. Come on now, It's time to get ready for the most important day of your life'.

Nancy put the finishing touches to Grace's outfit and stood back to admire her. Grace had chosen a dove grey silk dress with matching shoes and hat. She wore the necklace Daniel had bought her as a wedding gift. Rather than carry flowers, she decided to carry a prayer book with a small spray of pink rosebuds attached to it. She looked elegant, beautiful and radiant. Mrs. Fearon popped in to see if Grace was ready. When she saw her, she wiped the tears away from her eyes as she kissed her daughter and said 'You look beautiful darling, are you ready to leave?'

Daniel and Grace had chosen to marry in the chapel of the local Convent. It was small and private. They both thought it was the perfect place in which to take their marriage vows. As Grace walked down the aisle escorted by her father, she felt at peace and wonderfully happy. The final toasts had been said, the bride and groom left on their honeymoon. Soon the guests drifted away. Eventually, only Mr. and Mrs. Fearon and Michael were left. 'It was a beautiful wedding, wasn't it?, Grace and Daniel seem so right for each other, it was a celebration of their love. I hope they have a long and happy life together' Mr. Fearon said.

It was late afternoon when Grace and Daniel arrived at the hotel where they were to spend their honeymoon. They were shown to their room, the porter placed their luggage on the floor and handed Daniel the key. As soon as he left they put their arms around each other and held each other close. Daniel kissed her and said with a grin. 'Mrs. O'Reilly, I think we should unpack our clothes'. Later Grace held up two dresses for Daniel's inspection. 'Which one do you like best?' she asked. 'The pink one' he replied. Grace sat at the dressing table and put the finishing touches to her appearance. She dabbed as little perfume behind her ears and smoothed her hair. Daniel put his hands on her shoulders and kissed her on the nape of her neck. She reached up and caught his hand, kissed it and said. 'I adore you Daniel'. They left the room and Daniel locked the door behind them. Hand in hand Mr. and Mrs. O'Reilly went downstairs to dinner. They finished their after dinner drink and left the lounge for their room. Grace made her way to the bathroom and slipped the white chiffon nightgown over her head and then put her arms in the matching negligee, she was pleased with her reflection and walked to their bedroom where her husband waited for her. Daniel stood up and held his arms out wide for her as she ran into his arms and held each other close. 'I love you so much' he said. Looking up into his beautiful green eyes Grace moved closer to him and kissed him passionately. She led him to their bed, he kissed and caressed her with tenderness, love and passion, until their need to be ever closer to each other, reached a peak of desire. Their bodies united in the ultimate gift of love. Later, Grace fell asleep in his arms. He looked down at her face and kissed her very gently on the forehead, enchanted by her nearness. He freed his arm carefully, he did not wish to disturb her sleep, then lay down close beside her and drifted off to sleep.

Daniel and Grace took to married life like two ducks to water. They were truly happy. Grace made subtle changes in the home and both men loved the feminine touch, they had missed it. Sometimes, when Daniel was out on business she looked after the shop. It also enabled her to meet a lot more people in the neighbourhood. One evening she suggested to Daniel and Michael that they sell souvenirs. 'I've noticed quite a few holiday makers call into the shop, they expect to find a souvenir they can take home with them. They need not be expensive, however, if by chance we find an antique we can sell it as well'. 'What do you think and where would we put them, there's not much room left in the shop?' Daniel asked. 'I thought we should keep one window space free. People could see the items on display and if they liked what they saw, come into the shop and the price should be clearly marked' Grace suggested. 'Come with me tomorrow to the auction, you never know we may find a treasure and make a fortune' Daniel teased. Grace was delighted and the following morning she and Daniel attended an auction. Grace found what she wanted, some were a bit worse for wear, however, she knew how to restore them. By the end of the week everything was in order. She went outside to see what they looked like on display in the window. She had excellent taste, and every item was beautifully presented and ticketed.

James paid his annual visit and Daniel proudly introduced Grace to him as he greeted her warmly. 'I have looked forward to meeting you, Daniel is a very lucky man' he added. Daniel and James hiked around the countryside as they usually did and Grace helped in the shop. She found James charming and was fascinated by the depth of his friendship with Daniel. There didn't seem to be an age barrier. Grace had always been interested in antiques, and James was very knowledgeable in this area of the Arts. He promised to send her a book which would help her to identify and date any antiques she came across. She was sorry to see him go when it was time for him to leave and made him promise to extend his visit the following year. James smiled at her and kissed her on the cheek and promised to try. Michael shook hands with him then he and Daniel left so James could catch the train. 'He's a perfect gentleman, isn't he?' Grace said to Michael. 'Indeed he is, if there were more Englishmen like him, they would have no problems with Ireland', he replied.

In early September, the family received a letter from Finbar and Bridget.

Dear Grace, Daniel and Michael,

We hope you are all keeping well. We would like to come over and spend Christmas with you, if you haven't made other arrangements?. We would love to meet Grace, although we feel we know her already. Please write soon to let us know if this will be convenient. Now! We have some grand news for you. There are rumours going around that an agreement is on the cards regarding Ireland's Independence. We all have high hopes, Please God they will be realised. There has been so much innocent Irish blood spilt, we need to live in peace in our own country with our own Irish Leaders and not under the heel of England. Take care of each other and God be with you.

Bridget and Finbar.

Michael and Daniel discussed the possibility of Ireland gaining Independence from Britain. It was a subject close to their hearts. 'Do you think it will happen?' Daniel asked. 'Indeed I hope so, it's a few years since the Easter Rising, if Britain hasn't won the war, so to speak, by now, they will realise it will only drag on'. Daniel wrote back immediately inviting his uncle and aunt for Christmas with Grace's parents also invited, Grace was very excited about her first Christmas as Mrs. Daniel O'Reilly and was determined to make it a memorable one with all the family.

A week before Christmas Finbar and Bridget arrived laden with gifts, there was even soda bread for the men. There was great excitement at seeing one another, Grace and Bridget soon became friends. No one could really resist Bridget's sense of humour, to us the vernacular, 'she was a card'. The family attended Midnight Mass on Christmas Eve and afterwards walked home together in the crisp night air. While the others settled themselves before a huge fire Grace and Daniel slipped into the kitchen to prepare some food. When everyone had a drink in their hands, Michael proposed a toast to Christmas.

Grace's parents arrived early on Christmas Day, Grace, her mother and Bridget prepared the dinner. When all was under control, Bridget and Grace's mother returned to the living room and joined the men. Grace set the table for dinner. First the snowy white fine linen tablecloth, a wedding gift from Bridget and Finbar. Waterford Crystal glasses, a wedding gift from Michael, silver cutlery, a wedding gift from her parents and lovely china inherited from Grandmother O'Hara. The table looked absolutely beautiful. Finally all was ready, the food sat on the table except the centrepiece. Grace carried in the large golden brown goose, an orange stuck in its mouth, then the rich, dark Christmas pudding decorated with a sprig of holly and laden with scarlet berries. Well done! she thought and sat down to enjoy her first Christmas dinner as Mrs. Daniel O'Reilly.

January 1922 saw the official announcement of a Treaty between the British Government and Ireland, regarding Ireland's Independence.

'The Irish Free State' was declared.

When Michael and Daniel heard the news they were overjoyed. They believed that the 'Troubles' in Ireland were over. To some extent they were. However, it soon became apparent that there were divisions in their opinion of the Treaty. The six Northern Ireland Counties were not included. This led to a compromise treaty which gave nominal independence to Ireland but which made sure that Ireland remained economically tied to Britain. This Treaty was against the will of the great majority of the people in Ireland, particularly the partitioning of Ireland with the six counties of Ulster remaining under British rule.

The two men discussed the situation. Michael shouted 'It's a sell-out' sure they should have stuck together instead of agreeing to a divided Ireland. Indeed, I don't think Ireland will know peace after this. Why didn't Eamonn de Valera go over to negotiate, he was after all nominated The President of Ireland? Michael Collins was a soldier.' 'I agree with what you say but perhaps Michael Collins thought 'half a loaf' was better than none at all. Maybe, in time, the six Counties will unite with The Irish Free State?' Daniel said. Michael's view of the situation proved to be correct. The I.R.A. was formed and Civil War broke out in Ireland

Grace was somewhat restless. She had been married for over a year and wanted a baby, so far, no luck!. She and Daniel often talked about having a family and she knew he wanted a child just as much as she did. However, his response was always the same. 'Sure everything happens when it is meant to happen darlin. We'll have our family, don't worry about it'.

Some months later, Grace walked into the shop where Daniel was busy rearranging books etc., 'Daniel, I'm off to the shops. I'll be back in time for lunch'. Kissing him lightly on the lips she closed the door behind her. She finished her shopping then kept her appointment with Dr. Roberts, the local doctor. 'I have good news for you, Mrs. O'Reilly, you are pregnant'. A feeling of relief and happiness swept over her as she smiled at him 'That's wonderful news, my husband will be delighted'. 'I will need to see you every month, congratulations'. Dr. Roberts said.

Grace wanted to tell the whole world her good news. She felt she would burst if she didn't tell Daniel immediately, but then again, she wanted the moment to be special and private. I'll tell him tonight she thought. As she cuddled up to Daniel in bed Grace could keep her secret no longer. 'Darling, I have a surprise for you', she said. Daniel sat up and rested on one elbow, then looked at her. To tease him, she waited a little longer to tell him. 'Sure if you don't tell me soon, I'll nod off' he said with a grin. 'We're going to have a baby, I'm pregnant' she announced with a smile. Daniel flopped back on the pillow for a few seconds then took Grace in his arms. 'That's the best bit of news I've heard. It's wonderful, sure I can't tell you how happy I am', he said as he kissed her tenderly. Michael was delighted when they told him the good news. Of course Grace's parents were very excited, they had always hoped for a grandchild. Daniel wrote to his uncle and aunt in Ireland and to James. Preparations to welcome the baby began practically immediately. Grace and her mother, sewed, crocheted and knitted enough baby clothes and cot blankets to last for a year. Daniel left this aspect of becoming a father, to his wife. He did however, help to choose a suitable cot and pram. The whole family were delighted and looked forward to the baby's arrival. Grace enjoyed a very normal pregnancy, she was very healthy and happy.

Grace awoke with a sharp pain in her stomach. She lay quietly in bed and waited to see if it really was the beginning of labour, when she was sure, she shook Daniel. He was awake in a few seconds, he had been expecting it and jumped out of bed to help Grace lumber out of bed and dress. While he dressed, she checked her suitcase to make sure she had everything she needed, then closed it. She felt an intense excitement within her, she would soon hold their baby in her arms. As they left their bedroom, Grace said. 'The next time I sleep here, our baby will be in the cot'. When they reached the Nursing Home a nurse took Grace's case and led them to the room which had been reserved for her. As she placed the suitcase on the floor the nurse said. 'I'll leave you for a few minutes, then I'm afraid you will have to wait outside in the reception lounge, Mr. O'Reilly. 'Dr. Roberts will need to examine your wife'. 'Think about it Daniel, very soon we will have our own baby to hold, isn't it wonderful' Grace said. Daniel put his arms around her 'Indeed it is, I love you so much Grace'. As the Nurse entered the room Daniel stood up and took hold of Grace's hands and said. 'Sure I won't be far away if you need me'.

It seemed to Daniel he had waited for an eternity. As he lit another cigarette he wondered how much longer it would be, he was feeling very anxious. Then he saw Dr. Roberts walk towards him with a smile on his face. Daniel's spirits lifted, he knew it was good news. 'You have a baby daughter, mother and baby are fine. Congratulations! you can go in to see them now'. Daniel was amazed when he saw Grace, he didn't know quite what he had expected but he could see his wife looked radiant. He kissed her and then looked down at his daughter. All he could see was a tiny face, the rest of her was wrapped in a blanket. She was the most beautiful baby he had ever seen. Giving thanks to God for the gift of the tiny human who lay asleep before him, he said. 'Sure, she's the loveliest child I've seen'.

There was great excitement when the family heard the good news that the baby was born and that Grace was well. Grace's parents couldn't wait to see her and set off for the Nursing Home. Michael was the first member of the family to see the new baby and kissed Grace on the cheek as he handed her a lovely bunch of mixed flowers. 'You look radiant' he told her. As he looked at the tiny scrap of humanity asleep in the cot, he remembered the first time he had seen Daniel. It didn't seem all that long ago. Gently he made the sign of the cross on her forehead and prayed silently for her future well being. Daniel wrote to his aunt and uncle in Ireland and told them his daughter was born. He also wrote to James and told him the good news.Daniel and Grace decided to name the baby Alice. After a few days, Grace's room was filled with flowers and greeting cards. There was a telegram from James and a beautiful shawl from Bridget and Finbar. The atmosphere in her room was excitement, pleasant and friendly, the proud parents often wondered how they had lived without their baby daughter. Grace was so well, Dr. Roberts told her if she maintained her present state of health, he would allow her to go home the following week. Alice was now three weeks old and had taken to the breast very easily.

The telephone rang early one morning, Michael took the call. The Matron of the Nursing Home asked to speak to Mr. Daniel O'Reilly. Michael felt very anxious and wondered what was wrong, why had the Matron phoned at such an early hour? He shook Daniel to wake up then told him there was a call for him. He watched Daniel's face as he listened to the voice on the other end of the telephone. Putting the telephone down he said 'sure I have to get to the Nursing Home, Now! he ran into the bedroom and dressed quickly and was out of the house in a few minutes. Michael heard the front door bang after him and sat down in a chair to wait.

The Nursing Home wasn't very far away. Daniel pushed open the door and rushed inside. A soon as he saw Dr. Roberts face he knew there was something seriously wrong and wondered if Alice was sick. He followed Dr. Roberts into his office and sat down as requested and waited for him to speak. 'I'm so very, very sorry, Mr. O'Reilly to have to tell you, Grace died very suddenly a few minutes ago from a brain haemorrhage. I can assure you, we did everything we could to save her'. For a few seconds Daniel's body refused to function. He could see the doctor's lips moving, but he couldn't hear what he was saying Three words kept going around and around in his head. 'Grace is dead', 'Grace is dead', Grace is dead'.

As the doctor stood up Daniel automatically did the same and followed him down the corridor. The doctor opened the door to a room and stood aside to allow him to enter. Closing the door behind him he left Daniel alone with Grace. Daniel looked at her as she lay on the bed, head slightly to one side. She looked as though she was asleep. Kneeling beside the bed Daniel took hold of her hand, it was still warm, he lifted it to his lips and kissed her hand. The lack of response unleashed a torrent of sorrow within him; he lay his head next to Grace and sobbed uncontrollably. Sometime later, somehow, he functioned and left the room and met the Matron and asked 'Have you let Father Brennan know my wife is dead?' 'Yes!, he will be here in a few minutes would you like to wait in my office?' Daniel thanked her and telephoned Grace's parents. There was silence when he spoke to his father-in-law then put the telephone down. Daniel saw Father Brennan hurry inside and walked towards him. He accepted his condolences and led the way to where Grace lay and Fr. Brennan administered the Last Rites as Daniel knelt down and cried bitterly. Soon after they discussed the funeral arrangements. Daniel shook hands with Fr. Brennan and went in search of the Matron once again. She was in her office so he walked in and asked. 'When can I take my daughter home?. 'I think it would be best if we kept Alice here for at least a few days. We have to see how long it will take for Alice to take to the bottle. Sometimes it takes time for a baby to adjust. You can, of course, come into the nursing home as often as you wish to see your daughter. I'm so very, very sorry' she said. 'Thank you', he replied and left for home.

After their daughter was buried, Mr. and Mrs. Fearon remained with Daniel and Michael for some time. Mrs. Fearon took care of her granddaughter Alice and Mr. Fearon assisted with legal matters. Daniel worked hard but was very remote. The only time he showed any real emotion was when he nursed his daughter. He soon realised that his mother-in-law, could not look after Alice forever, she was no longer young enough and decided he would have to employ someone to look after Alice permanently. Daniel made enquiries and with the help of Father Brennan and Dr. Roberts, secured the services of a nurse called Peggy Brown who had been widowed during the 1918 War. She had worked in Germany before the War for a very rich German family and was quite fluent in German. When War broke out she returned to England and met and married a soldier. Daniel's bedroom was turned into a room for Peggy and Alice, he moved downstairs permanently. When Peggy had settled in to her new duties, Grace's parents returned home.

Late one evening as he nursed Alice, Daniel looked down on the face of his daughter. A deep feeling of resentment welled up inside of him. He felt so angry and devastated. The child he and Grace had wanted so much, was motherless. It seemed to him, that the female members of his family, whom he loved, and who had loved him, died and left him to grieve. Alice was now the most important person in his life, would she also die? he wondered. It was all too much, he surprised his uncle when he said he was off to the pub for a drink. It wasn't that he never went to the pub, it was something in his manner. He returned home well after midnight, blind drunk.

It was the beginning of another nightmare for the family. Daniel carried out his business duties routinely and every night he got drunk. When he was sober, Michael tried to reason with him to no avail. No-one in the family or friends could make any headway with him. Daniel seemed encased in a shell, polite as always when he was sober. They all knew it was a phase he was going through in his grief for Grace, and hoped he would soon be his 'old self' again. However, it was not to be. Daniel and the situation rapidly deteriorated.

Some months later, the telephone rang in the early hours of the morning and Michael answered it. A Police Sergeant asked him to come down to the local Police Station, Daniel was in custody. When Michael arrived at the Police Station he asked the Sergeant what had happened. He explained that Daniel had been brawling in the street and had caused a lot of damage. Fortunately for him, no- one except himself had been hurt. The Police Sergeant led the way to the cell where Daniel was being held. A cold shiver ran through Michael as he looked at him. Daniel was seated on a wooden bench, propped up against the wall totally dishevelled. His tousled hair was matted with blood on one side of his head and his eyes and face were swollen nearly out of recognition. Daniel's degradation was there for all to see. With sudden insight, Michael realised Daniel did not intend to stop drinking, his goal was to drink himself into oblivion.

The Police released him and Michael took him home and managed to get him into his bed. A forlorn hope stirred within him, that when Daniel saw the mess he was in, in the morning, it might have some effect on him. Daniel was ready to leave the house the following morning for an auction when Michael tackled him about the previous night. He listened politely and shrugged his shoulder, then left the house. Michael was angry and upset. He had tried, the family had tried to 'reach' Daniel without success. Mother of God! he thought, what's to be done?' Suddenly he thought of James. Hanging up a 'closed' sign on the front door of the shop he closed the door behind him.

When Michael reached the solicitor's office he asked the secretary if it would be possible for a message to be sent to Mr. James Smith He explained the matter was urgent, but would only take a few minutes of his time. He was lucky, a client had failed to turn up . Michael explained that their client, Mr. James Smith's friend, Daniel O'Reilly, was very ill and felt a letter would take too long and asked if it would be possible to contact Mr. Smith and ask him to telephone Mr. Michael O'Hara at home. 'I'll see what I can do, Mr. O'Hara, please wait' he answered and left his office. Michael waited anxiously and wondered whether James was even in London at the moment. Sometime later, the solicitor returned from his office and sat down behind his desk. 'I have been able to contact our client and I have given him your message, he will telephone you tonight Mr. O'Hara'. A very relieved Michael stood up and thanked him and left the office.

James telephoned as promised and Michael explained in every sordid detail the problem with Daniel. As he expected, James was very upset. 'I can hardly believe my ears, Daniel is such a very courageous young man. I'll catch the early morning train from London tomorrow. I should be extremely grateful, Michael if you would meet the train, we can discuss this matter privately'. 'Indeed, I'll be there' Michael answered and decided to surprise Daniel with James's visit.

The following morning, Michael waited on the platform for James' train to arrive. When it finally pulled in and the smoke cleared, he spotted James as he alighted from a carriage and hurried towards him. The two men shook hands and Michael led the way to the car. As he drove off, Michael said. 'Sure I'm very grateful to you James for coming so quickly, I know you are a very busy man'. 'Not at all my dear fellow, obviously the situation is very serious and warrants action, what action we have to determine. Perhaps we could stop at a hotel and order breakfast, I confess I'm absolutely famished'. Michael drove to a nearby hotel and the two men went inside. A waiter soon appeared and they ordered breakfast. Over bacon and eggs etc., they discussed the situation. Michael endeavoured to explain Daniel's drinking more clearly. 'Why do you think Daniel is behaving in this manner?' James asked. 'Indeed he is devastated by Grace's death, we know that, but there is something else, sure I'd like to know what?' Michael replied. When he is sober he is remote but polite. When he is drunk he is totally degraded. We've lost the old Daniel and my heart aches because I can't help him. As God is my judge, I believe his goal is to destroy himself, Michael explained sorrowfully.

Daniel smiled with pleasure when he saw James. James was shocked at the change in him. Both men greeted each other warmly and began to chat like the old friends they were. Later Daniel took him into the bedroom to see Alice. She happened to be awake and when she saw Daniel and James she smiled and held out her arms to be picked up. 'May I?' James asked as he picked her up and carried her back into the living room and nursed her. 'My word Daniel, she's a beauty, 'do I detect a little auburn hair growing on her head, and she has inherited your green eyes, congratulations Daniel' James enthused. Later, when Alice had been put back into her cot the two men chatted until it was time for dinner. Michael joined them. When the meal was finished, James and Michael waited to see if Daniel would stay at home or go the pub as usual. They didn't have to wait long to find out. Daniel stood up and lied convincingly. 'Sure, I'm sorry James, if I'd known you were coming I would have cancelled my appointment with some business acquaintances I have this evening. I'll be back soon'. James and Michael did not go to bed, they waited until Daniel returned. They heard him come in shortly after midnight and blunder his way to the bedroom. Then there was silence. For nearly a full week James assessed the situation. When Daniel left the house one evening for the pub James said to Michael that he had devised a plan to help Daniel. 'I think it is the only way we can help him. I'll explain it to you and if you agree we will go ahead with it. We both agree he needs help and we both agree the family has been unable to stop him drinking. Daniel needs professional help'.

James told Michael he had a Specialist friend of his who has a first class clinic for alcoholics, this side of London. ' He holds very advanced ideas in dealing with alcoholics and uses therapy to get to the underlying cause, which he believes, in most cases, is the root of the problem. Of course it does not always work. Daniel will be well treated. I'll ask my friend to give me a daily report on his progress and of course, I will pass the information on to you. When I am allowed to do so and I will visit him'. 'Holy Mother of God! James do we have to do this to him?' Michael asked dejectedly. 'Yes we do! I think we should act as soon as possible if we are to save him from himself. My dear fellow, I'm just as upset as you are Daniel means a lot to me. We must hope and you can pray to that 'God of Yours' that this solves his problem. When he is his old self again we must hope he understands and forgives us'. James added quietly.

With Michael's blessing, James made all the necessary arrangements with the Specialist. The following night, when Daniel returned home, drunk as usual, they were waiting for him. They bundled him into the back seat of the car and covered him with a rug. He muttered a few swear words but soon was snoring his head off. Michael and James climbed into the car and James drove off as fast as permitted towards London. When James drew up in front of the Clinic, two male nurses waited for them. Daniel was still 'hung over' and with Michael on one side of him and James on the other they managed to climb the steps to the entrance without mishap. James and Michael watched sadly as the two male nurses led Daniel away.

Michael's life was severely disrupted by Daniel's absence. It was compounded by the fact that he was so worried about him. However, he hired a young man to help him in the shop and attended auctions himself whenever necessary. Alice was his only consolation at this time, he adored her and spent as much time as possible with her. He found her resemblance to his dead sister, Clare, uncanny. Another worry he had was the possibility that if Daniel remained in the Clinic for a long time he would be a stranger to Alice and this would present another problem. She was growing very rapidly.

Six months had passed from the time he entered the Clinic, Daniel came home. There was subdued excitement in the family at the prospect of his return. They did not know what to expect. Peggy dressed Alice in her prettiest dress, and tied a satin bow in her auburn hair, there was enough hair now to hold it. Peggy kept telling her 'daddy is coming soon'. All was ready to welcome Daniel home. Michael was in his small office when James and Daniel arrived. He had a few seconds to really look at his nephew before he left his office to welcome him and felt relieved when he saw him. He was much thinner but that was the only difference he could see. He moved forward and Daniel put his arms around him and gave him a hug. Thank God! he has forgiven me he thought as he looked at James, who smiled wryly at him. Daniel led the way upstairs and stood still when he saw his daughter. The tiny baby he remembered was becoming beautiful little girl. Peggy said 'Go to daddy darling' as she handed her over to Daniel. Daniel took her gently in his arms as tears filled his eyes. As he held her close, he realised this was his reality, Alice was his future.

James stayed with the family for a week. He wanted to see Daniel in his own surroundings and hoped to resume their old pattern of hiking around the countryside. He was not disappointed. Daniel suggested they did that the following morning after breakfast. James was absolutely delighted. By the end of the week, James knew beyond all shadow of doubt the 'old Daniel' was back, he need no longer be afraid for him. He had also been completely captivated by Alice. Michael never knew what deep seated problems had caused Daniel's collapse, apart from his grief for Grace. He just thanked God it was all over. Daniel's life took on a new rhythm. The centre of it was his baby daughter, Alice. Although she had lost her mother, her maternal grandparents showered her with love and affection. Michael was like a grandfather to her also. Peggy took very good care of her and Alice brought happiness into the family.

The years passed, everyone grew older. Daniel soon realised when James paid his annual visit, he was too old to hike over the fells like they had done in previous years and instead, he took him on less strenuous walks around the countryside. Alice was now four years old. She was a beautiful child, a charming little girl full of life and mischief.

James arrived on his annual visit. When Alice saw him she ran over to him. He picked her up and hugged her then handed her a large parcel. She had difficulty in undoing the wrapping paper, so he helped her to remove the lid from the box. Inside was a beautiful porcelain doll. Alice stared at it, wide eyed. The doll was dressed in lemon silk and lace. Lifting the doll out of the box she hugged it. From then on she carried the doll with her wherever she went. The family were always sorry when it was time for James to return to London, he was part of the family, a great raconteur and very knowledgeable and they enjoyed his company very much indeed. He said his goodbyes and Alice put her arms around his neck as he kissed her on the cheek. James set her down on the floor and remarked, with a wry grin, 'I'm absolutely positive Daniel that your very charming little daughter has a splendid future ahead of her'. Daniel laughed and led the way to the car. James waved to the family as Daniel drove off to the railway station in time for James to catch his train to London.

Later in the year Daniel received a letter from Solicitors Jones and Roberts'. They asked him to call into the office as soon as possible; they had some matters to discuss. Daniel was anxious to find out what those matters were and called into the office the following afternoon. Mr. Jones was very polite and ushered him into his office and asked him to sit down. He shuffled some papers on his desk, then handed Daniel a letter. He recognised James' handwriting and wondered why he had not written to him at home. I'll leave you to read your letter Mr. O'Reilly, Mr. Jones said and left the office. Daniel opened the envelope.

My dear Daniel,

When you read this letter, I shall be dead and buried. To say 'thank you' for saving my life would be most inadequate. I have never forgotten the kindness you showed me on that occasion. You shared whatever you had with an unknown man. Our friendship has spanned many years and I have valued it most highly. I watched you grow from a rather lonely young man in a foreign country, to a mature and successful business man, loving husband and father. I enjoyed our fireside chats and our hikes around the countryside. Whenever I appeared on your doorstep you greeted me warmly and invited me into your family circle, for that, I am heartily grateful. It is my dying wish, Daniel, to help you realise your dream. I know you still cherish it. I have, therefore, instructed my solicitors accordingly. Perhaps you will say a prayer for me to that 'God of Yours'. Please say goodbye for me to the members of your family and lastly, give Alice big hug from me.

It is time Daniel! Goodbye my dear friend. Your sincere friend, James.

Daniel was shocked and distressed by the contents of the letter and couldn't quite grasp the fact that his old friend James was dead. Trying to wipe away the tears which were falling and blotching the writing in the letter, he blessed himself. A feint trace of a smile touched his mouth when he recalled the discussions they had over the years about that 'God of Yours'. Feeling very sad as he folded the letter, he put it back into the envelope and slipped it into his pocket. How like him, he thought, to be concerned enough to make sure I heard of his death this way. Sure I'll miss him very much. There was a knock on the door and Mr. Smith entered the office. 'I see you have read your letter. I have another matter to discuss with you, please follow me', he said. Leading the way into a much larger office he sat down behind the desk and asked Daniel to sit down also. Daniel remembered something in the letter about Solicitors but there was no time to dwell on it as Mr. Smith began to speak. 'As you are aware, our client, Mr. James Smith is now deceased. You are a beneficiary in his Will'. He opened a file on his desk and began to read from the document. *To my very dear friend Mr. Daniel O'Reilly, I hereby bequeath the sum of £30,000. pounds to enable him to realise his dreams.* Daniel heard Mr. Smith's voice, but it seemed to come from a distance.

'We have also been instructed to act on your behalf in this matter. To assist in anyway we can and to advise you'. Daniel was stunned, he just stared at the man. Too much had happened too soon, his normal world had been turned upside down. I have to get some air, he thought, or I'll suffocate, he stood up and thanked the solicitor. 'I'm sure you can understand how I feel at the moment. Indeed, these matters have been a terrible shock. I need time to think about what has happened and what to do about it. I will contact you in a few days'. Daniel shook hands with the solicitor and left the office. His mind was in turmoil so he just walked and walked until he felt tired. Sitting on a dry stone wall he read James' letter again. One sentence stood out. 'It is my dying wish ....' Daniel knew what he alluded to. It was his dream to own a hotel on Lake Windermere. They had discussed this imaginary hotel often and when he had said 'sure it will never happen', James had always responded in the same way. 'Pursue your dream Daniel'. Now he could realise his dream thanks to James. He wiped the tears from his eyes and set off for home. Thank you James, he thought, I'll never forget you. You will always be part of 'my dream' Rest in Peace. Daniel decided rather than tell his uncle Michael about James' death and legacy he would let him read the letters. It will certainly be a surprise, he thought. After their evening meal, Peggy put Alice to bed and left the house to visit friends. Daniel thought it was the ideal time to reveal his secret. Sitting down in his chair as Michael was about to light a cigarette, Daniel handed him James' letter. 'Sure I think you should read this'. Michael took the letter and after reading it, folded it and handed it back to Daniel. 'I'm very sorry, he was a good man. Indeed I'll miss him myself. Sure I know it's a great loss for you, you have been friends for most of your adult life. God rest his soul. Do you know when James died?' Michael asked. 'No, sure it must have happened soon after his last visit. I wish I had known, but I will never forget him or his friendship' he declared.

Daniel handed his uncle the letter which contained the details of James' legacy. Michael read the letter then looked at Daniel in disbelief. 'Holy Mother of God!' he exclaimed as he blessed himself. Sure he's left you a fortune, you're a rich man'. 'Sure I know that, but I can't quite grasp that fact yet. I know my life will be different. We used to talk a lot about the future and James always said 'Pursue your Dream' Daniel. I think he left me this money, many, many years ago'. 'What is your dream?' Michael asked. 'To own a Hotel on Lake Windermere', he replied. 'When I first arrived in The Lake District, it reminded me of Ireland, with the green fields and the rivers but I knew I couldn't go back home. When Michael heard him say that, he remembered the time when Daniel was a teenager, they had stood at the edge of the lake and he had said. 'One day, I'm going to own a Hotel on this lake'. At the time, it had seemed an impossibility but James has made it possible. I'll make an appointment with the solicitor to discuss details with him and I'd like you to come with me. You know more about property and money matters than I do'. Daniel said. 'Sure I'll do that' Michael replied.

The following week Daniel and Michael sat with Mr. Jones Details of the legacy were explained to Daniel. He was free to use the money in any way he chose. Thus, Daniel took the first step towards the realisation of the dream he had cherished, from the first time he had set eyes on Lake Windermere, as a seventeen years old youth.

The solicitor wrote to Daniel some weeks later and asked him to call into the office. They discussed financial matters and handed him a list of properties suitable for his purpose. Daniel decided to buy an old, run down hotel because of its position. It was built on top of a small hill. The rear overlooked the lake and the front faced the road. It stood in its own grounds and had access to a small private beach. Negotiations were completed very quickly and Daniel engaged an Architect to design the alterations he required He explained to him that he wanted a window in each room, so guests had a view of the lake and a suite of rooms for the family overlooking the lake. Another requirement was a boathouse to house the boats he intended to supply for the guests and a small pier and left the alterations in the hands of the Architect. Six months later the structural alterations had been completed. While the hotel was being painted, Daniel discussed the furniture and furnishings with the Architect, he didn't know much about furniture etc., but he knew what he liked so between them, the furnishings etc., were chosen. One piece of furniture Daniel chose himself was a beautiful shiny black piano. There was a piano in the farm house when he was growing up and he loved listening to the family playing on it.

During this time, the shop was put up for sale. All ornaments etc., of sentimental value belonging to the family and the antiques Grace has cherished, were taken to the hotel with them for their own personal use. Michael had a few regrets about leaving the shop. It had offered him a new and very different way of life. However, he looked forward with great anticipation to his new life in the hotel. Daniel, on the other hand was glad when the shop was finally sold. It held too many 'dark' memories for him. The 'shining' ones, he carried within him. Suitable staff had been hired, everything was in place. Most of the guest rooms had been reserved. The hotel was ready for business. Daniel went outside to admire his hotel, smiling with satisfaction as he read the name written in gold lettering above the oak panelled front door. 'THE JAMES HOTEL'

Twelve years had passed since Daniel opened 'The James Hotel' and many changes had occurred during that time. Daniel had extended the Hotel to accommodate the influx of visitors from Germany, Italy and France during the summer. Mostly, they were rock-climbers and hikers. Peggy had proved to be an invaluable asset because she spoke fluent German and had a smattering of Italian and French, she had also taught Alice to speak German and a little French. It added a personal touch with guests whose English was rather poor. Along with the row boats provided, boating was now a popular past time for the guests. Daniel was now a very successful Hotelier. Michael had grown too old to do any real work, however, he helped if necessary. He was now a very charming old man and chatted amiably with the guests in the evenings and made many friends.

It was a quiet time in the Hotel, most of the guests had left for their day's outings. Daniel sat down in a chair on the veranda and enjoyed the view of Lake Windermere. The water was not quite as blue now, it was nearly autumn. He watched a bird dive into the lake and emerge with a shining fish in it's beak and the fells provided the perfect backdrop. As usual, he felt at peace with himself. His thoughts turned to the day Alice started school, he remembered it vividly. Peggy had dressed her, then brought her to the lounge where he waited for her. 'Daddy' Alice cried, he had smiled broadly when he saw his small daughter dressed in her Convent school uniform. Panama hat, blue blouse and gym tunic, blue blazer, her black stockings and sturdy black shoes. Her beautiful auburn hair was tied back with a wide blue ribbon. Opening his arms for her, she ran across the room towards him. Picking her up, he swung her around over his head. As he set her down on the floor, he said 'Now darlin' let me look at you. Sure you look so grand, I hardly know you'. Alice pirouetted in front of him. 'Hurry daddy, we mustn't be late for school' she said. 'Indeed, we must not I'll just get my coat and we'll be off', he answered with a smile. Daniel felt a lump rise in his throat as he watched Alice walk away from him, hand-in-hand with one of the Nuns. She turned her head and smiled at him, then disappeared from view.

Daniel left the school grounds and got into his car. Lighting a cigarette he sat alone with his thoughts for some time. He drove for a few miles, then stopped the car and got out. It was a beautiful Autumn day. The sun was quite warm as he walked across the fields and over the styles. He climbed a small hill and stood on the edge of a wood. The 'sea' of bluebells had long gone.

They had been replaced by a carpet of autumn leaves. The trees were a blaze of vivid colour, ranging from crimson and scarlet to orange, yellow and brown. He dug his hands deep inside the pockets of his overcoat and walked through the wood. It was his special place and each season was a visual masterpiece. As he walked the dry leaves crunched under his feet, he was alone with his memories of the love of his life, his wife Grace. He remembered how she had looked when he asked her to marry him surrounded by a 'sea' of bluebells and wished she had lived to share this special day with him to watch their five year old daughter take her first steps into her unknown future. Wiping away the tears he returned to his car. As he drove along the winding lanes he knew so well, his thoughts turned to his old friend James, because of his gift to him, Alice would have the best education money could buy. The trend of his thoughts were broken when a waiter approached and told him the Architect had arrived for their appointment.

Daniel's aunt Bridget and uncle Finbar spent every Christmas with the family. In this way Daniel ensured they were part of Alice's life. Daniel took her over to Dublin as often as he could, he wanted her to know and 'feel' her Irish heritage. On one visit Alice persuaded him to take her to see the farm where he had spent the early days of his life with his granny. From the outside, the farmhouse looked much the same. The farm itself was much larger. More land had obviously been acquired. The old stone church was now a school. Daniel also took her to the graveyard where his beloved granny Kate, who brought him up and Martin his grandfather who died before he was born, were buried. Alice read out the inscription on the headstone and then placed a small bunch of pink rosebuds at the foot of the grave. She held her father's hand tightly as they said a 'Hail Mary' for them.

When Alice was thirteen years old, her maternal grandparents died very suddenly within a week of each other from a very severe bout of influenza. Daniel was upset and comforted Alice who loved them very much. His 'in-laws' had always been very close to him. Daniel had never forgotten their kindness to him as a young man. As there were no surviving relatives Daniel arranged the funeral service. Many of Mr. Fearon's colleagues and their wives attended the service. Alice clung to her father's hand during the service. A few weeks later, Daniel received a letter from his father-in-law's solicitor. They informed him that Alice was the sole beneficiary of their estate. Daniel learned that Alice's grandparent's house and contents, a large sum of money and all of her grandmother's jewellery belonged to Alice. Daniel explained to Alice that the household contents would be sold except for any item she wished to keep, also the house. The money would be placed in Trust for her, until she was 21 years of age. However, the jewellery, she could take with her.

Alice was not 15 years of age and had proved to be academically clever. Peggy had taught her to speak German and she had learned French at school. She had lots of friends and was a very happy well adjusted girl. Exams loomed very large in her life at this moment. She knew she had to pass the 'Matric' as the first step to a career as a Veterinary Surgeon. One evening after dinner she said 'Daddy! I've got a lot of studying to do and Cathy has asked me to spend the weekend at her parent's house so we can study together. I'll go home with her from school on the train, on Friday. Will you pick me up from school on Monday?' 'Indeed I will, Don't study all the time, take some time off to enjoy yourself'.

The weekend didn't go quite as they planned. Cathy developed severe pains on Sunday night and had to stay in bed. On Monday morning, she was still too sick to go to school. Alice declined Cathy's mother's offer to drive her to school. She explained that it was only a short distance to the railway station and she would enjoy the walk. Alice heard the train whistle and started to run down the hill, the ticket collector knew her and waved her though the barrier. Racing down the steps under the subway and up the steps to the platform on the other side of the station, she heard the train grind to a halt. As she reached the top step she tripped and fell face down on the platform, her school bag burst spilling the contents all over the platform. Alice scrambled to her feet and began to collect her belongings. She saw a group of male hikers not far from her, turn to look at her. She wished she could disappear from sight. Then she heard a voice say 'do let me help you'. Looking up into the face of a young man, very blonde hair and very handsome, she thought, smiled at her and handed her a pile of her exercise books. She mumbled something and they both collected the rest of her belongings. She heard her school friends call to her from the train to 'hurry up'. 'Don't worry, the guard saw you fall and he will hold the train for a few minutes' he said. It was then Alice realised what a sight she must look. She knew her panama hat was all askew on her head. She could feel it wasn't sitting correctly and she could see two large holes in the knees of her black stockings. However he smiled again and she noticed he had a most unusual mouth it was very thin and straight. He left her and returned to his group of friends. As Alice hurried towards the train, the door of the carriage was held open for her. She passed the group and heard them speak to each other in German. He must be German she thought? as she scrambled into the carriage and flopped down on the seat. Her friends closed the carriage door behind her, the guard blew his whistle and the train began to move. Alice's friends hung out of the window and called out, 'Goodbye!' Goodbye! and waved to the group of German hikers. She heard them answer, but was too busy tidying herself to take much notice. Boys were the last thing on her mind at that moment. Her friends withdrew their heads inside the carriage and closed the window and sat down opposite Alice and looked at her for the first time. They tried hard not to laugh at her, but it proved impossible, she looked so funny, rather dishevelled with two large holes in the knees of her black stockings. Fortunately, Alice also saw the funny side and they laughed themselves sick for the rest of the journey to school.

One Sunday morning, after Mass, Alice and her best friend Cathy, were in the lounge, listening to the radio. Suddenly there was a break in transmission. On the 3rd September 1939 a voice came over the air and informed listeners that The Prime

Minister of Britain, Mr. Neville Chamberlain would make an announcement.

They listened intently and when he had finished speaking, looked at each other and said. 'We're at War! We're at war with Germany. I wonder if daddy has heard the news, let's go down and find out' Alice said. running into the kitchen 'Daddy, did you hear the news?' 'What news?' he replied. 'Britain has declared War on Germany' we're at War' she said excitedly. 'My God!' he exclaimed! 'another War, sure it's only over 20 years since the last one, that's bad news, indeed it is'..

Almost overnight, the tranquillity of the Lake District was shattered by columns of army trucks full of soldiers on route to manoeuvres. Platoons of soldiers marched along the side of the roads in time to a tune they themselves whistled. Army, Navy and Air force personnel were very conspicuous. The 'Drill Hall' was headquarters for whichever Company of soldiers happened to be stationed in the district. Alice and her friends found the whole atmosphere very exciting. So did most of the single girls. Dances were held frequently in either the Scout hall or Church hall. Members of the Armed Forces made sure they attended whenever it was possible. The girls had a wonderful time; they had never been so popular. It was quite some time before the Casualty Lists began to affect families in the district. The truth of the cost of War, in human lives, became abundantly clear. Husbands, brothers and friends would never return.

It was 1941. Two years had passed since War had been declared. Alice was now 18 years of age. She had passed all her exams and tonight was her Graduation Ceremony. She finished dressing for the occasion and looked at herself in the Cheval mirror. Looking back at her was a tall, slim girl in a long white crepe dress trimmed with lace. Her auburn hair hung down over her shoulders. Hearing a knock on her door she called 'come in'. Her father entered the room and smiled when he saw her. 'You look lovely darlin, here now, I have something for you', and handed her a small blue velvet box. She opened the box and lifted out a solid gold locket. 'Daddy!, she exclaimed, it's lovely. Thank you so much'. 'I bought the locket for your mother shortly after we were married.. I kept it for you Alice. Here, let me fasten it around your neck'. She put up her hand and touched the locket, then turned to her father and laid her head against his chest as he hugged her.

People's lives had changed dramatically. Young people aged 18 years and over were now eligible for conscription in the Armed Forces. Rationing of food was in full swing, clothing coupons were needed to buy clothes, and the word 'Utility' became synonymous with goods manufactured during the war. Unofficially, an 'under the counter' system developed. Only those 'in the know' got a share of scarce commodities which were not rationed. A barter system also developed. People exchanged goods they did not want, for those they did. The clientele of The James Hotel changed. There were no longer visitors from Europe. Instead, most rooms were booked by servicemen of all ranks so their wives could visit them. Often honeymooners from as far away as London escaped to the comparative peace and quiet of the countryside. The atmosphere was totally different.

Alice was becoming bored, she had finished school and the hours dragged on for her. She helped around the hotel but the staff knew their jobs, she really wasn't needed. Most of her friends felt the same way. It seemed to them, that other people's lives were much more exciting. One by one her friends volunteered for the Service of their choice. She felt more isolated every day. Her career as a Veterinary Surgeon had been put on hold and she wondered what to do in the meantime. After much soul searching, she decided she would 'join up'. Alice wondered how her father would take the news, she thought he would be upset and waited for a suitable time to tell him. The moment arrived and rather nervously she explained to him how she felt and what she would like to do.

'Are you sure about this?' was his response. 'Your have never been away from home and your family, indeed army life will be very different from what you have been used to and you won't be able to change your mind'. 'I know that daddy, I know I will miss you all terribly. I've really thought it all through and I have some idea of what to expect from what Cathy has told me', she explained. Daniel looked at her for a few minutes then said. 'You're a sensible girl, if that's what you want to do you have my blessing'. 'Thank you', daddy Alice said as she hugged him. Daniel's thoughts retreated to the past history of his family in Ireland and how they were treated by Britain and thought to himself how things have changed.

Some months later Alice joined the W.A.T.S. and was sent to the Midlands for training. She found the lack of privacy the biggest challenge. However, she mixed well with her colleagues and made the best of the situation. After six months, she was selected for Officer Training and came through with flying colours. Some months later she was Commissioned and was now 2nd Lieutenant O'Reilly. Alice went home on leave, her father, aunt and uncle were all very proud her and delighted to see her. When she was posted to a 'Special Unit' outside London her intelligence and skill with languages were put to good use. Alice was good at her job and a year later promoted to Lieutenant and put in charge of a section.

Alice's 48 hours leave passed all too quickly. She thanked her hostess, her friend's mother, for her hospitality and walked down the hall to the front door. Sarah opened the door and instinctively they both looked up at the afternoon sky. 'I wonder if there will be an Air Raid tonight?', Sarah asked. 'I expect 'Jerry' will pay his usual visit but I should be back at the base before the event' Alice replied looking at her watch. She had five minutes to catch the bus into the City, shouting goodbye to Sarah she hurried down the street. As the bus neared the centre of London she heard the Air Raid Siren. The bus driver drove the bus to the nearest bomb shelter as quickly as he could, which happened to be the underground. As he stopped the bus the passengers got off and hurried to where the Air Raid Wardens directed the stream of people to the sandbagged entrance. Alice descended the flight of steps and reached the platform. She looked around her, hoping to find some place to sit. There were no seats in sight. Families with young children had already prepared for the night. Makeshift beds and blankets covered most of the floor and mothers dispensed sandwiches and drinks to their children. Threading her way through the crowd she settled for a small space. She leaned against the wall and lit a cigarette and wondered how long the Raid would last. Sometime later, Alice heard a man's voice. 'Excuse me! excuse me, oh! I am sorry I do beg your pardon'. She turned to see where the voice came from, it was an Army Captain walking towards her so she moved along a little to give him some room. 'That's very kind of you, a bit crowded tonight isn't it?. are you coming or going, on leave I mean?' he asked. 'I'm due back tonight', Alice replied politely. 'Let me introduce myself, Captain Charles Smith' and offered her his hand. Shaking his hand she replied, 'I'm Lieutenant Alice O'Reilly'. 'You're Irish?' 'Yes I am, I was born in England though'. It was two hours before the 'All Clear' sounded. By that time they were on a first name basis. People began to move towards the exit, so they joined the queue. Once outside the shelter it took Alice a couple of seconds to adjust to the blackout. She looked around to see if there had been much damage. 'My God Alice!, look over there' said Charles. Looking to where he pointed she could see an enormous fire in the distance. The flames leapt skywards in wild abandon. 'Come on, said Charles. I'll walk you to the train, things look very chaotic at the moment'. When they reached the railway station it was crowded.

Wives, girl friends, held hands with husbands and boyfriends before they said a tearful goodbye. Railway personnel moved around constantly and civilians just waited for a train home. There were queues for everything. The toilets, telephone, ticket office and the buffet. Alice decided she would try and find the Transit Officer to find out when the next train is due. She returned and explained there was a train due in about half an hour. 'That's jolly good luck, I say, how about a cup of tea?' he asked. Inevitably the buffet was crowded but they found two old rickety chairs at the back of the room and promptly claimed them. 'Gosh! it's good to sit down' Alice murmured. 'Tea, coffee?' Charles asked with a grin, 'tea please' Alice responded. By the time they had drunk their tea and smoked their cigarette the train was due, so they returned to the platform. Charles gently ushered Alice to the front of the crowd, he knew the train would be packed. The sound of the train drew nearer and a few minutes later reached the platform and ground to a halt. Charles saw a partly empty carriage and hurried forward to open the carriage door for Alice. Gratefully, she climbed in and placed her bag on a seat. After he had closed the door he waited until Alice rolled the window down so they could say goodbye. Alice leaned out of the window and offered Charles her hand. 'Goodbye. thank you so much for your company and your help'. Taking hold of her outstretched hand he asked if he could see her again, 'perhaps a show some weekend when we are both on leave?'. 'Yes, that would be lovely' she answered. 'Give me a telephone number where I can contact you', he asked. Alice found a slip of paper in her pocket and scribbled the number and handed it to him. The whistle blew and the train began to move. As Charles left the station he said to himself. I must see her again, she's a bloody beauty and bright with it, what a combination..

Meanwhile Alice settled down in the carriage. One solitary bulb was all the light there was, the windows were blacked out. She lit a cigarette and thought about Charles. He is rather good company, I wonder if he will get in touch with me? She knew from experience that friendships flourished very quickly in wartime and just as quickly died for many reasons. She closed her eyes and tried to sleep.

Charles telephoned Alice and followed up with a letter. He asked her to try and get 48 hours leave the following month so he could take her to his friend's wedding reception. 'Please try Alice' he asked. She managed to get the 48 hours leave and Charles arranged to meet her train. They set off for the Officer's Club, where the reception was to be held. Charles introduced her to the bride and groom, fellow officers and friends. The pianist began to play the piano and Charles asked her to dance. Soon it was time for the bride and groom to leave for their honeymoon. All the guests gathered around them and wished them well and especially, a night free from Air Raids.

Charles and Alice sat down and caught up with the news. They were in deep conversation when there was an enormous crash and the sound of shattered glass. Every head in the room turned in the direction of the crash, but gave a sigh of relief when they realised a waiter had knocked over a tray full of empty glasses. However, Alice's attention had been drawn to a tall, blonde officer standing with a drink in his hand at the bar. 'Charles, who is that officer at the bar, the tall blonde one?' she asked. Looking towards the bar he said 'That's Simon, Simon Chancellor, he's a friend of Freddie's, why are you interested?' he asked with a smile. Alice laughed and said, 'Not at all, he seemed familiar, but I can't place him'. Charles stood up and said with a grin, 'may I have this dance please?'. 'I should be delighted' she replied as she took hold of his hand and walked with him to the dance floor.

One night some months later, Alice awoke with a start and wondered why, so she lay in bed for a few minutes. In slow motion she saw Captain Simon Chancellor as she had noticed him at Freddie's wedding. Then the incident when she was a schoolgirl and tripped on the railway station platform and all her books etc., had spilled out of her school bag and scattered all over the platform. A young man had left the group of hikers he was with and helped her to pick them up. She had looked up into the face of a very handsome, blonde young man who had reassured her that the train would not leave without her because the guard had seen her fall. She recalled she had been surprised when walking pass the hiking group to hear them all speaking to each other in German but the young man had spoken to her without a trace of a German accent. She also remembered her friends had hung out of the carriage and waved to the group and called 'goodbye!. They had answered 'Auf Wiedersen Frauleins!'. Oh my God!, she exclaimed and shot out of bed. She put on her dressing gown and lit a cigarette. Is it the same man? she asked herself and again recalling the young man's face. Yes! It is the same man she decided. She was fully aware of all he implications, even civilians were bombarded with posters and slogans 'Careless talk costs lives. The Fifth Column'.

❝Alice served in a 'Special Unit', she knew stranger things had already happened. She thought about it for a long time and finally reached the conclusion that she would have to discuss the matter with her C.O. It would be his decision whether the matter should be taken further. She requested an interview with the C.O. immediately she returned to base. A few days later, she was summoned to the C.O.'s office. Alice saluted and waited for him to speak. 'Sit down Lieutenant'. 'You asked to see me?' he said. Alice explained the situation to him as succinctly as possible and waited for his reaction. 'Are you reasonably sure Lieutenant, the young man you remember as the German hiker and Captain Simon Chancellor are one and the same person?'. 'Yes Sir!' I am. 'Thank you Lieutenant that will be all', he said as he dismissed her. She saluted and left the office. A week later, she was summoned to the C.O's office, and waited for him to speak. 'Sit down Lieutenant. I have made preliminary enquiries regarding the matter we have previously discussed and have decided it does warrant further investigation. Captain Chancellor is in charge of a 'Special Unit'. Ostensibly, you will attend a Course he is conducting. During that time, you are to confirm that Captain Chancellor is German and investigate his family background, discreetly, of course', he ordered. Do you think he will recognise you? he asked. 'I very much doubt it Sir, I was a school girl and that is a few years ago' she answered. 'Quite so!. 'You will report directly to me when your Course is completed'. Do you understand?' 'Yes Sir', she replied. 'That's all for now' he said and dismissed her as she returned to her duties.

Some time later Alice attended the course conducted by Captain Chancellor and wondered if he would recognise her, perhaps from Freddie's wedding? but gave no sign that he did, not that it would have mattered too much. She concentrated on the course and got to know her colleagues. She soon discovered that whenever any of them were off duty for a few hours they spent them in the local pub. One night she and a colleague Terry had a few hours to spare, so off they went to the pub. Alice noticed that the pub staff often took telephone messages and passed them on when the person came in. If the person was in the pub, the member of the staff who took the call would 'call out' loudly. It gave her an idea.!

By the end of a few weeks, Alice had no doubt about Captain Chancellor, he was the same young German hiker who had helped her some years ago. The next step, she thought, is to get access to his personal file and find out about his background. She decided to wait for an opportunity to get into the office where the files were kept. As luck would have it, Allison, Captain Chancellor's Secretary, developed toothache, and Alice was delegated to look after the office while she kept an appointment with the dentist. She couldn't believe her luck. She pulled out Captain Chancellor's file and read it, noting the address and telephone number of his parents in London. There was nothing unusual in his file. He had been educated at an English Public School, both his parents were English. She made copies of the documents, replaced them in his file and returned it to its proper place in the filing cabinet and locked it. She then slipped the copies into a large envelope and sealed it. A few nights later when she had a few hours off she took the opportunity to find out more about Captain Chancellor's background. Slipping out of her room she walked quickly to the public telephone booth in the village. She dialled his parent's number and waited. A lady answered. Alice asked to speak to Mrs. Chancellor. 'Speaking', the voice replied. 'My name is Valerie Lengel my husband is a friend of your son Simon. They lost touch but we are in London temporarily and would like to contact him. Do you have a telephone number where he can be reached?' she asked. There was 'silence' as she waited for her reply. 'I'm so sorry, I don't remember your husband, Simon had so many friends. My son was killed in a riding accident' she explained.

Alice was shocked, 'Oh! I'm so sorry, I do hope I have not upset you? 'Not at all, it happened some time ago. Thank you for calling', the line went dead. Alice walked back to the base and wondered what his real background is? All doubts had now left her, she was confident she was on the right track. The Course was nearing the end but she knew she had to get more proof and had to hear him speak in German, she told herself.

It was her colleague Allison's birthday and most of the group who had attended the Course, wandered down to the pub to celebrate. A local chap played the piano and everyone gathered around it for a sing-song. Eventually, however, they all returned to their tables. One of her colleagues questioned 'why can't the British speak other languages as well as other nationalities, either we are all too stupid, which I doubt, or we just can't be bothered. Does anyone here speak a foreign language? I learnt French at school, didn't you? surely you remember, La plume de ma tante est sur la table, everyone laughed. 'How about you Simon?' Alice asked. 'I'm afraid not, languages are certainly not my forte'. he answered. 'I can understand that Simon, you are so obviously English, I suspect you believe all foreigners should learn to speak English'. Allison said. They all laughed, including Simon. That night Alice lay in bed and tried to think of a plan to prove Simon spoke German, even though he had denied it and came up with a simple idea. If it didn't work, there would be no harm done and if it did, she would have all the proof she needed. Some nights later Alice took the opportunity which had presented itself to her. She knew Captain Chancellor was in the pub with some colleagues and as she had some free time set off for the public telephone booth. She dialled the pub's number and waited. 'Rose and Crown', a voice answered. 'Is Captain Chancellor there at the moment?', she asked. 'Yes' came the reply. 'I would like to speak to him' she said. Alice waited. When she heard Simon's say 'Hello!' and held the receiver as far away from her mouth as was possible and said in German. 'It's me Simon, how are you, I haven't heard from you for a long time?' She brought the receiver quickly back and listened anxiously for his reply. 'Who did you say?' he replied in English. Holding the receiver well away from her mouth she gave it a shake. 'It's a very bad line, I'll ring again' in German, then put the receiver down. 'I've got him!, I've got him!' she told herself, he understood every word I said to him.

Walking back to the pub she joined her colleagues for a well earned drink and watched Captain Chancellor for any sign that he had realised he had given himself away. She saw no sign of it, he was his usual urban self. Alice finished her report on Captain Chancellor for her C. O. and slipped it into the envelope with the copies of the documents from his file. After sealing it she placed it in the bottom of her grip and returned to Base. A few days later Alice was summoned to the C.O.'s office. 'I have read your report on Captain Chancellor, it is very thorough. Well done! Lieutenant'.

A few months later, Alice and Charles were on leave and dropped into a Hotel for a drink. During the course of the evening Alice felt a tap on her shoulder and a voice asked. 'What you doing here?' Turning around to see who it was, she recognised Terry a colleague who had been on the same Course with her. Alice introduced her to Charles and asked her join them. Terry explained that she had arranged to meet a friend in the Hotel, but he was late. They chatted and caught up with any gossip or rumours that were circulating, then Terry excused herself to powder her nose. 'I'll come with you' Alice said. The two girls weaved their way to the powder room and found it deserted. While they freshened up, Terry asked. 'Do you remember Captain Chancellor's secretary?'. 'Yes, of course, her name is Allison, why'? Alice replied. 'I met her recently and she told me an odd story'. Terry explained. Captain Chancellor asked her to copy some documents and to leave them on his desk so they would be ready for him the following morning. She had to walk across the building to the general office and when she had finished copying the documents she happened to look out of the window overlooking the parade ground. She swears she saw Captain Chancellor escorted by two M.P.'s, then get into a staff car and move off. She thought it seemed rather odd, but dismissed it from her mind. However, the following morning when she reached her office, Captain Chancellor was not there, instead, another officer introduced himself saying that Captain Chancellor had been called away on urgent business and he would be taking his place for a few days. She hadn't seen The Captain since, that was a month ago'. 'What do you make of it?' she asked. 'Who knows what goes on in our Units, perhaps he has been transferred?. 'Come on, let's get back to our table'. Later that evening when Alice was alone in her room, she thought about the 'odd story' concerning Captain Chancellor and never doubted for one moment but that he really had been arrested and remembered what her uncle Michael had said when he would talk about Ireland 'There is nothing worse than an informer.. So ends that chapter, she thought!.

Nearly a year had passed since Alice and Charles had met during the air raid. |Over the months that followed they had written letters to each other and spent as much time as possible on the telephone. Their relationship deepened. So far, they had been unable to get leave together, apart from 48 hours which they spent with friends in London. On one occasion she was introduced to his parents and she found them very charming people.

When on leave Alice talked about Charles to her father. He realised how important he was to her, but so far, she had not said she loved him. Daniel was just as anxious to meet him as Alice was for Charles to meet her father. On one occasion, she discussed the subject of Irish/English relations and the fact that she was Catholic and Charles was not. 'Sure things are very different now Alice. The Republic of Ireland is a free country, now she makes her own laws. Indeed I know some English people resent the fact that Ireland has remained neutral in this War with Germany but so has Switzerland, why don't they resent that country? In a Democratic Society, Governments make decisions they consider are right for their own citizens, or at lease we hope they do? Sure, people would have plenty to grumble about if Ireland supported Germany. Perhaps they should consider that possibility'.

'Indeed, Irish men and women do sometimes have a problem outside of Ireland. To be Irish is synonymous with Catholicity. I agree with that supposition and the majority of Irish men and women are Catholic but there are many who are not and who fought and died for Ireland's Independence. Charles Parnell was a Protestant and he became a hero to the oppressed Catholics and was referred to as the 'Uncrowned King of Ireland and was the Irish Nationalist member of British Parliament and leader for the Irish People.. Charles knows you are a Catholic and I'm sure he has thought about the implications. It's something you will have to discuss with him whenever you think it is necessary. You know darlin the time comes for all of us, sometime in our lives, when we have to decide what we think is important and what is not. Indeed, I know from very painful experience, that only the person can make the decision. We have to be true to whoever we are, or think we are'.

Later in the year, Alice and Charles managed to get leave at the same time and agreed they would spend it at Alice's home. Charles looked forward to meeting her family and had heard a lot about them, especially her father. From what he had gained from her, he was very family orientated. Alice wrote to her father to say she and Charles would like to spend their leave with him. There was great excitement in the family at the thought of seeing Alice again and at last, they would meet Charles.

The day arrived and Daniel drove to the railway station and waited. He lit a cigarette and walked along the platform then heard the train whistle and shortly afterwards the train pulled into the station. Carriage doors were flung open and passengers alighted. Seeing Alice he hurried to meet her. He put his arms around her, gave her a hug saying 'Sure it's grand to see you again'. Alice slipped her arm through her father's and introduced Charles. The two men shook hands and took a good look at one another. Alice clung to her father's arm as he led the way to the car. As they reached the hotel Daniel dropped them off and parked the car, Michael and Peggy both waited for her. She put her arms around them as they hugged her, then introduced them to Charles. A young boy took their grips upstairs.

'It's a bit late to call it 'lunch', Daniel said but as soon as you are ready, join us in the dining room. Sure you both must be starving'. Charles seemed quite at ease and chatted pleasantly with everyone. The meal was nearly finished when Daniel said 'Ah! sure I nearly forgot, Cathy is home Alice, she hopes you can manage to see one another'. 'What luck!, I haven't see her for ages, can I borrow your car Daddy I would like to drive over to see her if only for a very short time?' Alice gave her father a kiss and she and Charles left. They would be back in time for dinner and would bring Cathy back with them.

It was a lovely Autumn day and Alice suggested to Charles that they take a long walk over the fells and have lunch in some little pub, he agreed and they set off. After they had walked for some time, Charles remarked 'It really is wonderful scenery around here, even the air is different from London's. It's so good to be with you Alice', she squeezed his arm and smiled at him. As they walked along the lanes, Alice stopped every so often to either pick or smell the last of the summer flowers still blooming in the hedgerows. Eventually, they reached a low stone wall and Charles asked Alice to sit down for a minute. Putting his arms around her he kissed her then reached into his pocket and brought out a small parcel then handed it to her saying 'This is for you darling, I hope you like it?'. She took the parcel and undid the wrapping paper and discovered it was a small jewellery box, sitting inside was a diamond ring sparkling in the sunlight. Alice looked at Charles slightly bewildered, she was unsure of what the ring meant. He reached over and took the box from her, then took out the ring and slipped it on the third finger of the left hand.

'I absolutely adore you, darling Alice, will you marry me?', he asked. She looked at him and said 'Yes, I love you too'. They fell into each other's arms and clung to each other. 'Alice, you are so beautiful, you have made me the happiest man alive. She moved into his arms as they kissed, secure in the knowledge of their love for each other. There was great excitement when Alice and Charles arrived home as she displayed her ring and declared 'Daddy, I'm engaged to Charles'. Daniel opened a bottle of Champagne which he had been keeping for a special occasion and filled everyone's glass. 'I propose a toast to the newly engaged couple. You have my blessing and my dearest wish is that you will share a long and happy life together, God Bless you'. They all drank to that!. 'Slainte' said Michael.

After dinner one evening, near the end of Alice and Charles's leave, Daniel, Alice, Charles and Michael went into the sitting room to sort through the photographs they had taken during the week. Most of them were very good, Charles was interested and took good pictures. Alice, on the other hand, was pretty useless with a camera and a few were only good for a laugh. In one, Charles's feet dominated the picture and appeared to be three feet in size. In another, Daniel and Michael were nearly decapitated. Alice took a large pile of photograph albums from a cupboard and placed them on the floor. She intended to fill any gaps with the new photographs.

Charles picked up an album and looked through it. Alice had told him about her family and was keen to see what they looked like. 'Darling, could you come over here and explain to me who everyone is in these photographs?' Alice sat down beside him. 'Who's this?' he asked. She looked at the photograph and explained. 'Oh! those are my grandparents, Clare and Declan, 'they died when daddy was a baby, Clare was uncle Michael's sister, he adored her. Evidently I have her green eyes and auburn hair'. They looked through a few more albums. There were plenty of photographs of Alice from babyhood to the present. Even a couple with her mother taken a few days after she was born. Charles closed the album and handed it to Alice. As he did so, some loose photographs fell out. He picked them up and handed them to her. 'Here's one of my maternal grandparents and here's one of daddy, uncle Michael and myself', she said.. 'Oh look!', she exclaimed here's one of daddy, his friend James and me holding a huge doll. I still have the doll, it has to be restored to its former glory one day'.

Charles took hold of the photograph and looked very closely at it for some time. It seemed to Alice that he couldn't take his eyes off it. 'Why are you so interested in that particular photograph?' she asked. 'I know it sounds absurd, but your father's friend looks very like someone I know', he explained, 'Really?' she replied. 'Excuse me a moment' he said and left the room. Charles returned with a pocket photograph album and sat down next to Daniel, Alice joined them. From his album he took out a photograph and placed it side by side on the table, with Alice's photographs.

Daniel was the first to speak. 'That's my friend James, how do you know him?' he asked in surprise. Charles looked at Daniel with a strange look on his face. 'Your friend James and my grandfather are obviously one and the same person', he said with a grin. 'What! your grandfather? he looked at Michael and then turned to Charles, are you sure?' 'I know my own grandfather' he laughed. They continued to examine the photographs until they were absolutely sure it was the same person in the two photographs. 'I can hardly believe it myself, no one is more surprised than I. We all agree that it is definitely the same man'. Daniel looked up and shook his head laughing and said 'sure the longer I live, the more I believe the old saying truth is stranger than fiction. James never spoke much about his family to me even though we were very close' said Daniel. There is something else I think you should know, Charles added. 'My grandfather was the Duke of Lancaster when you knew him Mr. O'Reilly, my father is the present Duke'. This new revelation, coming on top of the first, was an absolute bombshell. Daniel looked at Michael and Alice. Then Daniel stared at Charles in total disbelief. The room was full of a deafening silence.

Eventually, Alice found her voice and said, rather crossly 'Charles, I think you and I have to discuss everything you have told us' as she led the way to the garden. While Alice and Charles discussed their future, Daniel lit a cigarette and thought about his old friend. James had been a wonderful part of his life and was never very far from his thoughts. Tonight however, he felt very close to him and prayed silently that he would 'Rest in Peace' to 'That God of Yours' as he used to say. James had a very special childlike quality which enabled him to enjoy the simple things of life. Coupled with his knowledge of the world, it was a very powerful combination. They had talked about many things during their hikes around the countryside and had soon realised he always encouraged him in his endeavours to succeed. 'Pursue your dreams Daniel', was his usual turn of phrase. Because of the legacy bequeathed to him, he had been able to realise his dream and reap all the benefits that came with it. Now, his daughter Alice, was engaged to be married to James's grandson. She would marry the son of the present Duke of Lancaster.

The irony of the situation was certainly not lost on him especially what had happened in Ireland to his family by Charles' ancestors. He closed his eyes and thought about his old friend. In his mind's eye he could see his face, his bright blue eyes and the wry grin he knew so well. Chance had brought them together. They had come from totally different backgrounds, and yet their paths had crossed. It seemed as though their friendship had developed overnight and afterwards grew even stronger. Daniel asked himself the same question he had asked over and over again. Had he and James really met by fate or were they destined to meet? Alice and Charles returned to the room hand in hand, both looking very happy.

'Daddy, Alice said, Charles would really love to hear the full story of your friendship with his grandfather, would you tell him?' she asked with a smile. As they sat down Daniel began.

'It was a warm summer afternoon in late August when I was just a lad...............

HISTORICAL REFERENCES

'HEDGE SCHOOLS'

Hedge Schools are named after the clandestine schools run by the Irish during the time of the Penal Laws which not only forbade all teaching for Catholics, the law also prevented the Catholic Irish from holding office, or owning or purchasing land, and forbade them to educate their children by any means. 'Throughout those 'dark days' the hunted schoolmaster, with a price on his head, was hidden from house to house. In the summer he gathered his little class, hungering and thirsting for knowledge, behind a hedge in remote places, where, in turn each tattered child kept watch for the British soldiers, he fed to his eager pupils the forbidden fruit of the tree of knowledge.'

'THE FEVER / CHOLERA'

The disease' did not differentiate between rich and poor. At the time it was not known how Cholera spread, and there were fierce arguments about whether or not victims should be segregated from those who were not ill. (We know now that Cholera spreads through contaminated water, not by contact.) 'There is no reliable evidence of knowing how many died in these epidemics, but it was the final insult of the Famine period. The workhouses continued to manage the relief effort; many of the destitute ended up with nothing, and, therefore, found it very difficult to get out of the workhouses again. By 1849 – 1850 the workhouse had enough capacity to take appropriate care of all the destitute. Emigration also continued, although not quite at the levels of 1847. Approximately 200,000 per year left between 1848 and 1852 inclusive. Most of these traveled to America.

'THE BLACK AND TANS

The Black and Tans were mostly soldiers brought into Ireland by the government in London after 1919, the British Government advertised for men who were to 'face a rough and dangerous task'. Many former British soldiers came back to unemployment. There were plenty of ex-servicemen who were willing to reply to the government's advert. The first unit arrived in Ireland in March 1920. On arrival in Ireland it became apparent there were not enough uniforms for those who had joined up. They wore a mixture of uniforms. This mixture gave them the appearance of being khaki and a dark police uniform, hence the name 'Black and Tans'. The Black and Tans lacked self-discipline and all but terrorized local communities. For the Black and Tans, their primary task was to make Ireland 'hell for the rebels to live in'. The attitude of the Black and Tans is best summed up by one of their divisional commanders: 'If a police barracks is burned or if the barracks already occupied is not suitable, then the best house in the locality is to be commandeered, the occupants thrown into the gutter. Let them die there – the more the merrier. Should the order ('Hands Up') not be immediately obeyed, shoot and shoot with effect. If the persons approaching (a patrol) carry their hands in their pockets, or are in any way suspicious-looking, shoot them down. You may make mistakes occasionally and innocent persons may be shot, but that cannot be helped, and you are bound to get the right parties some time. The more you shoot, the better I will like you, and I assure you no policeman will get into trouble for shooting any man'. Lt. Col. Smyth, June 1920. There were many examples of them shooting indiscriminately at civilians. The government in Westminster quickly realised they were a liability as even public opinion in mainland Britain was appalled by a lot of what they did. The most infamous attack on the public came in November 1920. Many people had packed into Croke Park, Dublin, to watch a football match. In retaliation for the murder of fourteen under cover detectives by the IRA, the Black and Tans opened fire on the crowd, killing twelve people. The Black and Tans were pulled out of Ireland in ignominy. Their actions, however, did succeed in getting the republican cause a great deal of civilian support simply because of 'their acts'.

TENANTS AT WILL

The average tenant farmer lived at a subsistence level on less than ten acres. These Catholic farmers were usually considered tenants-at-will and could be evicted on short notice at the whim of the landlord, his agent or middleman. By law, any improvements they made, such as building a stone house, became the property of the landlord. Thus there was never any incentive to upgrade their conditions. The cottiers performed daily chores and helped bring in the annual harvest as payment of rent. Most of the Irish countryside was owned by English and Anglo-Irish hereditary ruling class. Many were 'Absentee Landlords' that set foot on their properties once or twice a year if at all. They held titles to enormous tracts of land long ago confiscated from the Irish. The landlords often utilized local agents to actually manage their estates while living lavishly in London or in Europe off the rents paid by Catholics for land their ancestors once owned.

IRISH POTATO FAMINE 1845

Beginning in 1845 and lasting for six years, the potato famine killed over a million men, women and children in Ireland and caused another million to flee the country. Ireland in the mid -1800's was an agricultural nation, populated by eight million people who were among the poorest people in the Western World.. Life expectancy was short, just 40 years for men.. The Irish married quite young at 17 or 18 and tended to have large families.. Infant mortality was quite high.

About the Author

Marie Shields was born 1921 in England, in the Furness Peninsula from an Irish Catholic background. Marie's parents were the first of their line to be born out of Ireland. Marie was a very talented woman and loved to write short stories for her grandchildren and great grandchildren.

'A Fateful Occurrence' is her first novel.

Marie was delighted to return to her roots in Ireland in the year 2000, where she lived with her daughter Maureen and son in law Joseph Purcell, her grandchildren and great grandchildren, in Co. Louth. Republic of Ireland.